TARGET FOR TREASON

LAURA SCOTT

Copyright © 2021 by Laura Scott

All rights reserved.

No part of this book may be reproduced in any form or by any electronic or mechanical means, including information storage and retrieval systems, without written permission from the author, except for the use of brief quotations in a book review.

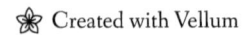

❦ Created with Vellum

CHAPTER ONE

January 30 – 7:10 p.m. – Washington, DC

Lina Parker paused for a moment, glancing up and down the street that was illuminated by streetlights and the full moon. The Metro station she'd recently exited loomed behind her. She told herself the Asian man watching her over the top of his book was nothing more than her overactive imagination as there was no sign of him now. A gust of cold wind made her shiver, and she broke into a brisk walk. Her stomach was knotted with a myriad of emotions, from anticipation to anxiety.

Tonight, she'd meet a member of her mother's family for the first time. Lina had been born in the US but was curious about her Chinese roots. She participated in several DNA websites, searching for family connections over the past two months, hoping to find someone she was even remotely related to. Having been born here in DC and losing her parents when she was young, she'd been raised by her father's family. She truly loved her Parker grandparents, but they weren't remotely interested in the Chinese culture. In fact, they'd given her the distinct impression they'd have preferred that she'd forget all about her mother's heritage.

Stumbling across her mother's sister was far more than she'd ever expected. It was exciting to meet a blood relative from her mother's side of the family, especially to find one here in Washington, DC. Yet it was difficult not to be concerned as Shu Yan Chen had wanted to keep this rendezvous a secret. That odd request, which Shu Yan had refused to discuss further except in person, was largely why she'd let her imagination run wild during the subway ride.

Clearly, she needed to stop reading suspense novels.

When Lina reached the next intersection, she turned right and headed up toward Turtle Park.

Not for the first time, she thought it a strange location for a meeting. The place was in the process of being renovated, the large track front-loader and dump truck sitting idle in the middle of winter. The recent storm dumped a three-inch layer of pure white snow, some of which had begun to melt.

As she entered the park, her footsteps slowed. The area appeared completely deserted, likely the reason Shu Yan had chosen it. The woman's need for secrecy was a bit concerning. Lina pulled the dark cap more firmly over her long dark hair as she searched for the trio of birch trees Shu Yan mentioned.

Turtle Park wasn't that large. After walking another few minutes, she caught a glimpse of the trees on the other side of a large excavator digging machine. She stopped for a moment to see if Shu Yan was there yet.

A dark shadow moved, but from this distance, it was difficult to see if the person was her aunt. It must be, who else would be here?

Lina hurried around the excavator. *Crack!* The sharp

report was louder than a firecracker, and it took her a moment to realize it was gunfire.

Someone was shooting at her!

Lina ducked beneath the excavator, using the steel machine for cover. Her palms were sweaty in her gloves, her heart pounding so loudly she couldn't hear anything else. DC was known for its high crime rate, but this was ridiculous.

From beneath the excavator, she noticed the dark figure lying on the ground, just ten feet away.

She sucked in a harsh breath. A Chinese woman was lying in the snow, blood oozing from her temple, staining the white fluff a horrifying crimson.

No! Shu Yan! Stunned, Lina tried to understand what was going on. Why on earth would someone shoot her aunt? Was this why Shu Yan had wanted her to keep the meeting secret? Because someone was after her?

Why had she been targeted?

Another crack of gunfire echoed loudly. She heard something ping off the metal excavator mere inches from her head. Frantic, she crawled farther beneath the machine until she couldn't see anyone or anything. Bile rose in the back of her throat as the seriousness of her situation hit hard.

The shooter hadn't just taken out Shu Yan. He was intent on doing the same to her! But who? And why?

Lina cowered beneath the excavator, silently praying for strength as she fumbled with her phone. She was wedged so far beneath the excavator that she could barely get the phone out of her pocket. After what seemed like forever, she managed to get the device out and used one hand to dial 911.

"Hello, what is the nature of your emergency?"

"I'm in Turtle Park, someone is shooting at me!" She spoke in a hushed whisper, hoping the female dispatcher could hear her. "The same shooter has killed a woman named Shu Yan Chen." Even to her own ears, the claim sounded incredulous. "I need help! I'm hiding beneath the excavator, please hurry!"

"I'll send a team of officers to your location," the operator said calmly. "Please stay on the line."

"I can't. They might hear me." Lina disconnected from the call, her heart pounding frantically as she strained to listen. The eerie silence surrounding her was not at all reassuring. This far under the excavator, she couldn't see anything, yet she felt certain the gunman was still out there, somewhere.

All she could do was pray the police would arrive before the shooter found a way to silence her, permanently.

JANUARY 30 – 7:18 p.m. – Washington, DC

Boyd Sinclair was doing his typical gym routine when his phone buzzed. He would have ignored it except for the fact that it was his new boss, Jordan Rashid from Security Specialists, Inc.

Muttering with annoyance, he halted his forty-ninth push-up to grab the device. He rolled to his feet, his biceps quivering from exertion, streams of sweat running freely down his face. "Sinclair."

"Boyd, we have a problem." Jordan Rashid and Sloan Dreyer were equal partners in Security Specialists, Inc., a company that offered a variety of special services to anyone willing to pay the exorbitant price they demanded. Based on several recent thwarted terrorist attempts, the company had received accolades from people as high up as the President of the United States and the Department of Defense along with the leaders in charge of the FBI, the NSA, and the CIA. In fact, the FBI and NSA were often the ones hiring the Security Specialists, Inc. team based on their skills in the field along with their language expertise.

He was the newest member of the team and eager to get to work. He'd met Jordan when the president had invited the entire Security Specialists, Inc. team to the White House to thank them for their service shortly after the threat during the inauguration last year. Jordan had overheard him speaking Chinese to a fellow agent and had instantly invited him to join his team. Boyd had turned down the offer, until he was forced to resign from the Secret Service. Now he was grateful to be able to continue protecting their freedom. While not perfect, the US government was better than anything else across the globe, and he'd sworn an oath, in the past and again now, to put his life on the line, to defend it. He toweled the sweat off his face. "What kind of problem?"

"Recent chatter from overseas indicates a possible but credible terroristic threat from a Chinese mafia organization known as the Six Red Dragons. Our company has been hired to dig into the threat."

Boyd guzzled a bottle of water, wishing Jordan would get to the point. "I'm aware of the concern, so what's the problem?"

"We've just learned of a professional hit against Shu Yan Chen, witnessed by Lina Parker who managed to call the police and escape unscathed."

He straightened, his instincts going on alert. "Chen is a very common Chinese surname," he cautioned. "This woman's death may not be related to the Six Red Dragons faction of the Chinese mafia. I know there are rumors of

Hui Genghis Chen being a part of the Dragons, but we don't know for certain he is related to Shu Yan Chen."

"Doesn't matter, we're taking this threat seriously. You need to get over to the Fifth Precinct and talk to the witness ASAP," Jordan said. "I need you to take Lina Parker someplace safe for at least the next twenty-four hours. I'm waiting for Clarence Yates, the Director of the FBI, to get me more intel because I have a really bad feeling about this."

"Got it." Boyd wasn't going to complain, after all, he'd rather be doing something constructive. The Secret Service had taught him patience, but he'd had just about all the standing around and watching he could take.

Not that his leaving the service had been a voluntary move on his part.

Keeping his military training sharp during the six years he'd been on the First Lady's detail hadn't been easy. The job demanded a lot of time, which hadn't provided lots of opportunities to hit the gym. After hearing what Jordan, Sloan, and Sun had been through over the past few years, he'd worked hard to get back in shape. This was a good time to put some of that training to use.

The urgency in Jordan's tone convinced him to bypass a shower in favor of heading straight to the precinct. As he drove, he tried to figure out why Jordan believed this incident to be related to the Chinese mafia. Granted, the name Chen was a possible connection, but the name wasn't unusual. There were tens of millions of Chinese citizens across the globe.

Unfortunately, gun violence had become commonplace across the country. What Jordan described wasn't what he'd consider a mass shooting. One victim dead and one witness didn't scream terrorist to him. Jordan's suspicions seemed a bit over the top. There was no indication Lina was connected to the mafia, and he couldn't fathom any reason why the Six Red Dragons would want to take out a woman. The Chinese mafia, much like the Chinese culture in general, didn't put much importance on their women. Men held all the power within their family, their government, and their criminal organizations.

Then again, they killed women without thinking twice, so maybe there was a connection. He didn't look Chinese, other than his dark hair, and his name was completely American. But he had spent enough time in China prior to his entering the military to know corruption was everywhere, even within the government.

And no matter what the president was trying to do, smoothing over the jagged relationship between their two countries, Boyd knew China was not really their friend and ally.

He made good time getting to the Fifth Precinct. Of course, the local cops weren't that happy to have him show up, but he insisted on being taken to Lina Parker. The only thing he truly missed about the Secret Service was having the authority and credentials to instantly slice through red tape. The Security Specialists, Inc. ID Jordan had given him meant nothing to anyone within the police department.

Returning to the ordinary status of civilian took some getting used to.

"She's in here." The cop gestured to a small square room. "We've taken her statement, so she's free to go."

"Thanks." Boyd opened the door and stepped in. For some reason, he was surprised to discover Lina Parker was a stunning Chinese American. Her almond skin was flawless, her green eyes bright. Her long, straight silky black hair must have come from her Chinese ancestors, but her facial features were definitely more American. She appeared pale and frightened, understandable considering the circumstances.

"Who are you?" She jumped to her feet, gathering her dark quilted jacket tightly around her torso. She had a black knit hat balled in her hand.

"Ms. Parker, my name is Boyd Sinclair." He smiled, which usually put women at ease. "I'm here to take you someplace safe."

"Safe?" She scoffed and tilted her chin. "Forgive me if I find that hard to believe. I just witnessed a murder, surely the police should be the ones to keep me safe."

He tried not to sigh. "I'll talk to the police about that, but you should know I work for a company that specializes in protecting people." He took out his lame ID and showed it to her. "Please come with me."

"No." She crossed her arms over her chest. "You're a stranger. For all I know, you're the shooter."

He arched a brow, unable to argue with her logic. If the situation were reversed, he wouldn't be so quick to leave with a strange guy either. "I'm not the shooter. What can I do to convince you my only goal is to keep you safe?"

She regarded him thoughtfully for a moment. "Get me some answers. The police refused to confirm that Shu Yan Chen is the woman who was shot despite what I saw with my own eyes. I deserve to know that much."

He nodded. "And who was Shu Yan Chen to you?"

"My mother's sister, although this was our first meeting. I found her using online DNA research sites."

DNA research site? That tidbit of information was new. As was her blood relationship with the victim. "Okay, stay here. I'll be back as soon as possible."

He left the room and found the cop who'd escorted him

back there. "Hey, who's in charge? I need information about the crime scene."

The cop smirked. "Captain Rugg is in charge, but you're not getting information about an active crime scene."

Again, he wished he had his Secret Service creds. "Where can I find Rugg?"

"That way." The cop jutted his chin to a small office marked Captain, then turned away.

Boyd crossed over and knocked on the partially open door. Without waiting for a response, he poked his head in. "Captain Rugg?"

"Yeah?" The guy scowled. "You better not be a reporter."

"No, sir." The captain's derision wasn't unusual, reporters were the bane of every government and civil servant employee's existence. After what had happened while he was in the service, Boyd shared the captain's feelings. "I've been asked to escort Ms. Parker to safety, but I'd like to know about the female victim you found at the crime scene. I believe she has been identified as Ms. Shu Yan Chen?"

The captain sat back, eyeing him thoughtfully. "You look familiar. Are you sure you're not a reporter?"

"Never. My name is Boyd Sinclair. I used to be with the Secret Service on the First Lady's detail."

"Ah, I remember." A gleam entered the captain's eyes. "There was a big write-up about how you failed to notice a crazy man who tried to stab her until it was almost too late."

"That's correct." He hoped his face wasn't turning red with embarrassment. Nothing like having your biggest failure put out for the entire world to see. *Thank you, media.* "I work for Security Specialists, Inc. now, and we have a vested interest in the female victim, Shu Yan Chen. If you could just confirm her identity and let me know when the autopsy will be completed, I'll get out of your hair."

"There was no victim." The captain's tone was blunt. "No evidence of blood either. There was a small snowman built near a trio of birch trees, which seemed odd, but nothing else to indicate a crime had happened. If you ask me, the so-called witness you're taking home is a nutjob. For all we know, she made the snowman."

Stunned, Boyd stared at him. "You're sure there was no victim and no evidence of a murder?"

"I still have techs combing the scene, but if they don't come up with something soon, I'm pulling them out of Turtle Park. Besides, who sets up a meeting in a park undergoing renovations anyway?" The captain waved an impatient hand. "I don't have time or manpower to waste on some crazy woman's imaginary problems."

"Thanks for the information." Grappling with this news, he turned and walked back to the small interview room. It didn't make any sense. Jordan had sent him to protect Lina Parker based on the victim being Shu Yan Chen and the possible connection to the Six Red Dragons faction of the Chinese mafia.

No victim meant no crime and no threat to the witness.

Only, he didn't believe it. The whole scenario carried the stench of a cover-up. Yeah, color him paranoid, but no way did he think Lina Parker made up this story. She wasn't wrong about what she'd seen. The stark fear in her eyes hadn't been fake, she'd clearly been terrified. And he felt certain the snowman had been created to cover the disturbed snow.

Thinking about it further, he remembered Lina's black jeans and jacket had been damp and stained with mud too.

She'd hit the ground for a reason, not because of some made-up story.

He quickened his pace and threw open the door to the small interview room.

It was empty.

Where was Lina?

Boyd spun on his heel and strode quickly through the police station. He'd left his weapon in the car, knowing they'd make him lock it up anyway, so he didn't stop until he was outside the precinct.

He swept his gaze over the area. Where did she go? How long had she been gone?

Bitter fear lodged in his throat. No way. This couldn't happen. He couldn't fail in performing his very first assignment in his new job.

He couldn't!

"Lina!" he shouted out of sheer frustration. Furious with himself for not anticipating this, he ran to his car, unlocking the door with the fob as he approached. Sliding in behind the wheel, he drove out of the parking lot, trying to think about which way she'd gone.

Did she have a car? Or had she taken the Metro?

He thumped the steering wheel with his fist, then turned left toward the closest Metro station.

Since DC traffic was notoriously bad, he hoped that meant Lina hadn't driven to Turtle Park. There was a Metro stop five blocks from the place. He couldn't help but agree with the captain on one point—the park was a strange place to hold a meeting.

But it may have been a really good place to set up a sniper to kill someone.

And if Lina didn't imagine the murder, that same

someone had worked very quickly to clean up any sign of the crime. No easy feat.

Using the hands-free function, he called Jordan. "Lina's in the wind." No point in beating around the bush. "Even worse, the police claim there is no murder because they haven't found the victim or any blood at Turtle Park."

"That's not right, I heard the 911 call Lina made. Because of the Chinese name of Shu Yan Chen, the call was routed to Yates with the FBI and then to me. The threat was real." Jordan paused, then added, "She's in danger."

"I know." Boyd was impressed with Jordan's swift access to information, wishing he could hear the 911 call too. "I'll find her, but I need her address and phone number."

Jordan rattled off the information, which he quickly memorized. Then he caught a glimpse of a slender woman with long dark hair running.

Lina!

Yanking the steering wheel hard to the right, he pulled off out of traffic and hit the brakes. He grabbed his gun and shot out of the car as Lina screamed, "Help me!"

A figure in a dark jacket and hood emerged from the trees a few yards behind her. It only took him a second to see the gun in the guy's hand, especially since he lifted it to aim at Lina. Boyd didn't hesitate to fire his weapon, his reaction quicker than the assailant's.

The hooded man instantly fell backward from the impact of the bullet, hitting the ground hard. Ignoring him, Boyd ran to Lina. "This way," he urged.

She didn't move, staring from the gun in his hand to his face, then back at the man lying dead behind her.

"No time to argue, move!" He barked at her as if she were a marine in his platoon. When she didn't respond fast enough, he took a step forward, grabbed her, then tossed her over his shoulder. Her phone fell from her pocket and hit the ground.

"Wait! My phone!"

He paused, then turned and stomped on it hard, smashing it into zillions of pieces, before carrying her to his SUV. "It's broken. Besides, you won't need it."

"But—" she sputtered.

He ignored her. Enough was enough. Failure was not an option.

He'd keep her safe, whether she liked it or not.

CHAPTER TWO

January 30 – 8:03 p.m. – Beijing, China

"I'm sorry to report the mission failed."

Failed! Anger spiked. How was that possible? The best team had been sent to the capital city of the US to perform one small task. These idiots had wasted the perfect opportunity to take out two birds with one stone.

Drawing a deep breath helped keep the anger in check. "Explain yourself."

"One target was taken down and removed along with all evidence of the crime as ordered. However, the second target escaped," there was a brief pause before the contact added, "twice."

"Twice?" Anger vibrated through the word. "Imbecile!"

"Yes." It wasn't difficult to imagine the contact standing with his head bowed down in deference to his leader and in response to his unforgivable mistake. If he were here, it would be tempting to kill him on the spot. But thousands of miles separated them, so the satisfaction of killing him would need to wait. "Of course, our plan is to keep searching for the target. We will find her."

"You had better find her, very soon. Time is running short. We have less than thirty-six hours from now."

"Yes." The easy agreement was annoying rather than reassuring. "I will call you when the deed is done."

"Soon." Unable to tolerate another second of the ridiculous conversation, the call abruptly ended. Throwing the phone against the wall would not help.

The Chinese New Year celebration was fast approaching. Everything that had been put in place many years ago would soon come to fruition.

One small woman could not be allowed to upset this master plan. They had one chance to complete the mission.

The future of China depended on the perfect execution of this plan.

Failure was not an acceptable outcome.

JANUARY 30 – 8:33 p.m. – Washington, DC

Lina wrinkled her nose and sat stiffly in the passenger seat of the SUV. The tall stranger sitting beside her reeked like a pair of old gym socks. While it wasn't entirely unpleasant, she turned to glare at him. "I don't appreciate being tossed around like a bag of bricks by a stinky stranger."

A flicker of remorse darkened his eyes for a nanosecond before he scowled. "Yeah? Not my fault. Standing around in the middle of the sidewalk with a gunman lying behind you was a stupid move. As was leaving the police station without me. Surely you must realize someone wants you dead."

He wasn't telling her something she didn't already know. The Asian man who'd jumped out of the woods had shaken her badly. Especially as she'd already managed to escape a different Asian man who'd started following her the moment she'd left the police station.

Remembering the gunfire at Turtle Park made her shiver. She cast a sideways glance at her so-called protector. "How do I know I can trust you?"

"You can't." His blunt response startled her. "I've explained who I work for, and that's all I can do." He turned to look at her. "Well, I also shot a man for you."

He had. And without a second's hesitation. His quick reaction had shocked her. She'd never witnessed something like that. Deep down, she knew there was nothing to stop him from killing her if he so chose. That he hadn't was a point in his favor. "Are you a cop?"

"No. Former marine and Secret Service."

"Secret Service?" The news surprised her. "Why did you leave that job?"

"It was time." His curt tone didn't invite further conversation. "Ms. Parker, I promise you that I'm here to keep you safe. And if I hadn't shown up when I did, you'd already be dead."

"I know." She closed her eyes for a moment, battling a surge of nausea. Two hours ago she was a normal person living a normal life. Now her mother's sister was dead, and men with guns were following her. But why? Was this all related to Shu Yan Chen? It was the only explanation she could come up with. "The police need to investigate why Shu Yan was murdered. I'm sure the same two men who'd just followed me were the same ones who killed her." Only one of them was alive now, though, thanks to Boyd Sinclair's quick reflexes.

"That's not going to happen."

She gaped. "Why not?"

"That's right, you left the police station before I could

fill you in on what I found out about your victim." The hint of sarcasm in his tone annoyed her. She wasn't going to apologize for not trusting a strange man claiming he wanted to protect her.

"Don't tell me they couldn't identify her as Shu Yan Chen."

"That's right, they could not identify her because she was gone, along with any and all evidence of the murder."

"Gone?" she repeated stupidly. "I don't understand."

Boyd shrugged. "I'm just repeating what the captain told me. No body, no blood, no evidence of a crime. He thinks you're some sort of crackpot."

"I'm not a crackpot!" She reached out to grab his arm. "I didn't make it up! I'm telling you, I saw her fall to the ground, the blood oozing from her head, staining the snow red. I saw the entire thing!"

"I believe you."

His words washed over her like a cold shower, dousing her fury. "You do?"

"Yes." He glanced at her hand on his arm, and she quickly let him go, belatedly realizing his muscles were rock solid. More so than any man she'd ever met before. Then again, she tended to hang out with nerdy scientists, not with surly bodybuilders. No wonder he smelled like old gym socks. "My boss listened to your 911 call. There was no mistaking the fear in your voice. And there was a small snowman built near a trio of birch trees, which may have been done to cover up the crime scene."

"I—thank you." She swallowed hard, trying to gather her thoughts. A snowman? It seemed ridiculous yet apparently effective. "Wait a minute, how did your boss listen to the 911 call?"

"He has connections."

She scowled. The removal of her aunt's body and all the corresponding evidence, along with making a snowman of all things, must have taken place after she burrowed farther beneath the excavator. When the police arrived, they'd called out to her that it was safe to come out. She'd crawled from beneath the excavator and ran toward them, unwilling to look directly at what was left of Shu Yan Chen. The police had quickly tucked her into the back of a squad, then fanned out to look for the shooter. One cop had taken her to the station to provide her statement, but no one had bothered to mention there was no evidence of a crime.

Something was wrong with this entire scenario. Very, very wrong.

They drove in silence for several minutes. She tensed when she realized they were heading in the opposite direction of where she lived. "Where are you taking me?"

He audibly sighed. "I've told you several times now that I'll keep you safe. We can't go back to your place, not after the near miss outside the police station. I know it's not easy, Ms. Parker, but you have to trust me."

Trust him? She didn't know him! She glanced outside at the full moon hanging low on the horizon. Then she lifted her gaze higher to the barely visible stars winking in the dark sky. Maybe she needed to trust in God's plan for her. It seemed obvious that this Boyd guy didn't intend to kill her.

She lost the energy to fight him. "Okay, I'll trust you. And my name is Lina."

"Lina." He nodded. "I'm Boyd. And I was at the gym when my boss called to let me know you needed protection. He said it was urgent, so I came straight over without showering."

Guilt assailed her. Normally, she wasn't so thoughtless and rude. "I'm sorry, I shouldn't have been critical. It's just

—this is all so inconceivable. I've never made anyone so angry that they'd come after me intending to shoot me. It just doesn't make any sense."

"How much do you know about your aunt?"

"Nothing, really." She shivered despite the warm temperature inside the vehicle. "We only spoke on the phone once, to set up this meeting. Most of our conversations were done via email."

"How do you know the woman you spoke to was really Shu Yan Chen?"

She turned to stare at him, feeling sick to her stomach. "I—don't."

"That was your first mistake," Boyd said firmly. "The second was agreeing to meet at a sketchy location. Turtle Park at night, while it's under construction? Basic common sense should have told you something was wrong."

Her cheeks burned at his rebuke. "Okay, maybe it wasn't the smartest move. But how was I to know that meeting my aunt about a DNA test meant someone would shoot at us? Attempt to kill us? Talk about insane. There's no reason. All I did was reach out to my mother's side of the family!"

"Whom you know nothing about."

All the air left her body in a silent whoosh. Because he was right. She didn't know anything about her mother's side of the family. That was the whole point of getting a DNA test and creating a family tree online.

The only relative to reach out to her had been brutally murdered.

Dear Lord in heaven, what had she done?

JANUARY 30 – 9:12 p.m. Washington, DC

Boyd felt a little guilty for being so blunt. Blame it on the fact that he hadn't spent much time dealing the opposite sex. At least, not in a close, personal, and intimate setting.

There had been female Secret Service agents, and even a handful of female marines, but those women were just as tough as he was. Sometimes more so. And getting romantically involved with them while working together was ill-advised.

He shot a sideways glance at the woman beside him. The slender and beautiful Lina Parker was about as far away from a marine or Secret Service agent as one could get.

He'd gone from being deployed overseas for two tours to serving his country as a Secret Service agent, neither occupation conducive to doing something as mundane as dating. Not from lack of interest but more so because his schedule had always been dictated by others without much downtime. This job was proving to be the same. He needed to get his act together, or Jordan would wonder why he'd taken the risk of hiring him after the debacle that defined his career.

Or lack thereof.

Thirty-three years old and washed up. How pathetic was that?

He pulled himself together with an effort. The motel he had in mind was just a few miles away. Once he'd gotten Lina settled, he'd call Jordan to let him know about the Chinese men who'd come after her. And the one he'd been forced to kill.

Not an auspicious start to my new job, he thought sourly. Then again, Lina was alive and with him, so he'd gotten that much right.

"You never said where we're going."

He glanced at her. "A motel. Just for tonight."

"Oh, no. Not happening." She thrust her chin out at a stubborn angle. "I'm not staying alone in a motel room with you."

Man, he was getting tired of arguing with her. No wonder he hadn't bothered dating. Lina might be beautiful in a way that tempted him more than he'd ever experienced before, but dealing with her was exhausting. "You'll be fine, it's not like I'm going to sleep. I'll sit in a chair near the door."

"You can't stay awake all night," she snapped. "Everyone needs sleep."

"It won't be the first time I've stayed up all night." His tours in Iran and Afghanistan had taught him to function on minimal sleep. And the Secret Service didn't exactly keep regular hours either. "Must you argue about everything?"

She opened her mouth, then closed it again. Turning, she stared out the passenger side window. Her silence was almost worse than her constant arguing.

Almost, but not quite.

He pulled into the motel parking lot, expecting to hear complaints about the less-than-optimal accommodations. The place wasn't high on anyone's list of places to stay, yet he knew that it was perfect for staying off the radar.

"Stay here. I'll be back in a minute." He pushed open his door and slid out from the car. Then he hesitated, wondering if she'd still be there when he returned. The way she'd ditched him at the police station still burned. He bent down and added, "Leaving will only put you back in danger. We can't neutralize the threat until we know where it's coming from. You need to stick with me, understand?"

She gave a brief nod. "I hear you."

He stared at her for a long moment, hoping she was

being honest with him. From the very beginning, she'd continuously asked why she should trust him.

It was time to consider whether he should trust *her*.

Boyd was able to secure a room for a little extra cash slipped under the table. Some things didn't change; money still worked to bend the rules. Pocketing the key, he quickly returned to the SUV, relieved to see Lina was still sitting inside.

Maybe he'd survive this job after all.

He parked the SUV in the darkest corner of the parking lot, then led Lina inside, flicking the small light switch to illuminate the dusty room. She wrinkled her nose at the musty scent, but thankfully, she didn't complain. He figured he didn't smell much better, another situation that wasn't about to change anytime soon. Oh, he'd love a shower, but there was no time for luxuries.

Without saying anything, Lina disappeared into the bathroom. He quickly called Jordan. "Hey, slight problem picking up Lina."

"Yeah, I heard about the dead Chinese guy," Jordan drawled. "Next time give me a heads-up a little sooner."

He grimaced. "I would have, but Lina wasn't exactly cooperative. I had to physically carry her away from the scene. And I doubled back several times to make sure we weren't followed."

"It's okay. I was able to take care of it."

"Get a name?" Boyd asked.

"Not yet. He had no ID and just a disposable phone with no information entered in it. His fingerprints didn't match anyone in the system."

"Professionals," he murmured softly. "Likely the same team that took out Shu Yan Chen."

"Yeah." Jordan sighed. "I've been talking at length to

Clarence Yates. The chatter we received from China seems to indicate the Six Red Dragons are targeting the US President. He's convinced Shu Yan Chen is related to Hui Genghis Chen, especially after learning about the sanitized crime scene."

"Shu Yan Chen is Lina's mother's sister. I have to agree with Yates. This hit could very well have been done by the Dragons."

"But that doesn't explain why they tried to kill Lina Parker. Just because she was meeting with Shu Yan?" Jordan's voice held doubt. "It seems like there's something more going on. Why call attention to themselves by killing Shu Yan Chen if they have a bigger plan?"

"I agree, something is off about this." It felt a little like doing a jigsaw puzzle with only a handful of the 100 pieces. "Did you have anyone check out Lina's apartment?"

"I just sent Mack and Sun over there now. I'm not holding my breath that they'll find anything useful." Jordan paused, then said, "I have to go, Sun is calling." He disconnected without saying another word.

Boyd pocketed his phone and crossed over to listen at the door. Hearing the sound of water running, he stepped back and looked around the small room.

There was one chair located near the doorway. It would be impossible to sleep in, but it would have to do. He paced the length of the room, waiting for Lina to emerge. When she finally did, he stood at attention near the door, the way he'd spent most of his days in the service. Always on guard. Always watching.

Always ready to jump in the line of fire.

Ironically, this was no different.

She eyed him warily.

"Try to get some rest," he advised.

"Okay, but what's the plan come morning?" She moved toward the bed. "I'm supposed to be at work by seven thirty."

He tried not to roll his eyes. What part of being in danger didn't she understand? "You're not going to work. Not until we know who's behind the murder of Shu Yan Chen."

"I can't just not show up for my job," she argued. "They'll fire me!"

"Call in sick. Once this is over, I'm sure your boss will understand."

She glared at him for a long moment before turning away. "Fine. But it seems to me you should be able to keep me safe at work. The place is secure enough."

"Wait a minute." He held up a hand. "Secure enough? Where exactly do you work?"

"The Institute for Nanoscience." At his blank look, she added, "You must know it's part of the US Naval Research Laboratory."

He slowly lowered himself into the chair. The nanoscience lab was a highly renowned institution, built within the past twenty years. And only the best and the brightest scientists were allowed to work there. He stared at her in shock. "What's your role within the institute?"

"I'm a scientist." She looked at him in exasperation. "You didn't know that? What sort of protector are you?"

He couldn't fault her criticism, this was clearly something he should have been told up front. Although he didn't think Jordan was holding back, more likely things were just moving too fast to keep track of all the moving parts. "What's your area of expertise?"

"I have a doctorate in biology. I use the high-powered

transmission electron microscope to perform research projects."

A biologist? Alarm bells clamored in his mind. Had they read the entire situation wrong? Was it possible the shooter had mistaken Shu Yan Chen for Lina Parker? "Does that mean you work with dangerous biological agents that could be used to create weapons of mass destruction?"

"No, of course not." She looked at him as if he'd sprouted three heads. "All the dangerous biological agents are held in a very secure facility jointly operated by the Department of Defense and the Center for Disease Control. Not our lab."

Her comment wasn't reassuring. "Then what does your work entail?"

"The easy answer is that we take biological specimens and enhance them to a level that allows us to study fine details that we've never seen before. We also perform various biological research studies with those specimens."

"What sort of specimens?"

She shrugged. "It's hard to explain. We're a research lab, so we get samples from all over the US. This transmission electron microscope isn't readily available to everyone, especially not the high-level one we have."

He drummed his fingers on the chair's arm, trying to understand what he might be missing. All this time, Shu Yan Chen was deemed to be the actual target.

But that assumption could be wrong. Even though he didn't quite understand what Lina was describing, just the fact that she worked for the Institute for Nanoscience, an offshoot of the US Naval Research Laboratory, was enough to make him consider her job as a facet of the attempts on her life.

Then again, the Six Red Dragons wouldn't be interested in a giant high-powered microscope. Would they?

Maybe. What did he know? Anything was possible.

He was about to call Jordan again when he heard a muffled thump.

With finely honed instincts, he jumped up, doused the light, and pulled his weapon. Two strides had him grabbing Lina's arm, shoving her behind him.

The problem with motel rooms is that there was only one way in and out. If the bad guys were just outside the door, they were sitting ducks.

A sliver of light shone from between the curtains. When a dark shadow moved across it, he pushed Lina to the floor between the bed and the bathroom wall, then hunkered down beside her. He yanked the mattress up a bit to help cover them.

His pistol was a semiautomatic with thirteen rounds, minus the one he'd already pumped into the Chinese man who'd tried to shoot Lina. Twelve rounds left. Hopefully enough to get them through this.

The door burst open. A barrage of bullets whizzed over their heads, peppering the walls, the furniture, and the bed. Beside him, Lina quietly sobbed a whispered prayer.

Using the mirror above the dresser, he factored in the angle and edged the muzzle of his gun around the mattress just enough to shoot twice. Both bullets hit his intended targets, dropping them where they stood. Good thing his aim remained true. The marines had taught him to shoot, and target practice was required by the Secret Service.

"Let's go." He grabbed Lina's hand and pulled her upright. Seconds later, he stepped over the two bodies of Chinese men. He didn't take the time to search them, fearing there were more waiting outside. He swept his gaze over the area. He didn't see anyone.

So far, so good.

He ran toward the SUV, dragging Lina with him. She was still praying between sobs, but she didn't resist when he lifted her into the passenger seat. He slammed the door and ran around to get behind the wheel, still keeping a sharp eye out for potential sources of danger.

Hitting the gas, he peeled out of the parking lot of the motel just as various motel occupants, including the manager, came running out to see what was going on.

They were safe, at least for the moment. Boyd gripped the steering wheel tightly as he tried to understand how they'd been found. He'd smashed her phone, so they hadn't been tracked that way.

Then how? He wasn't sure.

At this rate, he'd surely fail in his task of keeping Lina safe.

CHAPTER THREE

January 30 – 9:45 p.m. – Shanghai, China

CIA asset Sam King surreptitiously glanced at his watch, trying to ignore the itch crawling along the back of his neck. His contact, Jia Ling Ling, also known by her undercover name as An Ming Chen, was fifteen minutes late.

A highly unusual occurrence.

He'd known Jia for the past thirty years. She'd had been married to his best friend, Tony Parker, who'd been killed twenty-five years ago in a car crash that was meant to look like an accident but had been an attempt to kill Tony and Jia. Thankfully, Jia had survived and with the help of the CIA began working in China as an undercover operative for the United States. She'd been determined to seek justice for Tony's killers and over time had provided valuable intel, especially over the past few years. Sam admired her tenacity and courage to do the right thing.

Only now she was in trouble.

Another minute ticked by. The itch grew to the proportion of a tarantula dancing along his spine as his gut knotted painfully.

Something was wrong.

He was getting too old for this. Forty-nine, going on what felt like ninety-nine. Jia knew the risks, as did he. Still, he could barely quell the panic that threatened to overwhelm him. He couldn't stand the idea of Jia's cover being blown.

He silently prayed for her safety, even as another minute passed. And another.

With no sign of Jia.

Sam drew in a deep breath. Okay, there was still time for her to show. He edged along the side of the building located a few yards off the Yangzi River. Jia was good at being undercover, working hard to use various methods of transportation to attend their designated meetings.

In a city holding 22 million people, there was no escaping the traffic, wheeled or pedestrian. Bicyclists, rickshaws, motorcycles, and cars teemed around him.

One motorcycle approached, slowing as the helmeted driver turned to look at him. Then the motorcycle swerved to the curb and abruptly stopped. "Get on!"

"Jia?" He instinctively did as she asked. The second he threw his leg over the seat, gunfire echoed around them. He ducked down as far as he could as Jia hit the gas, the motorcycle leaping forward, the rear wheel burning rubber. He managed to hang on, grasping Jia's small form as he twisted around to find the source of the gunfire.

There was nothing to see. Whoever had shot at them was long gone.

Jia wove through traffic, breaking dozens of laws with careless disregard. She turned down one small alleyway and another in a zigzag pattern. After what seemed like forever but was probably only ten minutes, she took another alley and stopped the motorcycle.

He clamored off the seat. She ripped her helmet off and hung it on the handlebar. "Hurry." Without further explanation, she grabbed his hand and began to run on foot.

"I take it your cover has been blown?" He kept pace beside her.

"We need to get out of here as quickly as possible." Her answer provided all he needed to know. No reason to run unless the leader of the Six Red Dragons faction of the Chinese mafia had uncovered her real identity. "I have a boat waiting for the first leg of our journey."

Interesting that she'd taken the time to arrange the boat ahead of time. Maybe this wasn't a simple blown-cover issue. Then again, the gunfire had come dangerously close to hitting him.

Or her. Or both of them.

"What's our final destination?" he asked as they merged into a large group of pedestrians walking along the side of the road. The best advantage to a city this large was the mass of people. Easy enough to get lost among them, even though he looked completely American complete with blond hair that stood out like a beacon amongst the dark-haired Chinese, which was why he wore a baseball cap.

Jia waited a beat before answering. "Washington, DC."

JANUARY 30 – 10:13 p.m. – Washington, DC

He stood at the window overlooking the Potomac River, sipping his scotch. Soon, very soon, he'd have what he deserved. Take back what had been robbed from him.

His infinite patience was about to pay off. People would die, there was no way around that, but he didn't feel an ounce of remorse. Frankly, he'd done his best to avoid the situation they were currently facing.

Yet it always helped to have a plan B.

His disposable phone rang. With a frown, he answered it. "What?"

"They got away."

He spun from the window so fast his expensive scotch sloshed over the rim of the glass. "How is that possible? I gave you everything you needed to know. Eliminating two people in China shouldn't be so difficult."

"We're still looking for them," his contact replied. "And China being so big and highly populated makes it easier for people to disappear too."

He clenched his jaw in anger, tightening his grip on the glass. "It's critical that you find them, understand? Allowing them to live could blow this meticulous plan right out of the water."

"Yes, sir." The hired muscle disconnected from the call.

Muttering a curse, he tossed back what was left of his scotch, reveling in the fire that burned all the way down his throat.

It hadn't been easy to get the intel on a senior CIA operative and his undercover agent. To have the opportunity wasted was not good.

He still maintained a position of power, but time was running short.

The two operatives needed to be silenced permanently, before they could derail his master plan.

JANUARY 30 – 10:28 p.m. – North Bethesda, MD

Lina huddled in the passenger seat, shivering despite the heated cushions. Watching Shu Yan die had been difficult to witness, but the recent attack at the motel room had been worse.

Far worse.

She closed her eyes, trying not to hear the never-ending barrage of bullets, smell the cordite, or feel the bits of drywall, plaster, wood, and mattress stuffing that had rained down on her.

Why, Lord? Why?

Her prayers fell into an abyss of silence.

"Lina?" Boyd's voice was surprisingly soft rather than commanding. He was clearly a man who preferred to issue orders.

She drew in a deep breath in a vain attempt to calm her nerves. "Where are we?"

"Another motel." His gaze was grim. "Are you okay?"

"How did they find us?" She wasn't okay, would never again be okay. No way could a person return to a normal life after something like this. "H-how do we know we're safe here?"

"I don't know," he answered. She supposed she should give him credit for being honest. "Jordan is going to meet us here."

"Who's Jordan?" She shivered again. "What if he's the one who hired the shooters?"

"Jordan hired me to protect you, Lina." Boyd reached out to cover her trembling fingers with his large warm hand. "I know this has been traumatic. I'm doing everything possible to keep you safe."

"Yeah, that's what you keep saying." She didn't bother to hide her doubt in his abilities. Two Chinese men had barged into their motel room with guns, shooting indiscriminately to kill them. Granted, Boyd had managed to get them out without being hurt, but she still didn't understand how they'd been found at all.

Those men must have found a way to follow them. Not just to the motel but to their specific room.

The massive amount of firepower they'd deployed had been unbelievable.

No way could this all be related to a simple DNA test.

"I know. I'm sorry."

His quiet apology knocked her off balance. She lifted her gaze from their clasped hands to meet his gaze. "I didn't mean to sound ungrateful. I know we're only alive because of you."

He glanced away as if uncomfortable with her admission. "Jordan will help us get clean phones and a new ride. They must have somehow tagged my license plate after I shot that guy following you. This vehicle has been compromised. Once we have those two things, we'll find a different place to stay."

More driving? She swallowed a groan. "Clean phone? You said they tracked your license plate not your phone."

"I'm not taking any chances." He scowled. "The shooters are smarter than I gave them credit for. Or they have incredible access to resources."

Neither scenario sounded good. She tried to calm her racing heart. "Why are they all Asian?"

"Good question. I think a big part of what's going on is related to your mother's family."

"My parents are dead. I don't see how my mother's family could be involved. Shu Yan Chen didn't have to respond to my DNA query."

"Maybe Shu Yan mentioned the DNA link to someone else." He removed his hand from hers. "Or maybe she used the site to help hide the fact that she was reaching out to you."

"She did tell me to keep our relationship quiet until we could meet in person to talk." Lina blew out a breath. "Although now that you mention it, I was a little surprised that my aunt was alive and living in the DC area. I expected her to be somewhere else, like the West Coast or even in China."

"What do you know about your mother?"

"Not much." She tried to pull up the fragments of memories. "I was four when she and my father died. She used to read me bedtime stories."

"Was she born here in the US? Or did she immigrate from China?" Boyd persisted.

"I'm not sure. My grandparents told me that my mother was an only child." She frowned. "Which wasn't true since I found Shu Yan Chen on the DNA website and our DNA comparison proved she was a sibling."

"Did your grandparents tell you how your dad and mom met?"

"At college." She shrugged. "They took my dad's death hard. I tried to get more information, but they didn't like to talk about it. In the end, it was easier to let it go. I wanted to make them happy." She searched his gaze in the darkness. "They were the only two people I had left in the world. I knew a few kids who lived in foster care, and their stories did not always end well. I'm very blessed that my grandparents took me in."

"I'm sure they were happy to raise their only grandchild," Boyd said.

"Yeah." She hesitated, thinking back to those early days. "Although I sensed they didn't approve of my mom."

"Did they say why?"

"No." She sighed. "But they weren't very interested in the Chinese culture. Anything I wanted to know I had to find out on my own."

"Not being interested in the culture doesn't mean they didn't approve of her," Boyd said. "Maybe they were just a bit ignorant."

Bright headlights swept over Boyd's face as a car pulled up next to them. Her knee-jerk reaction had her ducking down in her seat, her heart pounding so loudly she couldn't hear anything else.

Keep us safe, Lord!

Boyd reached over to touch her shoulder. "Relax, Lina. It's only Jordan."

She didn't bother to point out that having never met the man, she wouldn't know Jordan from anyone else who'd wanted to kill her. She slowly straightened, noticing with some semblance of relief that the man who emerged from the vehicle wasn't Asian but had the darker skin and features associated with the Middle East.

Was Boyd right about her mother's family being involved in this? It seemed ridiculous, but the obvious Chinese features of the men shooting at them were difficult to ignore.

"We'll swap rides," Jordan said in lieu of a greeting. "I have a satellite computer, extra cash, and two disposable phones for you too."

"Thanks." Boyd slid out from behind the wheel. "Any idea what's going on?"

"Other than someone really wants Lina dead? No clue." Jordan turned toward her. "Sorry, I should have introduced myself. Jordan Rashid, co-owner of Security Specialists, Inc."

"Lina Parker," she said with a nod. "But I guess you knew that."

"Yes." A faint smile tugged at his features. "I'm sorry things have escalated so quickly. I want to assure you that Boyd is very good at his job. He'll protect you with his life if needed."

"I know." The way he'd taken down the two Chinese shooters at the motel proved that. Not to mention the guy he'd shot earlier. "But I still don't understand why your company is involved in this. Why did you send Boyd to come after me?"

Boyd and Jordan exchanged a glance. Finally, Jordan said, "Because the FBI hired my company to investigate a possible terroristic threat originating from the Chinese mafia."

Her jaw dropped. "The Chinese mafia?"

"Have you ever heard of the Six Red Dragons?" Boyd asked.

For an instant, the image of a red dragon flashed in her mind. She frowned, trying to place the image with a memory. Had it been just one red dragon? Or more than one?

Why couldn't she remember?

"Lina?" Jordan's voice pulled her from her thoughts. "Have you heard of them?"

"No." She'd never heard anyone refer to the Six Red Dragons, but the brief image niggled at the back of her mind. "Wait a minute, are you suggesting my mother was involved with this Six Red Dragons group?"

Jordan and Boyd exchanged another knowing glance but didn't say anything.

"Impossible," she said firmly. "No way. I refuse to believe it."

"Don't get defensive, we don't know anything yet," Jordan finally said. "It's just one of many possible scenarios."

Lina scowled and crossed her arms over her chest. "My mother died twenty-five years ago. Ridiculous to think that I've become a target over something that happened that far in the past."

"You're probably right about that," Boyd agreed. He turned to Jordan. "Thanks for the vehicle and the equipment. I'll be in touch soon."

"I pray you'll both be safe," Jordan said as he took the keys from Boyd's outstretched hand.

Lina followed Boyd to Jordan's SUV. As they left the motel, she brought the image up in her mind. After a moment, the image cleared. Not one red dragon but several, all twisted together in a mural. Closing her eyes, she counted the dragon heads in her mind.

She felt hot, then cold.

Six red dragons.

JANUARY 30 – 10:59 *p.m.* – *Beijing, China*

"They escaped once again."

The news was more infuriating than last time. He stared out the window at the crowded, teeming city below. "How?"

"They have help." A hint of defensiveness crept into his contact's tone. "A man with nerves of steel and the ability to shoot a bull's-eye without trying."

Anger seethed. "I suggest you find someone to do the same then. If you don't succeed next time, don't bother calling." Without waiting for a response, he disconnected from the call.

There was little hope these idiots would complete their mission. Which left only one alternative. He needed to call the man who'd hired him to get more assistance.

His failure would bring certain death.

JANUARY 30 – 11:01 *p.m.* – *Nantong, China*

Jia slipped money from the depths of her pocket to pay the boat captain when they reached their destination. She managed to keep her badly scarred forearm out of sight, fearing it would make her memorable. Unfortunately, greed and bribery tended to work both ways, making it an advantage as well as a disadvantage.

When Hui Genghis Chen discovered she'd been listening to Manchu's conversations while under the guise of being his housekeeper, she'd known her identity had been compromised, most likely because someone had paid an astronomical price by a man in a position of high power. She'd learned of a horrible attack against the US. Getting out of China, while trusting no one, was the only way to stay alive.

Sam jumped from the boat and offered his hand. She took it, trying to ignore the zing of awareness that rippled along her scarred arm. Inappropriate to notice him as a man while fighting the Chinese mafia. Especially since she had been forced to do terrible things to survive.

"Where to?" Sam asked as they left the oceanfront.

"The airport." She glanced at him. "I assume you have your passport?"

He frowned. "Yes, but it's under my alias not my real name. If our cover is blown, it's too risky to use it."

She ground her teeth together in frustration at the delay. Not that it was his fault. "Okay, then we'll have to fly to Beijing to get you a different passport. I hope you have lots of money because it's going to cost us."

"I do." Sam's expression was grim. "Are you going to tell me exactly what happened?"

"Later. Once we're out of China." She glanced around. "We need a ride to the airport."

"I'll take care of it." Sam had skills too, and it didn't take long for him to steal a car.

She stared out the passenger side window as he drove to the airport. To be honest, she would be glad to see the last of the country of her birth. The crowds, the corruption, the oppression. Once she'd been eager to help eliminate the bad guys, but these days, it was difficult to keep track of who the bad guys were compared to the not as bad guys. Getting rid of one bad guy just meant another stepped into his place.

Or maybe she was just tired of it all. Twenty-five years was a long time. She'd given up so much, had done far more than her fair share, hadn't she? And she had the scars, internal and external, to prove it.

The idea of going to Washington, DC, filled her with anticipation. She'd traveled back and forth to the US over the years, but never staying on US soil for very long. Despite the painful memories, she preferred living in the US.

And hoped that this time she'd be able to stay.

If they survived long enough to take a trip overseas, which wasn't a given. Even her backup fake passport may not be enough to get her out of the country.

Not with the price on her head.

Jia swallowed hard when she thought of the man she'd been forced to kill. She'd only lashed out in self-defense, but in China, a woman was not allowed to kill a man for any reason. Especially not one as powerful as Hui Genghis Chen.

She had no doubt Manchu would attempt to seek revenge. Her identity in China was over, but her job for the US government wasn't.

Not yet.

Sam pulled up to the airport and got out. "We're still going to need IDs to fly, even in the same country," he said in a low voice.

"I know." She debated using her secret fake passport, but she didn't want it associated with Sam's cover name in case he'd been compromised too. "We'll take the first available flight. Hopefully, we'll be in Beijing before they realize where we went."

Sam nodded grimly. "Whatever you think is best."

The responsibility of their survival weighed heavily on her shoulders. But what else could they do? Flying all the way to the US using Sam's cover name was too much of a risk.

They entered the airport and paid for their tickets. Jia scanned the area, making sure they weren't being followed.

The getaway in the boat had been clean. Yet the moment they'd purchased their airline tickets, they'd become possible targets.

Nantong was a third of the size of Beijing, but it was still a decent-sized city. Seven million people made it easy for the bad guys to blend in.

"Our flight is starting to board, do you want to grab something to eat?"

"No." Her stomach was a churning mass of nerves. They'd only been in the airport for fifteen minutes, but it already felt like fifteen hours. The back of her neck itched in warning. "Keep a look out for anyone tailing us. I feel naked in here."

The moment the words left her mouth, she caught sight of two men walking aimlessly along the concourse. They didn't look any different from the other countrymen and women waiting for flights, but the way they walked without talking, yet trying to look nonchalant, sent a chill down her spine. She thought one of the men looked familiar, as if she may have seen him with Manchu at one point. She grasped Sam's hand, tugged him toward her, and leaned up as if to kiss him.

"There are two men at your three o'clock," she whispered as her lips brushed his cheek. "I think they're on to us."

"Impossible," Sam murmured.

"Haven't you learned yet that nothing is impossible? We need to go outside."

"But our flight . . ."

She ignored his protest, tugging his hand and steering him toward the baggage claim. As they walked, they stuck close to other groups of people to blend in. Sam was wearing his usual baseball cap, but even that wasn't enough to disguise his blond hair. They'd have to dye it black before obtaining his new passport.

Five minutes later, they were back outside in the stolen car. "Just drive," she said with a sigh. "We'll have to find another way out of here."

"Are you sure this was necessary?" he asked as they left the airport. "Those guys could have been simple businessmen."

"No, they weren't." She couldn't explain how she knew, she just did. Instincts had kept her alive these past twenty-five years, she wasn't going to doubt them now.

Less than twenty minutes from the airport, a loud explosion rocked the earth. Sam wrestled the steering wheel as he glanced around. "What was that?"

To her right, she saw the fireball in the sky and put a hand over her stomach to stop from throwing up. "That was our plane."

CHAPTER FOUR

January 30 – 11:47 p.m. – Rockville, MD

Boyd managed to secure connecting rooms at the small motel in Rockville. When he handed one key to Lina, she looked up at him in surprise. "My own room?"

"Connecting rooms, but I would ask that you open your side of the door so I can keep you safe."

"Okay." She looked dazed, and he could tell the traumatic events were catching up to her. He only hoped she didn't have a major meltdown.

Not that she didn't deserve one because the average citizen wasn't used to running from constant danger. Still, he had no clue how to handle a weeping woman. And he didn't really want to learn.

True to her word, Lina unlocked and opened her side of the connecting door. He gave her a nod. "Thank you."

"I trust you to keep me safe, Boyd."

The words stopped him cold. Lina didn't know about his failure within the Secret Service. If she did, she might not be so quick to place her faith in him.

He forced himself to turn away. "I'll get the phones

ready." Leaving his smartphone in the garbage outside the last motel had been the right thing to do, but he didn't really believe his phone had been traced.

More likely, the SUV had been tagged when he'd picked up Lina from the sidewalk. He'd killed one Chinese operative, but the other could have gotten his license plate number. With the right resources, tracking his SUV was possible.

It was sobering to discover the Six Red Dragons were this sophisticated. Jordan was right about the faction being a critical threat against the US. Somehow, Lina Parker had landed in the middle of it.

Either because of her attempt to track down her mother's family or because of her role within the Institute for Nanoscience working with biological specimens and the high-powered microscope.

Possibly both.

He rubbed the back of his neck, trying to relax. After the precautions Jordan had taken, he and Lina should be safe here. After five minutes of pacing, he forced himself to take a quick shower.

For some ridiculous reason, Lina's comment about his being smelly had stung. Although why he cared was a complete mystery. She might be beautiful, but he wasn't about to let his guard down.

Never again, he silently vowed.

The hot water and soap helped. He didn't have clean clothes but told himself to get over it. He ran a towel over his damp hair, then went out to boot up the satellite computer.

"Boyd?"

He spun around so fast he nearly sent the computer

crashing to the floor. He took a deep breath. He really, really needed to get a grip. "Yeah?"

"I—uh, was hoping I could do something to help."

He scowled. "Help what?"

"Find whoever is trying to kill me." She crossed over to join him at the table. "I hate thinking my mother's family might be involved, but it's the only thing that makes sense. Shu Yan Chen wanted to keep our meeting secret for a reason. And your idea that she used the DNA site to contact me as a way to keep our communication secret also makes sense."

"I agree, it's the most likely scenario." He eyed her thoughtfully. "You mentioned your parents were killed when you were young. What do you know about that?"

"I was told they were in a terrible car crash." Lina sat beside him, too close for his peace of mind. Unlike him, she smelled like lilacs after the rain. "My grandparents told me I was fortunate not to have been in the car with them, or I would have been killed too. The car was completely destroyed." Her green eyes held sadness. "I wish I could remember them more clearly."

"I'm sorry for your loss." He forced himself to stay focused on the case, not her green eyes or beautiful features.

Could the car crash have been rigged? If so, why come after Lina now? Just because she searched for her family on a DNA website?

As Jordan had said, it seemed like a stretch considering Lina didn't know anything.

Unless someone thought she did? But why would they assume that?

Exhaustion pulled at him, but he pushed it away. There was no time to sleep. Not until he was convinced they were safe.

"Let's see if we can find Shu Yan Chen." He typed the name into the computer's search engine. "Maybe you can tell me for sure if the woman you saw at Turtle Park was really Shu Yan."

"Okay." Lina eagerly leaned forward, again too close for comfort.

Annoyed with himself for being so keenly aware of her, he scrolled down the page, searching for Shu Yan. "How old do you think she was?"

Lina considered this question. "My mother was twenty-two when I was born, so she'd be about forty-eight years old today if she'd lived." She shrugged. "I would estimate Shu Yan to be a year or two older or younger, although keep in mind it was dark at Turtle Park, and I only got a quick glimpse at her face."

"Understood." He switched over from the general search engine to try social media sites. After another ten minutes, he sighed. "I'm not finding anyone with that name on here."

"Maybe we should try to find her through a Chinese site?"

"I can, but this computer doesn't have the Mandarin alphabet." He drummed his fingers on the table. "I'm able to read and write Mandarin, but the US computer keyboard limits my ability to type in the information."

"You read and write Mandarin?" Lina stared at him with admiration. "I'm half Chinese, and I can't do that."

"I lived in China for five years when I was in middle school and into high school." He waved a hand, downplaying his ability. "Learning and understanding the language was pretty much a necessity. And I took it as a personal challenge to learn."

"Will you teach me?"

He blinked. "I—uh, maybe at some point." Teaching her Mandarin was the last thing he wanted to do. Getting close to her on a personal level was a bad idea. He needed to keep a professional distance like he had within the Secret Service. "For now, we need to focus on who is trying to kill you and why."

"Of course." A blush tinged her cheeks. "Can I use the computer for a moment?"

"Sure." He turned the device toward her.

Lina tapped the computer keys. "It might help for you to look at the DNA site where I met Shu Yan Chen."

"Good idea." He wasn't familiar with how the sites worked, but she had mentioned communicating with Shu Yan via email. "I'd like to see those messages too."

"Of course." She typed some more, then frowned. "That's weird."

"What?" He leaned over to see what captured her attention.

"I can't find my family tree." She typed more information, then waved at the screen in exasperation. "It's gone."

A warning tingle snaked down his spine. "What's gone?"

"All of it! My family tree, my DNA results, the messages between me and Shu Yan Chen." She turned to look at him. "It's all gone. As if it had never been there."

He grimaced at this news. "Did you print out any reports?"

Lina brightened. "I did! There was one report that I printed." Then her face fell. "But I didn't make hard copies of my emails."

He'd have to call Jordan to find out what, if anything, Mack and Sun found while searching Lina's apartment.

If the Six Red Dragons were involved in this fiasco, they were covering their tracks extremely well.

Too well.

Removing a dead body and evidence from a crime scene was one thing. To hack into a DNA website and remove all evidence of a family connection was a completely different level.

And he didn't like it one bit.

JANUARY 31 – 12:13 a.m. – *Yancheng, China*

Using back roads as much as possible, Sam drove from Nantong toward Lianyungang, normally a three-and-a-half-hour drive. Thankfully, the vehicle he'd stolen had a full tank of gas, which got them this far, but even as he filled up the tank in Yancheng, he glanced frequently over his shoulder.

"I don't think we were followed," Jia said reassuringly.

"They blew up our plane, killing everyone on board." He couldn't get over the explosion they'd barely escaped. If not for Jia's keen instincts, they'd both be dead too. "Why did they do that? Surely there's going to be an investigation. Someone is going to figure out the Six Red Dragons are involved."

"Sam, you know as well as I do that the Six Red Dragons have people in high places on their payroll. The investigation will go nowhere or be whitewashed as a mechanical failure. We need to stay focused on getting out of China." Jia covered his hand with hers, and he wished he wasn't driving so he could pull her into his arms. Then she removed her hand and tugged her tunic sleeve down to cover the scar. "I know it's difficult to move forward without looking back, but you know those innocent lives that were sacrificed today are not our fault. The Six Red Dragons are responsible, and they are seeking revenge against me for spying on them, and also for killing Hui Genghis Chen."

"I thought I'd seen it all," Sam muttered, knowing she was right. He believed in God's plan and prayed for safekeeping. Yet he also knew that fighting the bad guys put them in danger every day. "The horror never stops."

"Not until Bo Dung Manchu is arrested, convicted, and put in jail," she agreed.

Bo Dung Manchu claimed to be a private Chinese businessman, but Sam knew Bo Dung was the master behind the Six Red Dragons. Jia had spent years getting close to him. And she'd fed Sam plenty of information that helped to identify those working for the mafia, both here and back in the US.

Yet Manchu was still in a position of power. So much so that he blew up a plane.

Times like this made it difficult to maintain his faith. "I fear that will never happen."

"We have to make sure it does," Jia said firmly. "I heard the conversation with my own ears. We just need to get out of China."

Easier said than done. "Beijing is several hours away. Are you sure that's the only place to get a new fake passport? What about Zhengzhou?"

"I'm sorry, but I don't have a contact there. And the passport we get for you must be perfect, or we'll get stopped along the way. My contact will provide that for us."

He sighed. "Okay, then we'll need to steal another car at some point. The longer we drive this one, the more likely we'll get stopped." Sam didn't like breaking the law, but he would do whatever was necessary to survive.

Especially to keep Jia safe.

"We're going to get through this," she said softly.

He nodded. "We have God on our side."

She glanced at him in surprise. "God?"

"Yes." He paused, then added, "Tony believed in God. I thought you did too."

"Tony did, yes, and he taught me about his faith." Jia shrugged. "I haven't given God or religion much thought over the past dozen years."

He supposed that was understandable, even preferable considering she'd been living in China as a spy providing intel to the US. Practicing a Christian faith would have only put her in more danger.

As if Jia hadn't been in enough constant danger slowly wiggling her way into the Six Red Dragons organization. As much as he'd appreciated all the intel she'd given him, he'd worried about her nonstop.

"We could return to Shanghai and take the bullet train to Beijing," Jia suggested.

"No. What if they decide to blow up the train? I prefer we keep driving. I know it will take time, but it's safer for everyone involved." He watched the traffic in the rearview mirror. They may not have been followed from the airport initially, but he didn't doubt the Six Red Dragons had watchers everywhere.

When he came upon a crowded shopping area where there were many cars, he quickly boosted another one, silently asking for forgiveness and praying that God would find a way to get them to Washington, DC, safely.

As crazy as it sounded, considering their current circumstances, he wanted a second chance at a normal life.

One that included Jia Ling Ling.

. . .

JANUARY 31 – 12:28 a.m. – Washington, DC

"I want proof they're dead." After hearing about the earlier escape, he wasn't taking his contact's word that the plane explosion had successfully silenced them. He wasn't paying for false assurances.

He was paying for cold, hard facts.

"Understood. But proof will take time. Many other lives were lost as well."

"Stupid move on your part, then, wasn't it? Why didn't you just kill them both when you had the chance?"

"I will be in touch with the proof you desire." Before he could say anything in reply, his contact disconnected from the line.

Blowing up their plane had been a stupid move. Talk about overkill! He needed to get some sleep, tomorrow was a big day, but his anger and resentment made it difficult to relax.

If they were still alive—he swallowed hard and fought a wave of panic. No, he wasn't going to buy trouble. At least, not yet.

But if his contact had failed him, the man would be silenced. Which meant he'd have to swallow his pride and speak personally to Bo Dung Manchu. Between them, they'd find another pair of assassins to do the job.

Manchu would make him pay dearly for the mistake, but that couldn't be helped. At the end of the day, he and Manchu were on the same side. He didn't care if Manchu wanted to pretend to be more important.

Once their mission was complete, he could easily replace Manchu with someone more suitable.

For now, he had little choice but to take things one step at a time.

. . .

JANUARY 31 – 12:46 a.m. – *Rockville, MD*

Despite being physically exhausted, Lina couldn't fall asleep. The massive shooting at their previous motel continued to haunt her. She'd been scared to death out at Turtle Park, but having so many bullets aimed at her and Boyd had been beyond terrifying.

Boyd had been completely cool, calm, and collected, using only two shots to take out the Asian hit men.

Not just Asian but Chinese hit men. She squeezed her eyes shut. She was proud of her Chinese heritage and had actively sought out information about her mother's life and her culture. But there was no way to ignore that some very bad men from her mother's homeland were trying to kill her.

First, they'd gotten rid of the evidence of Shu Yan Chen's murder, and then they'd eliminated her DNA results, her family tree, and the emails she'd exchanged with her mother's sister.

Completely covering their tracks. If their goal was to make her look crazy, she was very much afraid they'd succeeded. If not for Boyd and Jordan believing in her, she'd already be dead.

She drew in a deep breath and let it out slowly. Adrenaline continued to race through her bloodstream even though they'd been safe for the past hour.

A harsh laugh bubbled up in her throat. Wow, one whole hour of safety. Gee, must be time to do a happy dance.

Her mirth faded as quickly as it had come. Her emotions were all over the place. It felt good to be alive, but she couldn't say her future looked bright.

She doubted she had much of a future to look forward to at all.

The sound of a deep male voice caught her attention. She swung up and off the bed, moving silently toward the connecting doorway. Realizing Boyd was on the phone, she lightly knocked and pushed the door open.

He glanced over, his blue eyes locking on hers. The impact was enough to make her knees go weak. Giving herself a mental shake, she ignored the sensation and came in to hear the conversation.

After all, it was her life on the line. Boyd's too because he clearly took his role as her protector very seriously.

"You're sure there was no DNA report in her apartment?" Boyd asked.

She sank into the closest chair, stunned to realize that the Chinese men who'd tried so many times to kill her must have also gone to her apartment.

Boyd had made the absolutely right decision to bring her to a motel. No wonder he'd been annoyed with her arguing about it.

Then again, she doubted Boyd had truly anticipated a shootout at the O.K. Corral. For the first time, she wondered what the police had thought about what had happened there. Maybe now that police captain would believe her about Shu Yan Chen's murder.

"Hmm. That is interesting," Boyd said. "Anything else?"

She wished Boyd had the call on speaker so she could hear what Jordan was saying. What else had they discovered at her apartment? At this rate, she'd never be able to relax enough to fall asleep.

"Got it. Keep me posted." Boyd set down his phone. "Did I wake you?"

She shook her head. "No, I couldn't fall asleep. Too

many memories, too much adrenaline." She waved a hand. "Tell me what you know."

Boyd looked grim. "Sun and Mack, two members of the Security Specialists, Inc. team, went to check out your apartment. The place had been thoroughly searched, but it wasn't a sloppy job. In fact, Mack described it as meticulous. The way they knew that anyone had been there was because of the items that were clearly missing."

She paled. "Like what?"

"Your computer and any backup drives you may have had." Boyd shrugged. "Based on how they erased your DNA results and your emails, that isn't really a surprise."

Maybe not to him, but it was a shock to her. "What else?"

"No sign of the printed DNA report you mentioned."

"They may have missed it," she said. "I have a complicated filing system."

The corner of Boyd's mouth quirked in a half smile. "I know you're a brilliant scientist, Lina, but both Mack and Sun are members of the Mensa society. They're just as smart as you. They didn't miss the report because there weren't any files in your desk."

"What?" She stared at him. "No files? You're saying the Chinese men took every single file I had?"

"Exactly. It seems they weren't willing to take any chances on missing something important."

She felt as if she'd been punched in the abdomen. They'd taken her computer and every single file she owned, even the mundane ones like her credit card file, her phone bills, her mortgage information.

"Lina, I have to ask, did you ever take your work from the institute home with you?"

"Huh? Oh, no. That wasn't allowed. All the work had to

be done in the lab for security reasons." Then she abruptly straightened. "Wait. I am able to access my work email from my personal computer by using a secure network."

Boyd reached for his phone. "Jordan? We have a problem. There is a possibility that someone could use Lina's laptop to access her work email. You need to get your FBI contact to shut it down ASAP along with deactivating her credentials."

"When?" she asked when Boyd finished the call.

He raised a brow. "When what?"

"When did they break into my apartment?" she demanded. "How long have they had my computer?"

"We believe the apartment was searched during or after the Turtle Park incident," he acknowledged. "But Mack and Sun were there before the recent gunfire at the motel."

At least two hours, maybe more. She felt sick at the possibility of a security breach that would not only ensure she lost her job but would put key information into the wrong hands.

And used against the United States of America.

CHAPTER FIVE

January 31 – 1:11 a.m. – Beijing, China

"My men have failed." These were not easy words to say.

A string of curses filled his ear. "Time is running out. This problem needs to be taken care of immediately."

"I need more information to go on." He tried to deflect some of the man's anger. He understood the man had hired him to do a job, but he needed help. "Without a phone or vehicle to track, there is no way to know where they are staying."

"And what am I paying you for?" The man's voice was low and dangerous.

"Providing the muscle." He did his best to remain calm. "Without information, I'm afraid there is nothing more I can do."

"It's the middle of the night! I can't very well call the Feds at this hour to fish for sensitive information. It's going to be difficult to get anything more out of my contact anyway. Besides, I'm paying you a premium to find them!"

"I understand, and I wish very much to help."

"Wait a minute, Security Specialists, Inc."

He'd never heard of this. "Who?"

"A company that my government has used to help track terrorists in the past." There was a long pause. "I will see what I can come up with."

Before he could respond, the call was disconnected.

The abrupt silence enveloped him like a thick woolen blanket. He feared that his job of providing the muscle may no longer be needed.

Then again, why not? Using a contact in another country provided some secrecy. And he was normally very good at his job.

He told himself to wait. To be patient. The boss man would call again, and this time he would find a way to succeed.

Several minutes passed when he heard a knock on his door. A wave of trepidation hit hard, but he forced himself to cross the room to answer it.

He saw the gun a moment too late. The report was muffled by a silencer, but pain hit hard in the center of his chest, knocking him to the floor.

Then he saw nothing at all.

JANUARY 31 – 1:28 a.m. – Washington, DC

"Jordan Rashid. Yes, he must be the key." He nodded to himself, a surge of anticipation soothing his previous anger. The idiot who'd failed him twice now had already died for his sins.

He logged into his computer with a renewed sense of urgency. Why hadn't he thought of this before? Of course, the Feds would have called for reinforcements. He was high enough in rank to know that the US government was constantly under attack. After all, that's exactly what he'd been counting on.

Thankfully, he had access to information that others didn't. Doing so was a risk as security had been tightened significantly over the past year since the last failed attempt to assassinate the President of the United States. But he had secretly obtained inside access. The trail would not lead to him. At least, not right away.

His plan must succeed. It had been set up years ago and was finally about to come to fruition.

They only had one chance to get this done. If this opportunity was blown, there wouldn't be another. At least, not with the precision that this current plan had been created.

Yes, he thought as he logged into the secure site, it was time to place all his cards on the table.

The end result would be well worth it.

JANUARY 31 – 1:54 a.m. – Lianyungang, China

Jia couldn't ignore the sense of urgency. This decision to drive to Beijing hadn't been the smart move. The trip would take too long. They were fortunate enough to have made good time after escaping the plane explosion.

But they needed another plan ASAP.

"Sam, we need to either take the bullet train to Beijing or find a fast boat." Not a small fishing boat like the one they'd used to escape earlier, but something sleek and fast. The coastline wasn't straight; they'd have to go out of their way to get around the point. Not to mention, Beijing wasn't located on the water. After getting off the boat, they'd still need a ride into the city. "We cannot waste any more time."

Sam looked as if he wanted to argue but then slowly nodded. "You're right. Which do you think is best?"

"The train is easier. Finding a suitable boat will take too long." The freedom of using a watercraft was preferable over the railway, but they absolutely needed to get out of China. And for that, Sam needed a new passport.

One with a name that wouldn't be traced back to either of them.

Time was of the essence. Jia glanced at her watch. "We must hurry. The bullet train will be leaving for Beijing shortly."

"Let's go then." Sam drove straight for the train station. They quickly ditched the stolen vehicle, then boarded the train with barely five minutes to go prior to its departure. If she was a believer, like Tony, she'd have thought God might have been guiding them.

But she wasn't convinced. So much had happened in the years since she'd lost her husband and had given up her daughter that she couldn't find solace in her husband's ever-enduring faith. The deep ragged scar along her arm was only part of what she'd suffered.

No time to dwell on the past. The good news about the bullet train was that they could simply pay without showing identification. Jia's nerves remained on edge until the train began moving, then quickly picked up speed as this was a direct connection between the two cities. There were no scheduled stops along the way.

"It seems as if we're finally safe, at least for now," Sam murmured. "But we're still several hours from Beijing, even via the high-speed rail."

"I know." She tried to relax back against the seat. Soon the ticket master would stop by, requesting their tickets. Which, of course, they didn't have. But she knew from experience that doubling the fee and using cash would be enough to smooth things over.

No ticket required.

Sure enough, doubling their fares worked. Jia offered the money with her left hand, keeping the scar on her right arm well hidden. The ticket master slipped the money into his pocket. He moved on to the next group of passengers without saying a word.

It never failed to amaze her that greed and corruption could work both ways.

"When we reach Beijing, we'll need to dye your hair prior to finding my contact to obtain a new passport." She kept her voice low to prevent the nearby passengers from overhearing. "Black hair will allow you to blend in with the crowd."

"It will help some," he acknowledged. "Although I'm still taller than most of the Chinese population."

"Your features aren't Asian either," she agreed. Personally, she thought Sam to be incredibly handsome with his light hair and pale gray eyes.

Not that she had any business allowing his looks to distract her from their mission. Sam had been a good friend for a long time. Nothing more.

Jia was under no illusions that getting to the US would solve their problems. Manchu would never rest until she paid for killing his second-in-command. And for betraying his trust.

She'd spent years and years infiltrating the Six Red Dragons faction of the Chinese mafia, inching her way closer and closer to the inner circle of the leaders in charge. She'd witnessed enough to know Manchu was an evil, ruthless man.

Bringing him to justice would be the defining point of

her entire career. Of her entire life's work. Taking on this role to avenge Tony's death had meant giving up everything, even her own flesh and blood, to get to this point.

They were so close.

She and Sam needed to succeed in this endeavor, even if that meant sacrificing their lives to accomplish their mission.

JANUARY 31 – 2:27 *a.m.* – *Rockville, MD*

Boyd awoke with a start, every sense on alert. During his two deployments as a marine, he'd survived by following his instincts. He didn't dare ignore them now.

Jackknifing off the bed, he reached for his weapon and moved silently to the motel window. Noises outside a motel weren't uncommon, but it was the middle of the night, and he wasn't about to take any chances.

Not when Lina was smack in the center of a killer's crosshairs.

He'd parked Jordan's SUV off to the right side of Lina's room, which was to his left. He found himself second-guessing that decision now. Boyd peered through the narrow opening between the heavy curtains and scanned the parking lot.

Everything looked quiet. Too quiet.

Something was off. He wasn't sure how or why, but he firmly believed they needed to take action. He moved away from the window and took a moment to pack up the satellite computer, slinging the bag over his shoulder. Then he silently crept into Lina's room. She was stretched out on the bed, her beautiful face peaceful in sleep. When he lightly touched her shoulder, she bolted upright, glancing wildly around.

"Shh," he warned.

"What's going on?" To her credit, she didn't scream, cry, or whine. She bent over to slide her feet into her thick-soled boots, then stood. She was so close her lilac scent surrounded him. He had to stop himself from pulling her into his arms.

Why was he so hyperaware of Lina? The sensation was irritating. This wasn't the time or the place for this nonsense. Staying focused wasn't easy, but he managed to grasp her hand and guide her toward the door. "We're getting out of here."

"Why?" She still kept her voice low, but her stubborn streak was back as she dug in her heels, refusing to budge. "I barely got any sleep."

She'd gotten more than he had, but he didn't bother to point that out. A slight movement past Lina's window caught his eye. Reacting instinctively, he pulled her across the threshold of their connecting rooms and quickly closed and locked the door.

The silence was deafening, but he knew someone was out there.

Peering through his window, he saw two Chinese men standing on either side of Lina's door. His gut clenched when he saw they were both holding guns. The guy closest to him also held something small in his right hand. It took a moment for the object to register in Boyd's mind.

A grenade!

He pulled Lina closer and whispered in her ear. "Stay calm and quiet. We'll have a chance to get out of here the instant they make their move."

This time, she simply nodded, her green eyes wide with fear.

Boyd eased the door open just enough so he could see

them. Thankfully, their attention was centered on Lina's room. The man across from the guy holding the grenade used a key to unlock Lina's door. Boyd wondered how they'd obtained the key and hoped the motel lobby manager wasn't lying dead behind the counter. As the Chinese man pushed the door open, the grenade guy stepped forward. In a smooth motion, the Chinese man pulled the pin and launched the grenade through the doorway. Then he and his partner backed away.

Now! Boyd quickly opened the door the rest of the way and aimed his weapon at the two men. He pulled the trigger twice, easily nailing both assassins where they stood. Before they hit the ground, he burst out of the motel, dragging Lina with him.

Go! Go! Go! His inner mind screamed. There was no time to waste! They had to move! They needed to get away from this motel before the grenade . . .

Kaboom!

The explosion shattered the motel room windows and blew out the door, which slammed into the SUV Jordan had provided them, smashing the windshield into a giant spiderweb of broken glass. The force of the blast knocked them onto their backsides. Boyd landed awkwardly on the satellite computer he'd been carrying over his shoulder.

Pain ricocheted through him, but he ignored it with the ease of long practice. It was minimal compared to what he'd experienced while being deployed to Afghanistan. Without hesitation, he rolled to his feet and reached down to help Lina up.

"Are you okay?" He noticed she appeared to be in pain too. "Can you walk?"

"I'll manage." Her voice was faint, but there was a flash of steely determination in her eyes.

"Good. We need to hurry." He led the way down and around the back of the motel. He raked his gaze over the area, searching for a way out. Then he spotted the black SUV that was parked in the corner. The vehicle had been backed in as if to enable a quick getaway.

Did it belong to the two Chinese men? He veered over toward the vehicle, Lina coming along beside him. Looking inside, he noticed the interior was meticulously clean. He felt certain it belonged to the Chinese assassins.

The screech of first responder sirens filled the air. The cops would be swarming the area around the motel any second. He swallowed a surge of frustration. There was no time to go back to the two dead men to grab the key. Still, he took a moment to memorize the license plate, then reached for Lina's hand.

"We'll have to go on foot." He didn't have a firm destination in mind, other than to get away from the motel and the resulting police and fire response.

Lina gave a weary nod. He tried to set a reasonable pace, sweeping his gaze around for any sign of another threat. At some point, the people coming for them would increase their manpower. Instead of sending a two-man team, they'd up the ante to four or six men. And if there had been two more men stationed along the perimeter, he and Lina probably wouldn't have escaped at all.

The grim realization hit hard.

Keeping Lina safe was proving to be more difficult than being assigned to the First Lady's detail. This was the fourth attempt to kill her in less than five hours. At this point, they'd be lucky to be alive come morning.

No. He would not fail Lina Parker.

He continued guiding her for several blocks, taking a zigzag pattern to avoid anyone following. At this hour of the morning there weren't many people out and about, so thankfully, they didn't come across anyone. After they'd been on the run for about fifteen minutes, Lina stumbled, falling against him.

He easily caught her, relishing the opportunity to hold her close. "What's wrong? Are you injured?"

"A little. My hip is killing me." She winced and rubbed her right side. "When that bomb went off, I landed hard."

A grenade was similar to a bomb, so there was no point in correcting her assumption. "We need to go a little farther yet." The sirens were too loud and too close for his peace of mind. "I'll carry you."

"No, I'll walk." She pulled away from his embrace and stepped forward, moving with a limp. He hated knowing she was in pain, but it was more important to stay alive. She took a few steps before asking, "Why can't we call Jordan? I'm sure he'd be willing to bring us another vehicle."

"We'll do that later." He slid his arm around her waist. "Lean on me."

She rested against him as they continued walking. Their pace was agonizingly slow, but he told himself to get over it. Moving at all was better than remaining stagnant. Yet sooner or later, he'd have to call for backup.

Yet he wasn't convinced contacting Jordan was the right decision. He'd parked Jordan's replacement SUV near Lina's motel room, and that was the same room the two Chinese men had gone to. They'd flanked the door and tossed the grenade inside, no doubt expecting to kill her outright. A different approach after the failed attempt to shoot at them like ducks in a pond at the previous motel room.

Securing connecting rooms had saved their lives.

Yet how had they been found? Especially so quickly?

The only answer he could come up with was that Jordan's SUV had been compromised. Somehow, the vehicle had been traced, enabling them to be tracked to the motel.

While he didn't know Jordan or Sloan very well, he couldn't imagine either man had turned traitor. Not after the way they'd saved the country from terrorism, not just once but on three separate occurrences. They'd put their lives on the line over and over again.

Besides, if they were traitors, why bother to hire him to protect Lina in the first place? No, he knew Security Specialists, Inc. was a high-powered and highly secure company. He didn't believe Jordan, Diana, Sloan, Natalia, Mack, or Sun were the leak.

But it could be that someone higher up in the food chain knew Jordan's company was involved in protecting Lina. After all, there was still a potential link between Shu Yan Chen's murder and the Chinese mafia terrorist threat. Maybe those in charge of the Six Red Dragons were aware of the relationship between Security Specialists, Inc. and the US government.

Jordan had mentioned talking to Clarence Yates, the Director of the FBI. Maybe he or someone close to him had turned traitor.

If so, calling Jordan wouldn't help their situation. Now that they were safe, he was secretly stunned at how close those men had gotten. If he hadn't woken up, Lina would already be dead.

Boyd took his role of protecting Lina very personally. He couldn't fail her the way he'd failed in protecting the president's wife.

He couldn't help but wonder if he and Lina would be better off staying completely on their own.

. . .

JANUARY 31 – 3:13 a.m. – *Richmond, VA*

Where was she?

Seventeen-year-old Kali blinked, trying to see through the darkness. Her mouth was horribly dry, and her head throbbed painfully. She didn't drink or do drugs, but she felt the way some of her friends had described as being hungover.

Kali pushed herself upright, frowning as she realized she was lying on a bed. Panic hit hard, and she quickly patted herself, somewhat reassured to find she was still dressed in her high school uniform. Hopefully, that meant no one had tried to sexually assault her.

Her stomach churned with fear and worry. She didn't understand what was going on. Why was it so dark? What time was it? She couldn't seem to get her bearings.

When she moved her legs, she realized there was something hard around her ankle. The darkness was so complete she couldn't see what it was. She bent over and used her fingers to feel the area.

A cold metal band encircled her ankle.

She shivered and squelched a surge of panic. Why was she here? Why was she chained to a bed?

Where was she?

"Help," she croaked through her desert-dry throat. She desperately wanted a glass of water. Her queasy stomach rebelled against the thought of food, but water. She instinctively knew that she needed fluids in order to flush whatever drugs she'd been given out of her bloodstream.

She put a hand to her head, trying to think. The last thing she remembered was leaving her last class and heading to the pep rally for the upcoming basketball game.

She was science partners with Kevin Larson, who played center for the team. Her parents weren't keen on her dating, but she'd felt certain Kevin was going to ask her to prom.

But she didn't remember the pep rally.

Or anything else either. There was a blank fog where her memory should be. She recalled that she was walking down the hallway past the restrooms, but nothing after that. She frowned. Wait a minute, where was her detail? The Secret Service shadowed her every move. Surely, the agents assigned to her have noticed she'd been taken.

Kidnapped.

The reality of her situation sank deep. There was no other explanation. She'd been kidnapped to use as leverage against her father, the most powerful man in the country.

"Help me!" Her second cry went unanswered.

Shivering in the darkness, Kali collapsed back onto the bed, tears streaming down her cheeks. How long would her kidnappers keep her here?

Would they come to release her after whatever ransom they'd demanded had been paid?

Or would they return to silence her for good?

CHAPTER SIX

January 31 – 3:40 a.m. – Bullet train heading to Beijing, China

Nerves on edge, Sam scanned the passengers seated around them. It was disconcerting to have several of them move from one train car to the next as if changing seats would make their ride more comfortable.

Maybe he was being paranoid, but he didn't trust anyone seated around them. What was to prevent one of them from leaping out in an attempt to stab them with a knife or shoot them with a gun? The Six Red Dragons had support from Chinese leaders in high places; their reach was far and wide.

He scanned the interior of their train car, looking for cameras. There wasn't anything obvious, but that didn't mean they didn't exist.

"Relax," Jia murmured. "We'll be in Beijing before you know it."

Sam drew in a deep breath, then slowly exhaled. She was right. They were already over ninety minutes into their five-hour trip.

The doors between their train car and the one in front of them opened. Two young Chinese men, roughly in their late twenties, came through, walking slowly down the narrow aisle. Sam straightened in his seat, his muscles tense as he watched them approach. The pair did not look him directly in the eyes, but that was not unusual in the Chinese culture. Keeping your gaze lowered, especially when approaching your elders, was a sign of respect.

Even as that thought registered, though, one of the two young Chinese men lifted his head and boldly locked his gaze on Sam. The simple gesture told him these two men were not casual train passengers.

Jia must have noticed as well because she rose from her seat and moved in front of him toward the aisle. He tried to hold her back, but it was too late.

The Chinese man who'd arrogantly met his gaze moved toward Jia. She responded swiftly, turning and thrusting with her hand. Somehow, she'd snatched the knife from his hand and turned it against her attacker.

The arrogant one let out a hiss as the tip of the blade pierced his skin. Jia turned toward the second man, who was eyeing her warily.

She nodded at him. "Stay back or I will defend myself to the death. I will kill you both without hesitation," she said in fluent Mandarin. Then she repeated the sentence in several other Chinese dialects.

The other passengers murmured amongst themselves, but no one came forward to interfere in the altercation.

The arrogant one glared at her but kept his distance. Seconds later, the two Chinese men turned and retreated to the train car they'd come from. The one she'd almost stabbed had kept his hand over his puncture wound.

Stunned, he drew Jia down into her seat. "I don't understand," he whispered. "Why didn't they continue attacking?"

"I believe they retreated to save face," she said with a shrug. "Better to let us go than to risk losing the fight to a woman."

"They're not part of the Six Red Dragons?" It was inconceivable that the Chinese mafia would send low-level manpower to take him and Jia out of service.

"I don't think so," Jia murmured. "I believe they noticed you as an American and decided to steal from us. They were young and stupid. I was able to take their knife easily enough. And they know I could have easily killed them."

Great. Just what they needed, another target on their backs. "Unbelievable."

"It's okay," Jia assured him. She rested her hand on his arm. "I don't believe they will cause us any more trouble."

He wasn't sure that was true, but what could he do? This particular high-speed train didn't have any scheduled stops. Looking out the windows, he could see they were crossing some desolate countryside. China was the most highly populated country in the world, but the Chinese citizens flocked to the cities to live and work. Few remained in the rural areas farming rice and other produce.

Several of the passengers around them sent furtive glances their way as if trying to figure out who they were. Sam rubbed his hands over his face. Their attempt to fly under the radar of Manchu's men wasn't working very well. If questioned, these people around them would readily identify them.

He hoped that this little altercation wouldn't cause Manchu's men to be waiting for them at the central train station in Beijing.

How long could they survive before the bad guys found and killed them?

JANUARY 31 – 3:50 a.m. – *Rockville, MD*

Lina's hip screamed in agony as she leaned against Boyd. They'd been walking for what seemed like forever. She wanted to beg him to stop, but the memory of the explosion of her room made her grit her teeth and push on.

It was difficult for her to wrap her mind around the series of events. There had been so many attempts to kill her.

And she didn't understand how they kept finding them. Especially at a small motel in a city outside Washington, DC.

"We'll rest at the train station up ahead," Boyd said as if reading her mind. "Try to hang on for a little longer."

"Okay." She focused her gaze on their destination. She highly doubted the Metro ran all night, at least it didn't in DC, but she'd be thankful for the opportunity to sit and rest. For the past thirty minutes, she'd wondered if Boyd had planned for them to walk all the way back to the city.

They hobbled to the train station. She practically collapsed onto the closest bench, closing her eyes in relief. Boyd dropped down beside her, setting the computer bag on the ground between his feet before pulling her against him.

"How bad is it?" he asked, his voice a deep rumble near her ear.

"I'm fine." She wasn't really, but whining wouldn't make her hip feel any better. And clearly, they'd needed to get far away from the two dead Chinese men at the motel. "Tell me again why you haven't called Jordan?"

Boyd was silent for a long moment. She angled her head

up to look at him, not surprised to note he was scanning the area. Finally, he said, "I want you to know I trust Jordan and his partner Sloan. They've done great things for our country, but I also believe the SUV Jordan swapped with us was somehow tracked to that motel. I was an idiot to park it near your door. The fact that the two men flanked your room and tossed the grenade inside meant they knew you were in there."

She swallowed hard, feeling sick. "If that's true, why would you continue to trust Jordan and Sloan? Anyone can turn traitor for the right price."

"Not those two," he said firmly. "They interceded and prevented three different terrorist threats against our country at great personal risk to themselves and their loved ones. Their security company is very well regarded at the highest level of our government, the president himself has praised Jordan and Sloan for the work they've done to protect him and those around him."

The president? She couldn't help being impressed. "Okay, but not talking to Jordan won't help us figure out how we were found."

"I know." His chest rose and fell on a deep sigh. She rested her head in the hollow of his shoulder, wishing she could stay there until the bad guys were caught and sent to jail. "It could be that whoever is behind these attacks assumed Security Specialists, Inc. had been hired to keep you safe. I believe the SUV is listed as belonging to the company, which means it could have been tracked to the motel."

She blanched. "Is that really possible?"

"Anything is possible," Boyd responded grimly. "Especially if someone very high up in the government is involved in this."

"Someone in our government?" she echoed. "You mean someone close to the president is planning to commit treason?"

"Yeah," Boyd said. "That's the only thing that makes sense. Your average bad guy wouldn't have access to track and find a vehicle listed as being owned by Jordan's company that quickly."

She lifted her head to look at him. "All the more reason we should call Jordan. They must be working other cases, right? He needs to know that it's likely his company has been compromised by someone with high-level security access."

"I will." Boyd stared deeply into her eyes for a long minute. "I just want to be in a different location when I make the call. Just in case the Rockville police are looking for us."

"Looking for us? Oh, because of the two dead guys."

"Yeah, that." Boyd rubbed the back of his neck. "Pretty sure we're going to be blamed not just for killing two men but for the explosion and any other crimes that were committed. They had a key, which makes me think they hurt the guy at the front desk too." The flash of guilt in his eyes tugged at her heart.

"You killed them in self-defense," she whispered. She reached up to lightly cup his face. "I owe you another debt of gratitude for saving my life, Boyd. You're truly amazing."

He didn't answer, but his intense gaze spoke volumes. He wasn't interested in her gratitude. His gaze dropped to her mouth in a way that convinced her he wanted something different.

She was exhausted, hungry, and sore, but she'd never been so attracted to a man the way she was right this minute. They were connected deep down where it counted.

Without allowing herself a chance to think it through, she leaned forward and kissed him.

Their lips brushed, then clung. For a moment, he held himself back, but then suddenly he was kissing her with a banked desire she'd never experienced. He crushed her close, and she reveled in the strength and gentleness of his arms.

Car headlights washed over them. Boyd abruptly broke off the kiss and jumped to his feet, turning to watch as the vehicle passed by. "We should keep walking," he said as if the brief embrace had never happened.

She tried to gather her scattered thoughts. "But—the train station opens at four fifty, with the first train running at five."

He glanced down at her, then looked away. "We can't sit here for that length of time. We'll need to leave for a while, then come back."

She grimaced but nodded. "Can we find something to eat? I'm hungry."

"Sure." He held out his hand to help her up. She almost moaned as her hip throbbed painfully. "Lean on me."

She did as he suggested, but despite his support, the easy camaraderie between them had disappeared. Her impulsive kiss had changed things between them and not in a good way. Lina inwardly sighed. Part of her wished she hadn't kissed him, but deep down, she wanted nothing more than to kiss him again. Boyd's courage, his willingness to do whatever was necessary to keep her safe, made him extremely attractive.

Yet she'd read him wrong. It was clear he didn't reciprocate her feelings.

Which was okay because she could understand why a

man of action like Boyd wouldn't be interested in a nerdy scientist.

Once this nightmare was over, she doubted she'd ever see him again.

JANUARY 31 – 4:13 *a.m. – Washington, DC*

He paced the length of his suite, unable to relax or get some badly needed sleep.

No response from his teams was not good. They should have contacted him by now, letting him know the deed was done.

How could it be so difficult to kill two people? Especially as they'd had the element of surprise on their side.

He paid for competence, not for idiots who couldn't seem to do anything right.

Why hadn't he heard from them?

Spinning away from his view of the Potomac, he grabbed the remote and turned on the television. He flipped to the news, hoping to find the information he desperately needed.

The meteorologist droned on about the weather for a full five minutes before the news anchors took over.

"We have breaking news out of Rockville, Maryland," the anchor said. "We have a report about an explosion in a small motel. We know that at least two men have been declared dead, although the police have not yet released their names. We will continue to bring you details as we learn more from the active crime scene."

Two men? Not a man and a woman?

No! He threw the remote against the wall, smashing it into dozens of tiny pieces. The woman and her protector were still alive!

They'd failed again!

JANUARY 31 – 4:32 *a.m.* – *Rockville, MD*

Boyd eyed the restaurant as they approached. Lights were on and staff were moving around inside, indicating it was open for business. For that he was immensely grateful.

Every cell in his body was hyperaware of Lina. Their explosive kiss had changed everything.

He'd never experienced such an instant attraction to a woman. He couldn't get her sweet, enticing taste out of his head. Couldn't forget how perfect she'd felt in his arms.

And couldn't think of anything but kissing her again.

No way. Not happening. Allowing her to distract him from his job was unacceptable. He couldn't adequately protect her if he was emotionally involved. It was the first rule the Secret Service had drummed into him. One of the reasons they gave nicknames to their protectees was to keep them at an emotional distance.

The president's nickname had been Eagle, and the First Lady had been Peacock, their teenage daughter had been Orchid. The names weren't meant to be degrading but a way to talk about the presidential family amongst those assigned to their protective detail.

In his mind, he'd tried to assign Lina the code name Lilac.

Enough. Stay focused. Boyd pulled himself together and steered Lina a.k.a. Lilac toward the restaurant. She hadn't uttered a single complaint, but he could tell by how heavily she was leaning on him that she was still in a lot of pain.

Her injury complicated things. Not that they weren't complicated enough already.

Inside the restaurant, there was a wide variety of open tables to choose from. He picked a location where he could sit with his back was against the wall and both the main entrance and the kitchen doorway were both in his line of sight. He slid in first, then set the satellite computer on the seat beside him.

Lina dropped into the other side of the booth with a low moan. "It feels so good to sit down."

He grimaced. "I'm sorry we had to walk for so long. I'm sure your hip is killing you."

"Not your fault." She drew the plastic menu toward her. "I'll be fine. But for some reason, I'm really hungry."

"All that adrenaline rushing through your bloodstream can have that effect." He glanced over to the server who was coming toward them carrying two coffee mugs and a full pot.

"Coffee?"

"Yes, please," he and Lina said at the exact same time.

Lina let out a small laugh. He smiled because she was so much more beautiful when she laughed.

Then his mirth faded as he realized she didn't deserve to be in this horrible situation. To be chased from one city to the next by the Chinese mafia. She was innocent, her only crime had been to try to find her mother's side of the family.

Now it seemed these assassins wouldn't stop until she was dead. Even if that meant taking him out too.

He couldn't, wouldn't let that happen.

Their server took their order, then returned with more coffee. When they were alone again, he braced his elbows on the table and leaned forward. "When we're finished eating, we'll head back to the Metro station."

She winced. "I was hoping you'd call Jordan. I figured

that if you called him now, he'd be able to get here by the time we're finished eating."

He hesitated, knowing her hip was really hurting her. Should he do that? Would it matter if they waited here for Jordan compared to arranging a meeting in another location, like the next Metro stop?

"Okay, I'll call him now." He pulled out his phone and dialed Jordan. His new boss answered on the second ring.

"Rashid," he answered sleepily.

"We were found at the motel, narrowly escaped being blown up by a hand grenade." Boyd got straight to the point. "Lina injured her hip as a result of the blast, but we managed to get away. We're on foot, the SUV you loaned us is still at the motel with a shattered windshield."

"How in the world did that happen?" Jordan demanded, seemingly wide awake now. "You and Lina should have been safe there."

"Good question." Boyd hoped Jordan would be able to figure out the possible connection to his company on his own. As the newest employee, he didn't relish pointing fingers at his boss's lack of subterfuge.

"Wait a minute. You think they tracked the SUV?" Jordan asked.

"I'm afraid so."

"I didn't leak the information, and neither did anyone else on my team," Jordan said hotly.

"I never thought you did, but someone might assume that your company would hire a guy like me to keep Lina safe."

There was a long silence. "Clarence Yates hired us for this job, and I've trusted him with my life over the past two years. No way did he blow your cover."

"Again, I didn't suggest that. But what if someone found out the SUV was owned by Security Specialists, Inc.?"

Jordan whistled. "It would take significant security access to get that information and to track it to a motel in Rockville."

"It's the only explanation," Boyd insisted. "Oh, and by the way, we need a lift."

"I'll be there as soon as possible." Jordan paused for a moment, then added, "I'll make sure the next vehicle has no ties to my company or to any of our names."

"Thanks." Boyd disconnected from the call and slipped the phone back into his pocket, glancing at Lina who was watching him closely. "Jordan is on his way."

"I'm glad." She offered a slight smile. "I'm sorry to slow you down."

"No need to be sorry." He scowled. "It's my job to keep you safe."

Her smile faded, and she stared down at her coffee for a moment. "I'm beginning to wonder if I'll ever be safe again."

Her words broke his heart. He reached across the table to take her hand. "You will be safe, Lina. We'll get through this, together."

"I hope so." She didn't look convinced.

Their server arrived with their meals. He'd ordered a meat lovers omelet, while Lina had requested two eggs over easy with toast and fruit. He picked up his fork to dive in when he noticed she'd folded her hands together and bowed her head. It took a second to realize she was praying.

"Dear Lord, please continue to keep us safe in Your care," she whispered. "Guide us and help us find those responsible for these terrible crimes. Also bless this food we are about to eat. Amen."

He sat frozen until she was finished, then cut into his food. Feeling her curious gaze, he looked at her. "What?"

"You don't believe in God?"

He shrugged. "My parents took me to church when I was young, but I drifted away from religion when I lived in China. Although several of my marine buddies were believers." He remembered being impressed by their faith.

"I'm sorry to hear that, Boyd, because I truly believe the only reason we've gotten this far without being seriously hurt is thanks to God's grace in protecting us. I've been praying ever since Shu Yan Chen was murdered at Turtle Park. And look at how well we've managed to escape one crisis after another."

He wanted to dismiss her claim, but then he thought about that moment in the motel room when he'd woken up, sensing something was wrong.

At first, he'd assumed his finely honed instincts had alerted him to the danger. But thinking back, the two Chinese men had left their SUV hidden behind the motel and hadn't made a sound.

Was Lina right? Had God awoken him in time to avoid being killed?

It was an intriguing thought. If not for the close call, he probably wouldn't be so quick to believe. Yet there was no denying that he'd woken just in the nick of time.

Hopefully, for Lina's sake, God would continue guiding them. At this point, he'd take all the help he could get.

And then some.

CHAPTER SEVEN

January 31 – 4:53 a.m. – Rockville, MD

Lina dug into her meal, a little sad to learn Boyd didn't believe in God. The casual, emotionless way he spoke of his parents gave her the impression he wasn't very close to them. She was curious about his background, his family. His life.

Maybe because of the incredible kiss that he'd abruptly ended. The one she couldn't seem to get out of her mind, no matter how hard she tried.

After a few minutes of eating in silence, she asked, "What happened with the Secret Service?"

Boyd's gaze shot to hers. "Why? Does it matter?"

Clearly, it was a touchy subject. Still, she didn't back down. "Not really, I've already told you I trust you to keep me safe. You've proven yourself more than capable of doing that. But it occurs to me that I don't know anything about you. You could be married, engaged, have children, or . . ."

"I'm not married, engaged, or have children," he swiftly interrupted. "And you need to understand I'm not interested in any of those things. I'm here because I have a job to do. My only goal is to keep you safe."

She eyed him curiously over the rim of her coffee cup, wondering who he was trying to convince. Her? Or himself? She suspected the latter but let that subject go. "You mentioned living in China for five years, was that with your parents?"

"Only with my father." He took another bite of his omelet.

"I'm sorry for your loss."

He sighed and glared at her. "What loss? My parents divorced. They fought over me like I was some shiny object but then couldn't wait to get rid of me. I bounced between them like a ping-pong ball, and frankly, they reveled in arguing over me."

That sounded worse than what she'd been through. "I'm sorry to hear that, Boyd. But I don't understand how you ended up living in China."

He stared at her as if debating how much of his life to reveal. Finally, he said, "My father had business in China, and when my mother announced she was getting remarried, he took me with him overseas. It didn't take long for him to find a beautiful Chinese woman to marry. He tried to send me back to the US; my mother resisted having me intrude on her new marriage. I was a third wheel, for both my parents. As soon as I was eighteen and finished high school, I joined the marines. From there, I did several tours in Iraq and Afghanistan, then came home and went to college. The moment I finished my degree I was recruited to join the Secret Service."

She waited for him to expound on that a bit, but he didn't. "I take it you don't see either sets of parents very much?"

"No." His tone didn't invite further questions. When his phone rang, he pounced on it with relief. "Hey, Jordan. Tell me something good."

She couldn't hear the other end of the conversation, but soon Boyd nodded.

"Okay, twenty minutes works. See you then." He set the phone aside and continued eating.

Lina suppressed a sigh. Boyd was all business, and she couldn't blame him. The poor guy had gone above and beyond the call of duty in keeping her safe. In fact, it was truly horrifying that he'd been forced to kill so many people, even if it was in self-defense.

The attraction she felt toward him wasn't his problem. She'd have to find a way to get over it. The way he'd mentioned his father marrying a Chinese woman made her believe even more so that he wasn't interested. Maybe if she didn't look Chinese, things would be different. Yet as she eyed him across the table, taking in his dark hair, his muscular build, and his blue eyes, she wished for something more.

Stupid to even think like that, considering she had the Six Red Dragons faction of the Chinese mafia gunning for her.

Wait a minute. She mentally smacked herself in the head at the fact that she'd never told him what she'd remembered. "Uh, Boyd?"

"Yeah?" he answered between bites.

"I—think you might be right."

"I'm always right," he said, the corner of his mouth tipping up into a tiny smile.

She couldn't help grinning in response, even as she rolled her eyes. "Highly doubtful, except in this case. You were right about my mother."

Now she had his attention. "What about her?"

She licked her suddenly dry lips. "I remember seeing a large mural of red dragons. Their bodies looked more like snakes or serpents, but their heads were definitely dragons." She paused, then added, "And I'm fairly certain there were six of them."

Boyd's gaze clung to hers as he lowered his fork to his plate. "Do you remember where you were when you saw them?"

"No. You have to understand I was only four years old when I lost my parents." She toyed with her toast. "But I must have seen the mural because of my mother, right? I mean, who else would have taken me to see something like that?"

"I don't know," Boyd admitted. "I'd like you to keep going back to that memory, see if you can't bring out more details. Maybe you'll remember something that will give us a clue as to where this mural is located."

"I'll try." She didn't think there was anything else in her mind. Even remembering the six red dragons had been a minor miracle. "I had no idea that my mother's family was involved with them. Maybe if I'd known, I wouldn't have tried to find out about her family."

His gaze turned gentle. "It's not your fault, Lina. As you said, you were four years old when they were killed. You're not responsible for anything that happened back then. Thanks for sharing that information with me. I'll let Jordan know when he comes to pick us up."

She nodded and took a bite of her toast. Her earlier hunger had vanished. For the first time, she understood why her grandparents hadn't encouraged her to learn about the Chinese culture.

It was possible her mother's involvement in the Six Red Dragons had gotten both of her parents killed.

Leaving her an orphan.

She thought again of her aunt, Shu Yan Chen. The woman must have risked reaching out to Lina to warn her of the danger. It would explain why Shu Yan had been murdered.

Yet she didn't understand why she had become a target because she didn't know anything. A simple memory of a mural containing six red dragons wasn't enough to kill all these people.

Was it?

Or was there even something more sinister going on?

Lina felt her strength and resolve slipping to the point she feared she'd break down sobbing. So much death over what? Money? Power? Fame?

She closed her eyes and reverently prayed.

Dear Lord, please keep us strong and safe in Your care as we find those responsible for killing so many innocent people. Amen.

JANUARY 31 – 5:02 a.m. - Washington, DC

Clarence Yates woke when his phone shrilled in his ear. Muttering under his breath, he reached for the device. When he saw Jordan's name on the screen, he quickly answered. "Yates."

"We have a problem," Jordan said tersely.

"We have many problems." Yates rubbed a hand over his balding head. He was getting too old for this. "Which one in particular?"

"Someone traced my Security Specialists, Inc. SUV to the motel where Boyd had stashed Lina. They managed to escape without sustaining serious injury but left two dead bodies and a blown-up motel room behind. Oh, and let's not forget the dead motel front desk guy, likely taken out by the two assassins."

Yates scowled. "They must have been followed."

"Boyd said they weren't, and I believe him." Jordan's tone was firm. "You and I both know all the information about my company has been listed as classified, which means someone high up in the FBI, the NSA, or the CIA accessed and leaked the information. Now every one of my team's missions is at risk. I have Sloan and Natalia working on that most recent Russian intel, and Mack and Sun are working on this current threat. Do I need to pull Sloan off his current project?"

Rashid was right. This was a big problem. Yates stood and began to pace. "I'll have the NSA see if they can track the person responsible. Anyone accessing classified information would leave an electronic trail." He hated the possibility of yet another traitor in the ranks. Every investigation into a potential terrorist threat had revealed insiders aiding and abetting the criminals involved. As if they didn't have enough bad guys to track down, there were those who were supposed to be good guys helping them. It was getting mighty old. "We'll find the person responsible."

"I have a better idea, let's let Sun and Mack do that. I'm not sure we can trust the NSA." Jordan was not happy. "Keep them out for now, let's let Mack do his thing instead. I'm on my way to pick up Boyd and Lina now, using a rental that can't be traced back to me or the company. Sloan will follow me with another rental too. I'm planning to call everyone in to start over with untraceable vehicles, IDs, and computers. A breach like this cannot happen again."

"I'll pay whatever is necessary to make sure you're

successfully covered from this untimely exposure." Yates didn't have much choice, Jordan's company had proven to be the best asset money could buy, and his team was his best chance at finding those responsible for this new terrorist threat. "Lina and Boyd are really okay?"

"Boyd is doing a great job of protecting her," Jordan said. "He's just as good as Sloan and Sun. From what I'm hearing, his instincts are impeccable. But they need our help not more leaks."

"Yeah, I got it." Yates couldn't help feeling defensive. He didn't like having leaks within the organization any more than Jordan did. "Listen, I've learned the Chinese leader, Xi Jin Ping, is still planning to attend the president's Chinese New Year party at the White House tonight, despite the terrorist threat. We need to know if Shu Yan Chen is linked to the Six Red Dragons faction of the mafia and why assassins were hired to take her out. If there's a plan to disrupt the festivities tonight, I want to know about it."

"I understand," Jordan assured him. "Mack and Sun are digging for every bit of information available regarding the Six Red Dragons. As soon as we find something significant, I'll let you know."

"Thanks." Yates disconnected from the call and dropped heavily into the closest chair. He'd tried to tell the president this upcoming event was a bad idea. But the guy was convinced this step was necessary to open communication channels with China. The president claimed it was time to form a stronger alliance between their two countries. Yates wasn't convinced, then again, the president was relatively new in his role, just voted in a year ago, and very young to be in the office at all. In fact, the president's rapid rise to power had stunned everyone, especially the older cadre of senators and congressmen. Not to mention the old guys like him and the others in charge of keeping their country secure.

Lots of money had been poured into President Copeland's campaign, starting way back when he was a freshman congressman, barely in his midthirties. Since that time, Copeland had gotten only more and more powerful.

Maybe too powerful.

He sighed and tried to quell the panic clawing up the back of his throat. The White House was the most secure place in the city. Yet knowing that didn't make him feel any better about the upcoming Chinese New Year celebration.

If something terrible happened to the President of the United States, or to Xi Jin Ping, the backlash could send the entire country spinning into a third world war.

One in which the United States may not win.

JANUARY 31 – 5:05 a.m. – Richmond, VA

Kali slid out of bed, wincing when the metal cuff pulled tightly around her ankle. She explored the room with her hands, finding the portable commode located in the corner of the room. She was able to reach it by pulling the chain tight, but she was not able to find a door.

Sobbing over the past couple of hours hadn't helped. If anything, she felt thirstier than before. She feared her captors would keep her here, without food or water, until she died.

Maybe that was their plan. To force her to experience a slow, painful demise.

After using the commode, she tried once more to reach the door. She stretched out on the floor, tugging at the chain restraining her movements. Wiggling her fingers, she attempted to reach the opposite wall.

Nothing.

Kali swallowed a sob and told herself to keep trying. There had to be a way in and out of the room. Even a jail cell had a doorway. A locked doorway was better than nothing. She angled herself along the floor in a slightly different direction than before and tried again. And yet again.

Still, she felt nothing but air.

After two more attempts, Kali gave up. Her captors had taken great care to keep her locked up without even the slightest chance to escape. She hadn't been able to find a door or a window, only the bed and the commode.

The dark silence crushed her hope of getting out of there. Sure, she wanted to believe her detail had reported her missing and that right now there were dozens of FBI and Secret Service operatives out searching for her. Her dad always said the smartest and brightest people worked for him. They must be smart enough to find her.

But what if they weren't?

No, she couldn't allow herself to lose all hope. Not yet. She wasn't sure how much time had passed, but certainly it had only been hours and not days.

She crawled back into the bed, tugging the thin blanket around her, desperately wishing she had some idea of what time it was.

How long would her captors keep her here without food or water? Until she was nothing but skin and bones?

Kali shivered, lowered her head to her knees, and prayed to God that someone would rescue her before it was too late.

. . .

JANUARY 31 – 5:12 a.m. – Bullet Train to Beijing, China

Jia didn't dare sleep but sat with her eyes closed, her senses remaining on alert. She jerked her head up as the train began to slow down. This wasn't right. The bullet train between Lianyungang and Beijing did not have any scheduled stops.

"What's going on?" Sam asked in a low voice. "We still have another ninety minutes to travel before we reach Beijing."

"I'm not sure." Her instincts were clamoring at her. She pressed her face to the window, horrified to realize they were approaching a bridge stretching over the Chaobai River. It stretched along the eastern portion of the city of Tianjin, going all the way along the edge of Beijing. There was absolutely no reason for the train to stop over a river. "This is bad," she whispered.

Sam tensed. "An unscheduled stop is never good."

"We need to get off this train as soon as possible." She rose and took his hand, tugging him upright. "Follow me."

"I hate to ask, but what exactly is your plan?" Sam asked as he followed her down the center aisle, passing occupants who eyed them warily.

"You'll see." She tried not to look directly at any of their fellow passengers, although she could feel their gazes boring into her back. After the altercation she'd had with the two young Chinese men, she'd half expected the People's Armed Police to storm the train and haul her out in handcuffs.

For all she knew, that was still Manchu's plan. Stop the train in the middle of nowhere to capture them. Yet she thought it was odd for them to make a move at this point, near a bridge just past Tianjin. In her opinion, it would have been better for them to have waited until they reached Beijing.

Maybe rather than the People's Armed Police, the Chinese government had sent the People's Liberation Army. One thing the People's Republic of China had was a seemingly infinite number of well-trained soldiers. Being employed by the government was a well-paying job, although it was also one in which each soldier knew their lives would be sacrificed in the blink of an eye.

For the greater good.

Still, even knowing that, each soldier would obey the leader's command without hesitation or argument.

If that was the case, she and Sam wouldn't be arrested and tossed in jail for the next few decades.

They'd be killed.

No. She was not going to allow that to happen. Not after all these years.

Not after coming this far.

Jia passed through the doorway at the end of the car and kept going. They needed to get to the back of the train to find a spot to jump off.

They passed the two young men who'd tried to stab her with a knife. She noticed the two men had earbuds in and studiously ignored them as they moved past. Good. At least she wouldn't have to deal with them.

Just dozens of soldiers within the Chinese army, she thought grimly.

The train was slowing down even more now, and she knew time was running out. The soldiers or police officers would board the train at every possible entrance.

When they reached the last car, there were several people sitting there. Ignoring them, she found an empty seat. The train was already heading over the bridge.

She took a deep breath and executed a roundhouse kick that broke through the window. Ignoring the screams and cries from those nearby, she used her booted heel to get rid of the glass shards.

Then she crawled up onto the seat and slid her head and shoulders out the window.

The train had slowed, but not nearly enough to make this an easy escape. The bridge was narrow, but the water would be like concrete.

Even as she hesitated, the train slowed a bit more. She glanced back at Sam who came up next to her.

"Are you sure about this?" His gaze was full of concern.

"Yes. I'll see you on the west side of the river." Without waiting for him to respond, Jia got her feet beneath her and jumped.

CHAPTER EIGHT

January 31 – 5:17 a.m. – Rockville, MD

Boyd mulled over Lina's memory of the six red dragons mural as they waited for Jordan. Trusting the recall of a four-year-old child wasn't smart, but it was still interesting that Lina had seen it. Or at least thought she had.

He eyed her over the rim of his coffee mug. He didn't trust easily, a by-product of his tours as a marine and later as a member of the Secret Service. Still, he didn't believe Lina would hold back vital information at this point. Not after the series of attacks against them.

"You're sure you don't remember anything else about your mother's family?"

A flash of irritation darkened her gaze. "If I did, I'd tell you. Do you think I like knowing Shu Yan Chen died because of my reaching out to her?"

"Shu Yan must have put her DNA into the database for a reason." He abruptly straightened. "Maybe she was trying to find you."

She gaped. "But I'm the one who reached out to her."

"I know." His thoughts whirled. "Yet you wouldn't have

been able to do that if she hadn't uploaded her DNA, correct? I mean, you would have needed that information to know she was a relative."

"Yes," Lina agreed, looking shell-shocked. "I guess I hadn't thought of it that way."

His phone buzzed. Seeing Jordan's name on the screen brought a sense of relief. "Hey, where are you?"

"Five minutes out. Where do you want to meet?"

Glancing around the empty restaurant, Boyd didn't see a reason to leave, especially since Lina was injured. "We're at a café about a mile from the Metro." He gave Jordan the restaurant's name and address. "Do you want a coffee to go?"

"No thanks, I'm good. See you soon." Jordan disconnected from the call.

He waved down their server and paid the bill.

"Where are we headed now?" Lina asked wearily. He understood she was probably exhausted and in pain. "I feel like we'll never be safe again."

"We will be," he said firmly. He reached across the table to take her slender hand in his. "I'll do everything possible to protect you."

She nodded and gripped his hand tightly. "I wouldn't be alive if not for you, Boyd."

Her gratitude was unnecessary, so he didn't say anything. While deployed overseas, he'd experienced this same sort of gratitude from many of the Afghan people. He understood the dependency Lina was feeling toward him. So much so that she'd kissed him. It was typical hero worship and didn't mean anything. Once things went back to normal, she'd move on with her life.

All the more reason to make sure she understood he wasn't interested in anything personal, no matter how much he wanted to kiss her again. No matter how attracted he was to her strength and sheer stubborn will. She had to remain Lilac in his mind, not Lina. "Hey, don't stress. Jordan and the rest of the team will get to the bottom of this, you'll see."

A pair of headlights caught his eye. He tensed and rose, pulling Lina along with him. He pushed her behind him until he was able to verify the driver of the SUV was Jordan.

His phone buzzed, and he lifted it to his ear while watching the SUV. "Is that you?"

"Yeah, I'm here. Leave the satellite computer behind."

He eased the case off the bench seat and onto the floor. It was off, so it couldn't be used to track them. He stood and eased toward the door, Lina following close behind. "You sure you weren't followed?"

"I took every precaution," Jordan assured him. "Oh, and ditch the phone."

"Okay." He disconnected from the line and tossed the phone into the garbage before heading outside. "Toss yours too," he told Lina. After she did as he asked, he raked a keen gaze over the area before ushering her toward the SUV. "Sit in the back, okay?"

She didn't argue. He jogged around to the passenger door. The moment he was seated Jordan hit the gas. The SUV lurched forward.

"I spoke to Yates," Jordan said. "We're officially going off-grid from this point forward. This SUV along with all vehicles being used by the rest of my team will have no ties to the company. None of our equipment will either."

"I'm glad to hear it." Boyd could tell Jordan was seriously ticked. "I'm sorry it had to come to this."

"Yeah, well, the worst part is that only someone with a high-level security clearance would have been able to find the information. Which means there's a serious leak within the NSA."

Boyd nodded grimly. "I figured as much."

"How high?" Lina asked.

Jordan met her gaze through the rearview mirror. "A senior adviser or above. But try not to worry. I have Mack and Sun tracking the possible link. And Yates is paying to cover the extra expense."

"Yates is the director of the FBI," Boyd explained to Lina. "We can trust him." He couldn't help being impressed by Jordan's contacts within the bureau. That Security Specialists, Inc. reported directly to Yates was reassuring. Although knowing the leak was that high within the US government was a serious problem.

"I hope you're right," Lina murmured.

"Have Mack and Sun found anything significant related to the Six Red Dragons?" Boyd asked. "They must be involved in this. It's the only thing that makes sense."

"I heard from them on the way over," Jordan said. "They learned the CIA has an asset working within the Six Red Dragons faction in China. The asset is the one who warned of a terrorist attack against the president."

Boyd whistled between his teeth. "That's good to know. I assume the president has taken precautions?"

"Some, but he hasn't canceled the visit with the Chinese leaders."

That wasn't good. "Still, having an asset helps. That person must be feeding us intel on what we should expect, right?"

"Wrong," Jordan countered grimly. "Unfortunately, the asset and her handler are in the wind. In fact, we don't know at this point if they are alive or dead."

· · ·

JANUARY 31 – 5:32 *a.m.* – *Chaobai River, China*

The shocking cold water stole Sam's breath. He pushed hard to reach the surface despite his sore muscles. Hitting the water had hurt, even though he'd tried to go in feet first to absorb the blow. The impact had jarred his entire body, from his heels all the way up to the top of his head.

Gasping for air, he swiped the water from his eyes and frantically searched for Jia. For a moment, he couldn't tell which way was east or west until he finally caught a glimpse of the tall buildings of Tianjin located to the west. Turning around, he saw the bullet train had come to a complete stop on the bridge.

Taking a deep breath, Sam disappeared under the water. He swam in what he hoped and prayed was the right direction toward the west side of the river. He had no way of knowing if Jia had survived her plunge but did his best to stay positive. Jia was one of the most resourceful women he knew.

She'd make it to the west riverbank. Or die trying.

No, she couldn't die. Not now. Not when they'd come so far.

When his lungs felt as if they might burst from the pressure, he risked going up to the surface to take another breath. Thankfully, he'd made some progress, and the river's current helped take him away from the bullet train.

Still no sign of Jia, at least not close by. Taking another deep breath, he went back under again. He did this again and again and again until he finally reached the river's edge. And even then, he didn't immediately get out of the water.

There was no way to know who was looking for them, but he knew it was likely the People's Liberation Army. Dozens of Chinese soldiers were likely fanning out to look for them right now. Best to stay in the water for as long as possible. And where was Jia? His chest tightened with fear as he searched the area. She'd jumped a few minutes before he did, so he told himself she was likely already on the shore.

If she'd survived at all.

Please, Lord. Please keep Jia safe in Your care!

When he felt as if he couldn't swim another meter, he grabbed a scrubby bush and pulled himself from the water. He collapsed on the ground, thankful to be alive. Fear for Jia's well-being quickly spurred him into action. Pushing himself to his feet, he walked along the river, continuing to move away from the train.

The wrong direction, considering they needed to get to Beijing. But it couldn't be helped.

Tianjin would have transportation they could use to get to Beijing. If they could reach the city before being caught by the People's Liberation Army.

A rustling noise caught his attention. Sam froze, his heart lodged in his throat. He expected to be surrounded by soldiers, but when the slim figure emerged from the brush, he nearly cried out with relief.

"Jia!" His voice was hoarse from all the river water he'd swallowed. He rushed toward her just as she threw herself into his arms.

He held her close for a long moment, ignoring the river stench and reveling in the fact that she was alive and well.

"I've been watching for you," Jia whispered. When she pulled out of his arms, he reluctantly let her go. "I even prayed that God would provide for your successful escape."

Her confession made him smile. "I prayed for you too, Jia. And God has answered our prayers."

"Yes." She took his hand and tugged him forward. "We

must hurry. We need to purchase replacement clothes and find a way to get to Beijing."

Neither task would be simple, but he found himself grinning like a fool as they made their way toward Tianjin.

Jia had hugged him. Had prayed for him.

He felt certain God would continue to watch over them, guiding them back to Washington, DC.

JANUARY 31 – 5:48 a.m. – Washington, DC

"The People's Liberation Army has been deployed to bring them in."

He wanted to scream at his new contact on the other end of the phone. The army? To capture two people? Talk about inept! He struggled to remain calm. "And have they been found?"

There was a long pause, indicating the news was not good. "They managed to escape by jumping off the train."

He frowned. "The bullet train travels at a fast rate of speed. Surely the jump had killed them."

Another long pause as his contact carefully chose his words. "The train was slowing as it went over the Chaobai River. We believe they jumped into the water."

What nonsense was this? "How could you be so stupid?" he raged. "Why didn't you take them in a deserted stretch of the country? There are plenty of less populated areas to choose from."

"We will find them," his contact said firmly. "We have many soldiers spreading out across the country. They will be found and captured."

"Killed," he swiftly corrected. "I want them eliminated. Do you understand? Kill them!"

"Yes, sir." His contact disconnected from the call,

putting an end to his ranting. He threw the phone onto the sofa and paced the room.

They'd deployed the Chinese army to find two measly people. The news should be reassuring.

It wasn't.

In fact, he was beginning to worry that Jia and Sam would manage to get all the way back to the United States. He didn't trust that his new contact had everything under control. He wasn't proving to be any better than the one he'd disposed of. Quite the opposite. He needed to find a way to make sure they'd be taken out the moment they landed on US soil.

Things must move forward according to plan. A plan that had been years in the making.

He retrieved his phone and made another call. No way would he allow two people to get in his way.

He'd find his own men to take over the task, should they make it this far. The pair would be dealt with, permanently.

JANUARY 31 – 6:01 a.m. – Washington, DC

Lina stared at the traffic surrounding them. "Why are we back in DC? I thought the point was to hide from those who are trying to kill us?"

"That is the goal, yes. Going through the city is a temporary measure," Jordan explained. "We won't stick around for long."

Lina tried not to think about how she would normally be getting ready for work. It felt as if she was living in an alternate universe. Like she'd been dropped into a terrible warlike video game, only she wasn't given a weapon to use against her enemies. And they were firing real bullets and hand grenades, not fake ones.

Not that she'd know how to use a gun if she'd been given one. She'd probably shoot herself in the foot.

She sighed and tried to think of something other than the Six Red Dragons who'd targeted her.

Lina shifted in her seat. Despite being physically and emotionally exhausted, she couldn't seem to relax. Not just because her hip still throbbed.

She glanced out the window, seeing bad guys behind the wheel of every car around them. So far, those who'd come after her had been Chinese.

Would they stick with that tactic? Or deploy someone else?

"Lina? Are you okay?" Boyd's dark gaze held concern, so she forced a smile.

"Yeah, fine." There was no point in complaining. All that mattered was that she and Boyd were alive.

"I think we should head to Arlington," Boyd said.

Lina frowned. "That's awfully close to where I live."

"Exactly." Boyd shot a glance at her over his shoulder. "The last place they'd expect us to go, right?"

"I don't know, Boyd." Jordan's tone held doubt.

"You said this vehicle is clean, so it shouldn't be a problem," Boyd reminded him. "And I think we should consider a possible link to the Institute for Nanoscience or the Naval Research Lab."

"Wait a minute, what are you saying?" Lina leaned forward in her seat. "You thought my mother's family was involved with the Six Red Dragons. My family has nothing to do with my work. Besides, it isn't anything related to national security. I told you before, I'm just a microbiologist."

"I don't think there's anything simple about what you

do, Lina." Boyd offered a wan smile, then shrugged. "It's still a possibility, though."

"You could be right," Jordan agreed. "I'll get Mack and Sun to dig up more information. If there's a link between the Six Red Dragons and the research lab, they'll find it."

She scowled. "Don't you think I would be in a better position to do that? It's my job after all."

"Normally, yes," Jordan admitted. He met her gaze in the rearview mirror. "But these guys are desperate to get to you, Lina. I can't risk anyone tracking you via computer."

"We've been using a satellite computer," Boyd pointed out. "And you brought another one, which should be safe as it's not tied back to the company."

"I guess you can try," Jordan said.

Lina sat back in her seat. The idea of her work at the research center being involved with the Six Red Dragons was preposterous. However, she also knew that it was important to consider every possible angle. Her security clearance was high, but not at NSA levels.

If nothing else, it would behoove her to prove there wasn't a relationship between these men determined to kill her and her job.

"Jordan, do me a favor and drive past the institute," Boyd said, craning his neck to see out the window.

"We need to find a motel for the two of you," Jordan protested.

"I just want to eyeball the place." Boyd glanced back at her. "How far do you live from the center?"

"Just a few miles. I walk in the summer and take the Metro in the winter." She gestured toward the landscape outside. "We're still about ten minutes out, but when we get closer, you'll be able to see my apartment building off on the north side of the highway."

Boyd and Jordan exchanged a glance. Jordan said, "Mack and Sun have been there already, remember?"

"I know," Boyd said. His tone made her wonder if he was second-guessing his decision to come to Arlington.

The traffic was picking up now, even this early in the morning. It was the reason she used the Metro or walked rather than owning a car. Well, that and parking fees were ridiculous.

She caught a glimpse of her apartment building off in the distance. Seeing it made her long for home. Not that her apartment was anything special, but to be surrounded by her things, her books, her family pictures, her plants.

It made her wonder if she'd ever see her place again.

She purposefully tore her gaze from the building. No point in wanting something she couldn't have. Rather than focus on what she'd lost, she needed to stay positive over what they'd accomplished.

Dear Lord, thank You for continuing to keep us safe in Your care. I ask that You please guide us on Your chosen path as we trust in You, always. Amen.

The silent prayer brought a sense of peace. She noticed a sign advertising a chain motel. "Jordan, do you have a motel in mind?"

"I need one with a manager that I can convince to take cash," he replied dryly. "So don't expect too much."

"I'm not picky."

"You've been great about all this," Boyd said quietly.

His praise made her blush. "I'm thankful to be alive."

"How is your hip?" Boyd asked.

"Better." It ached like crazy, but at least she wasn't walking on it. She was grateful for that much.

Jordan's phone rang. He answered using the hands-free functionality. "Rashid."

"It's Sun. There seems to be something going down at the Institute for Nanoscience."

"Like what?" Boyd demanded.

"I'm not sure, but the place is undergoing an urgent evacuation. It's all over the news, looks like there are dozens of police surrounding the place."

"Bomb threat?" Jordan asked.

"Either that or a gas leak. Regardless, I just wanted you to know." Sun quickly disconnected from the call.

"Turn around," Boyd urged. "We need to get far away from the area."

Before Jordan could reply, a massive booming sound rang out, literally shaking their vehicle from side to side.

Lina gasped and glanced in the direction of the Institute for Nanoscience, her workplace. Where the building should be was nothing but a large cloud of dark smoke.

Someone had set off a bomb in the building!

CHAPTER NINE

January 31 – 6:42 a.m. – Tianjin, China

Jia led the way into the city of Tianjin, her gaze constantly moving from side to side. How much time did they have before the People's Liberation Army found them? She didn't doubt they'd come to Tianjin to search as it was the closest city to the train.

Avoiding the curious gazes focused on their wet clothes, she quickly found a clothing merchant. Her money was wet, but that didn't hinder the transaction. Not in a country where there were so many poor people struggling to make a living.

She and Sam hastily changed into their dry things. Thankfully, she was able to find another long-sleeved tunic to help cover her scar, knowing Manchu and others would use it as a way to identify her.

They quickly moved toward the center of town to find transportation. The urge to hurry was strong; she fully expected a sea of soldiers to surround them at any moment.

Claiming the first rickshaw they came across, she and

Sam sat huddled together. What they really needed was a car or a motorbike to get to Beijing.

"Where are we going?" Sam asked in a low voice.

"Beijing is our ultimate destination," she whispered. "But we're currently heading to the north end of the city."

Sam nodded and wrapped his arm around her waist. His presence beside her was both reassuring and problematic.

His American looks were too noticeable. Even after they'd dyed his hair black, it wouldn't be easy to disguise him. He was tall and broad-shouldered, far more than the average Chinese man.

If it wasn't so critical to get out of Tianjin, she'd suggest they stop long enough to dye his hair here. Catching sight of a uniformed police officer made her tense. It took every ounce of willpower to ignore him.

Had the Army disseminated their photographs to the People's Armed Police? She felt the urge to pray to God, the way Tony had believed, to help them escape the city without being caught.

The rickshaw trip was slow and arduous. Traffic teemed around them, vehicles and motorbikes coming close to hitting them on several occasions. When she was satisfied that they'd gotten close enough to the northern side of the city, she jumped out of the rickshaw, gesturing for Sam to follow.

After paying the driver, she slipped into the crowd. Pedestrians swarmed the streets and walkways. Keeping a hold of Sam's hand, she wove her way through the street markets. When she spied a motorbike propped against the side of a building, she made a beeline toward it.

"Wait, what are you doing?" Sam slowed his pace, holding her back. "We can't just steal it."

"Do you have a better plan?" She understood his reluctance to break the law, but they desperately needed to get out of the city.

"Find the owner, we can pay him or her for it," Sam said.

Two armed police officers strode purposefully through the crowd. Jia tensed again, fearing she and Sam were the target. There was no time to find the motorbike's owner. She knew how to hot-wire the engine, but as she grew closer, she noticed the key was in the ignition.

Any owner stupid enough to leave the key in their motorbike deserved to have it taken. *Probably a tourist*, she thought. Rushing forward, she threw one leg over the bike and cranked the key. The engine sputtered to life.

Thankfully, Sam quickly joined her. Maybe he'd seen the police too. She steered the motorbike away from the Armed Police and tried to remember where to find the closest highway.

There! She drove rather recklessly between the cars, desperately trying to get out of the city as fast as possible. No one seemed to pay them any attention, most motorbike drivers did the same thing. Street laws were rarely enforced; therefore, no one paid them any attention. Besides, the amount of traffic crowding the streets made speeding impossible.

Several loud shouts echoed behind them. Gunfire punctuated the air. Jia pushed harder, continuing to weave a path between the cars so close that her knees and Sam's hit the sides of the vehicles.

"Do you think they're looking for us?" Sam asked, his voice near her ear.

"Yes." She couldn't afford to assume otherwise. The Six Red Dragons had a reach that was far and wide. Both the army and the police would be searching for them. Maybe they'd been spotted or maybe the police had been alerted to their stealing the motorbike. Or maybe someone had noticed her scar and reported it. Either way, it was imperative to get out of the city.

Concentrating on the task at hand, she gained speed, taking treacherous turns to escape. As she drove, she was surprised to hear Sam whispering a prayer over and over in her ear.

Dear Lord, please guide us to safety!

JANUARY 31 – 6:57 a.m. – Arlington, VA

"We need to get off the highway!" It wasn't the first time Boyd had said these words to Jordan, who was doing his best to do just that. The traffic had been at a dead stop for nearly ten minutes before it began to creep forward inch by inch.

"I'm trying." Jordan's tone remained calm, although his expression was grave. "Everyone else is attempting to do the same thing."

"I know." He blew out a frustrated breath, inwardly reeling from the explosion. Turning to look at Lina, he noticed she was still pale and shaky. "I guess it's a good thing you couldn't get to work today."

His attempt to lighten things up fell flat. "How many are dead?" Lina asked, her voice trembling with emotion. "How many of my colleagues did I lose today?"

"I don't know." He reached back to rest his hand on her knee. "I'm hopeful many were able to be evacuated prior to the blast."

"Even if they were outside, they might be dead," she whispered.

"I'm sorry, Lina." He hated feeling helpless. And he still

didn't understand why the Institute for Nanoscience had been targeted in the first place. Lina had assured them the lab didn't handle biological weapons. So what was the point of setting a bomb?

Simply to send a message? It didn't make any sense.

"I'll try Yates again," Jordan offered even though he'd already called the director twice. "Maybe he has some answers."

Boyd listened as Jordan left yet another message while fighting traffic. They edged closer to the exit, although once they got off the highway, traffic was just as gnarled.

At this rate, they'd never get anywhere near a motel room. He didn't like being out in the open like this. With the car moving at a snail's pace, they were vulnerable to an attack. He was keeping a careful eye out, but they were literally surrounded by strangers.

When the phone rang, he startled badly. Jordan lifted a brow as he hit the button to answer. "Rashid."

"It's Yates. Are you really in Arlington?"

"Yes, and we saw the explosion at the institute," Jordan confirmed. "What's going on?"

"The intel is sketchy, there are dozens of casualties so far," Yates admitted. "You need to keep Lina Parker safe."

"Yeah, we know that's our mission," Jordan drawled. "But you must have some idea of why the institute was targeted."

There was a brief pause as if Yates was considering how much information to give them. "Right before the bomb threat, there was a claim that the institute's security had been breached."

"A security breach?" Boyd echoed. "Who and why?"

"That is still under investigation. But you should know

that Lina's ID and thumbprint were used to access the building late last night."

"What?" Lina's voice rose in shock. "My ID and thumbprint? How is that possible? I wasn't anywhere near the place."

"I'm aware of that," Yates said calmly. "Before we could investigate further, the bomb threat came, and then the device was activated. We think they stole your ID from your apartment and lifted your thumbprint from there too. We also believe the bomb was planted by whoever accessed the building."

"Why wasn't Lina's ID deactivated?" Boyd demanded. "We told you to shut down her computer access and her ID."

"We did shut down her access and deactivate her ID," Yates said testily. "It could be they managed to get in before that took place. As I said, we're still investigating how this happened. Your job is to keep Lina safe and to continue investigating the Six Red Dragons threat, understand? I've deployed FBI agents to the scene of the institute and military intelligence is involved too. When I know something more, I'll let you know." Without waiting for a response, Yates abruptly disconnected from the call.

Boyd blew out a frustrated breath and glanced at Jordan. "That was a big mistake not deactivating her ID right away."

Jordan nodded slowly. "An unusual one. Makes me think the system was rigged somehow."

"It had to be," Lina chimed in. "The security is fairly tight. Both the ID tag and the thumbprint are required to access the building. If they deactivated my information, someone must have found a way around that."

"How?" Boyd demanded.

Lina was silent for a long moment. "My best assumption is that the security system was hacked and the deactivation reversed. Then they could have used my stolen ID and my fake thumbprint."

He turned to look at her. "You're saying that whoever did this targeted you? They wanted the world to think you set the bomb?"

She nodded slowly. "The only logical conclusion is that I was set up to take the fall. And the worst part? If not for you two keeping me safe, providing me an ironclad alibi, I'd likely already be arrested for treason."

JANUARY 31 – 7:12 *a.m.* – *Washington, DC*

Having been summoned by the president, he stood in the Oval Office, waiting for the news he already knew.

"The Institute for Nanoscience has been bombed," the president said. "I have the FBI and military intelligence working on the case, but I need to know your thoughts. You have more experience than I do, so I'm looking for advice." He paused, then added, "Personally, I don't see how it's possible this bombing could be related to our international guests and upcoming celebration, but what is your opinion?"

"I believe it's a random act of violence, not targeted to anyone in this office," he said. "I'm sure it's just a way to get attention."

"Domestic terrorism? As if there isn't enough of that coming at us from overseas?" The president was clearly irritated. "The timing is terrible."

"Yes, sir." He couldn't deny feeling a stab of annoyance as well. The bomb had been a secondary plan, one that should not have been necessary. Clearly, these people he'd been told were the best were far from it. There was nothing he despised more than failure. He cleared his throat. "If you cancel this evening's festivities, the domestic terrorists win. We cannot let that happen."

"People died today," the president snapped. "They've already won!"

"Yes, of course the loss of life is tragic," he hastened to add. "But we cannot allow these people to hold us hostage to their will. We must move forward. You, sir, are the greatest and most powerful leader across the globe. All will be watching how this unfolds. And your alliance with China is a necessary partnership for your agenda."

The president abruptly stood and turned to stare out the window. "I don't like this. Something isn't right. It feels as if there's an impending storm brewing, and there's nothing I can do to stop it from hitting us hard."

A niggle of concern crept under his skin. He'd heard claims about the president having a sixth sense for danger, and listening to him now, he believed it. He strove to sound reassuring. "Sir, I understand your concern, but why not wait to find out what the FBI and military intelligence information reveals? No need to call anything off this early. I'm sure everything is under control. More facts related to this despicable bombing will be forthcoming."

The president continued to stare out through the window for a long moment. Finally, he turned back to face him. "I will, thanks. That's all."

It irked him to be dismissed so abruptly, but he didn't allow his emotions to show on his features. He turned and left the White House, ignoring the frantic staffers running around. He had no doubt the press secretary would have her hands full. Outside, he checked his phone. Nothing. He swore under his breath, wanting to hear some good news from his new contact in China.

Silence indicated something had gone wrong.

He scowled as he waited for his car to arrive. The celebration was scheduled to kick off at eight o'clock tonight.

Thirteen hours to go. Thirteen hours before he became the most powerful man in the world.

He would not allow a couple of CIA agents or one annoying loose end of a woman get in his way.

JANUARY 31 – 7:18 a.m. – Arlington, VA

Lina couldn't believe her ID badge and thumbprint had been used to access the Institute for Nanoscience. She understood her thumbprint could have easily been picked up from her apartment, likely when members from the Six Red Dragons had gone in to steal her computer and destroy her printed DNA report. Still, it was mind-boggling that they'd gone to all this trouble to frame her even as they'd sent multiple teams to kill her.

Because of her mother? That simple explanation wasn't logical any longer. There wasn't enough of a connection between her attempt to find her mother's family and a bomb set at the institute.

Wait a minute. She sat straighter in her seat. It did make a sense if she could be linked directly to the Six Red Dragons. Her mother's family must have been involved with them. Maybe the Six Red Dragons had even been responsible for killing her parents. Had they been around that long? Twenty-five years?

Was she crazy to think along these lines? She'd been born here in the States. She was an American citizen.

Anyone who knew her personally would know she didn't belong to a faction of the Chinese mafia.

Then again, it could be that most of her closest colleagues were dead and unable to vouch for her.

A chill snaked down her spine. Government officials would be quick to place the blame, not just for the security breach but for the loss of American lives.

A half Chinese woman would be the perfect target for treason.

"I think it might be better for us to walk from here." Boyd's deep voice broke into her thoughts. "I can't sit here much longer."

"Didn't the Secret Service teach you to have patience?" Jordan asked. "You're safer in here than on foot."

"Don't count on it," Boyd grumbled. He glanced back at her. "How's your hip?"

"Fine." If he wanted to walk, she'd manage.

"Looks like there are several cops stopping cars up ahead," Jordan said with a frown. "Wonder what that's about?"

The chill along her spine turned to ice. "What if they're looking for me?"

Boyd and Jordan exchanged a long glance. "Maybe you should head out on foot," Jordan finally agreed. "But take the replacement satellite computer and the new phones." He reached into his pocket and handed Boyd a large roll of bills. "Call me if you need more."

"Will do," Boyd agreed.

Seeing the computer bag beside her, she handed it up to Boyd. Seconds later, they were both out of the car and moving away from Jordan's SUV.

Ignoring her hip pain, which thankfully wasn't as bad as it had been, she hastened to keep up with Boyd's long strides. He took her hand in his and led the way past several streets until they stumbled across Penrose Park.

"This way." He took a jagged path through the park, using the trees as cover.

Lina risked a glance over her shoulder but didn't notice any police officers following them. Then again, she wasn't about to bank her life or Boyd's on what she couldn't see with her eyes.

This constantly running from armed men was making her seriously paranoid.

She tripped and would have fallen if not for Boyd's hold on her hand. He slowed his pace enough so that she could stay at his side.

"Let me know if you need me to carry you."

"I'm fine." No way was she going to be tossed over his shoulder like a bag of grain again. She'd find a way to keep up with him, injured hip or not.

They emerged from the other end of the park. A few blocks later, they found a motel. It was well before the usual check-in time, but that didn't stop Boyd from heading into the lobby.

"Stay back," he whispered. "I'll handle this."

She gave a nod and dropped into a saggy chair. The middle-aged woman behind the counter seemed to have eyes only for Boyd.

"Ma'am, I know it's early, but I really need a room." He flashed a smile so dazzling the woman practically melted. "My friend is running from her abusive husband, we just need a place to hide out for a while."

Abusive husband? Lina lowered her eyes and tried to look like someone who'd been recently traumatized. Not a stretch, considering what they'd been through.

"It will cost you extra," the woman said, barely glancing at Lina.

"I'll pay you double if you take cash." Boyd laid several bills on the counter. From where she was sitting, Lina couldn't tell how much he'd given her, but the woman didn't hesitate to scoop them up.

"Room 103," she said, giving Boyd a key. "Check out time is ten o'clock tomorrow."

"Thank you." Boyd turned from the counter and nodded toward the door. Lina quickly joined him.

The room was better than the last one they'd been in, and she didn't complain about the fact that he'd only gotten one instead of two rooms. So far, they hadn't stayed in either of the motels for long and she felt certain Boyd didn't plan to stay here the full twenty-four hours either. He dropped the satellite computer onto the table and dug out their disposable phones.

She collapsed onto the edge of the bed and reached for the TV remote. Before she could turn on the local news, Boyd snatched it from her hands.

"Don't. It won't help."

A wave of fury hit hard. She leaped to her feet and spun to face him, thumping her fist against the rock that was his chest. "People are dying, Boyd! Because of me! The whole world will think this is all because of me!"

"Shh." He surprised her by wrapping his arms around her. "Don't do this, Lina. It's not your fault."

"I did the DNA search! I set up the meeting with Shu Yan Chen! It is my fault . . ." She closed her eyes against the sting of tears.

Boyd cradled her close, murmuring words of comfort. Her anger toward him quickly evaporated as she clung to his muscled strength.

"The world is quick to hate the Chinese," she finally whispered.

"Only the ignorant ones lump all Chinese together," he assured her.

Ignorance was rampant throughout the country, and Washington, DC, was no exception.

She tried not to cry all over Boyd's shirt, but it was impossible to hold back her emotions. Her life as she knew it was gone forever. Even if she and Boyd managed to get out of this alive, she doubted she'd be granted the security clearance she'd need to do her job.

Research work she enjoyed. What would she do when this was over? She had no idea.

"Please don't cry," Boyd said, his voice sounding hoarse. "I can't stand it."

That made her chuckle, although she doubted that was his intent. She pulled out of his arms and looked up at him. She was about to thank him for being understanding when his intense blue gaze focused on her mouth.

And then he was kissing her, hard and deep as if he might never stop.

CHAPTER TEN

January 31 – 7:44 a.m. – Arlington, VA

He'd lost his ever-loving mind. It was the only explanation for kissing Lina. Yet once he'd started, he was unable to stop. The lilac scent of her would forever be embedded in his senses.

Finally, she broke off the kiss, taking gulping breaths. "Wow. That was—wow."

The purely male part of him wanted to smile with satisfaction, but he forced himself to push those ridiculous emotions out of the way. His decision to use the code name Lilac wasn't working very well. "I—That shouldn't have happened."

"Yeah, I think that's what you said last time." Lina's luscious mouth curved into a smile. "But it did. Twice."

She was right. How was it possible that their second kiss was even more powerful than the first? He needed to get a grip. "I shouldn't take advantage of the situation."

She narrowed her gaze. "Maybe I'm the one taking advantage of the situation. I can honestly say I've never been drawn to anyone the way I am to you, Boyd. I think God brought us together for a reason."

And there was the crux of the matter. For someone who relied heavily on logic and science, her believing in God was anything but. He forced himself to take several steps back from her despite how every cell in his body wanted nothing more than to pull her back into his arms.

"God didn't bring us together, I was hired by Security Specialists, Inc. to protect you." He silently willed his heart rate to return to normal. He felt as if he'd finished his usual fifty push-ups and weight-lifting routine, followed by a five-mile run. Which might be why his emotions have suddenly run amok. He normally kept himself centered by pushing himself physically. Something he hadn't been able to do since he'd been tasked with protecting Lina.

"God knows all, Boyd. He is in charge, not us. We need to depend on God's grace and strength to get through this."

He could see by her serious gaze that she honestly believed that. And some of their very narrow escapes had made him wonder if there wasn't a higher power helping them out. Yet he also knew that he couldn't just depend on the possibility of God watching over them. No, he had to use every skill he possessed to keep Lina safe.

He cleared his throat and glanced at the satellite computer, reaching for it as if it were a lifeline designed to save him from drowning in the depths of Lina's green gaze. "I need to get to work. There must be some way to find out information related to the Six Red Dragons."

"I'll help."

No! He swallowed hard and forced himself to nod. At this point, he couldn't afford to ignore her assistance. Not after the way her ID tag and thumbprint were used to access the institute. "I think we should try to find the mural you saw as a child."

"Okay." She stepped forward to join him near the computer. Her lilac scent drifted toward him, and he had to stop himself from lowering his face to her hair.

Work, he told himself sternly. He needed to stay focused on what was important.

As he booted up the satellite computer, he knew the scent of lilacs would remind him of Lina for the rest of his life.

JANUARY 31 – 8:03 *a.m.* – *Richmond, VA*

Kali heard a door open. She immediately jumped off the bed, but it was too late. The door closed within seconds.

She sniffed the air, her mouth watering at the scent of eggs and toast. She crouched down on her hands and knees, moving across the dark room, feeling for what she felt certain was a tray of breakfast that had been left for her.

Once again, she stretched out on the floor, reaching as far as she could with the iron cuff around her ankle. The tips of her fingers brushed the edge of a tray. She gasped and forced herself to extend farther. With the edges of her fingernails, she managed to draw the tray closer. The darkness made it impossible to see what was on there, but she felt a plastic cup of water, the softness of scrambled eggs, and the crusty toast.

She lifted the plastic cup to drink, then hesitated. What if they'd drugged the water? Or the food? Maybe she shouldn't eat any of this. Yet her mouth was so incredibly dry she couldn't stop herself from taking one tiny sip. Then another. Her stomach churned, so she nibbled on the edge of the toast.

Slowly, she ate everything on the tray, going as far as to lick the crumbs off the paper plate. She told herself it didn't matter if the food was drugged. What was the worst that could happen? She'd fall back to sleep. Not the worst fate considering there was nothing else to do but worry about what was happening outside the dark room.

Unfortunately, she accepted that escaping her captors was impossible. She couldn't reach the door or a window if there was one.

She left the tray nearby and crawled back onto the bed. Kali tried to envision her mom and dad, to imagine they were getting updates from the Secret Service and the FBI about how the search to find her was going. Surely they'd find her. Wouldn't they?

Her stomach felt better after eating the meal, but her eyelids grew heavy. Duly, she realized they had drugged her again. No doubt to keep her quiet and cooperative. She wanted to scream and yell at the top her lungs, but it was no use.

Within minutes, she succumbed to the darkness.

JANUARY 31 – 8:14 a.m. – Beijing, China

By some sort of miracle, Jia and Sam made it to Beijing without being captured. They were currently in a cheap hotel, finishing up the dye job on Sam's hair. Jia secretly preferred his natural color but knew the black coloring would help them escape the country.

Jia glanced down at her newly purchased disposable phone. She'd left a message for her contact who specialized in creating fake passports thirty minutes ago but hadn't heard back.

It was difficult not to succumb to panic. To have come

so far, all the way across China, to end up stuck and stranded in Beijing was terrible. Bo Dung Manchu was looking for them, along with the People's Liberation Army and the People's Armed Police. Oh yes, let's not forget those seeking to avenge Hui Genghis Chen.

Hiding in a city as highly populated as Beijing would only work for so long. Eventually, someone would see them and readily turn them in for easy cash. Bribery worked better than anything else in the city.

Besides, time was of the essence. She desperately needed to get to Washington, DC, to prevent the attack she knew was imminent.

And maybe even to find her daughter.

"He'll call," Sam said, reading her thoughts.

She forced a smile. "I know. It's time to rinse your hair."

"Okay." Sam rose and headed into the bathroom to shower. When the door closed behind him, she stared down at her phone again, debating whether or not to try again.

What if Hu Zhen had been arrested? Or killed? She didn't know of anyone else who would be able to create a fake passport for Sam.

The earlier plane explosion was proof they needed another identity.

She could leave him here.

The moment the idea popped into her mind, she thrust it away. Leaving Sam behind would be signing his death sentence. He wouldn't be able to survive without her.

Could she get him to the American embassy? Maybe. It was a risk as she suspected there were enemies within the embassy. She couldn't afford to trust anyone.

When her phone rang, she was so startled she dropped it. Feeling like a clumsy fool, she quickly scooped it off the floor and answered in Mandarin. Thankfully, Hu Zhen skipped the customary pleasantries and got right down to business.

"Document can be ready in one hour after I receive the required photograph," he said tersely. "Double the fee."

"Double?" she echoed in spite of herself. "That is quite an increase from a mere six months ago."

"I take much risk for you. My life and those of my family. Double the fee," he repeated.

She couldn't argue the risk. Treason against the People's Republic of China was dealt with swiftly and severely. "Agreed."

Minutes later, she had the information she needed to find Hu Zhen. The cost would be exorbitant but necessary.

Getting out of Beijing alive was worth that price, and more.

It was worth everything.

JANUARY 31 – 8:35 a.m. – Arlington, VA

Lina watched over Boyd's shoulder as he searched various sites to find a mural with six red dragons. It took all her willpower not to lean against him to absorb his strength. His broad muscles stretched the T-shirt across his chest, one that had been both soft beneath her cheek and firm beneath her fingers.

He'd kissed her, but he obviously wasn't happy about it. He'd claimed he wasn't married, engaged, or seeing anyone, but that didn't mean there wasn't a woman out there who still had a hold of his heart.

Lucky woman, she thought wistfully.

"Wait." She grabbed his arm. "That looked familiar."

He glanced at her, then increased the image on the

screen. Seeing the entire picture made her catch her breath. "That's it," she whispered.

"It's a mural painted on a building in Beijing, China." Boyd glanced at her. "Your parents took you overseas?"

"I—don't remember." She couldn't look away from the mural. It was very similar to what she remembered, although these dragons weren't all the same shade of red as she thought. The reds were dark to light, so light it was almost a pinky-orange color.

"You would think you'd remember a long plane ride," Boyd pressed. "And being in a foreign country."

Casting back to the blurred memory, she tried to recall if she saw it in person or as a photograph. "I don't think I went to China," she finally admitted. "I think it may have been a photograph." Then she shook her head. "No, it was big. Really big. Not a picture but likely a recreation of the mural somewhere here in the US."

"Where did you grow up?"

"In Fairfax, Virginia, why?"

"Makes me wonder if the mural is in Fairfax," Boyd said.

"I highly doubt the Six Red Dragons painted a mural outside their building, announcing their presence for the entire city to see," she retorted. "That would be a tad obvious, don't you think?"

"Yes, that's true." Boyd turned back to stare at the screen. "Do you still have family there?"

"No. My grandparents moved to Phoenix, Arizona, a few years ago." Her stomach knotted. "Do you think they're in danger?"

"No, I doubt anyone would consider your grandparents a threat, especially since they're not even in DC." He offered a smile. "Try not to worry."

It hadn't occurred to her that her Parker grandparents might be targeted to get to her. Despite the fact that she hadn't lived with them since she'd turned eighteen and headed off to college, they were still vulnerable.

Lina abruptly stood and grabbed the disposable phone Boyd had given her. She punched in her grandfather's cell number, holding her breath until he answered.

"Who is this?" he demanded.

"Grandpa, it's me. Lina." She closed her eyes on a wave of relief. "Are you and Grandma doing okay?

"Yes, of course. Your grandmother is still sleeping, it's pretty early here." She winced remembering the time zone difference. "Why do you ask? And why are you using a different phone?"

"No reason in particular, I lost my old phone." She glanced at Boyd who was clearly listening. "I just wanted to check in on you, that's all."

"We know you're busy, Lina," her grandfather assured her. "You're welcome to come down for a visit anytime."

Her last trip to Phoenix had been over Christmas, and they'd encouraged her to come down any time to escape the snow and cold. "I don't mind the winter, Grandpa."

"Trust me, someday your old bones will hate that cold, damp weather too," he said wryly.

That made her smile. "You're probably right. I'm glad you and Grandma are okay. Take care, Grandpa. I love you."

"Love you too, Lina."

She lowered the phone and let out a heavy sigh. "They're okay."

"I'm glad to hear that," Boyd said. "I'm sure they'll be fine. I'll have Jordan get someone out to watch over them, just in case. But there's no reason to go after them. Not if they have already framed you for the bombing of the research lab."

She nodded, hoping he was right. Her grandparents may not have embraced her Chinese heritage, but they had mourned the loss of her parents, raising her as if she were their own.

They were all she had left in the world.

If anything happened to them because of her, she'd never forgive herself.

JANUARY 31 – 9:12 a.m. – Washington, DC

Yates waited outside the Oval Office for the president. He'd gotten very little sleep since this nightmare had started, and he didn't see that changing anytime soon.

He was the only one who knew the truth about the bombing, other than the ones who'd masterminded it. He knew that Lina Parker had been framed to take the fall. Yet he had to be careful who he talked to about this. Only someone with high-level security access, possibly within the FBI or the NSA, could have made that happen.

Once again, he was in the dire position of not knowing whom he could trust.

The president? Ideally, yes. But that didn't mean that someone close to the president, one of his advisers, his chief of staff, or even a house representative or congressman wasn't complicit in this. Experience had taught him that even those high up in the government could be lured by greed and thirst for power.

A wave of exhaustion hit hard, and he leaned against the wall for support. He was too old for this. His goal had been to groom one of his men to take over, but so far, he hadn't been overly impressed.

Too bad Jordan Rashid and Sloan Dreyer had left the agency. He'd hand the reins over to either man in a heartbeat.

Not that the FBI hierarchy would allow such a thing. In his humble opinion, it was that stupid political hierarchy that created half the problems they'd faced in the past two years. Far too many men craved money and power. A dangerous combination when the security of the entire country was at stake.

"Director Yates?" The president's chief of staff strode toward him. "I'm sorry, but the president isn't going to be able to make this meeting after all. I've rescheduled your session for three o'clock this afternoon."

Yates scowled. "This is a matter of national security," he said sharply. "The president can't be doing anything more important than that."

"I'm sorry, sir." The chief of staff didn't look the least bit apologetic. "His meetings with Xi Jin Ping have gone longer than planned. How about I let you know if an earlier time opens up? I'll do my best to shoehorn you in."

Yates felt his fingers curl into fists, wanting nothing more than to wipe the smirk off the younger man's face. He straightened and leaned forward, pinning the guy with a fierce look. "Did you tell him it was important?"

"No, because he left strict instructions that this meeting cannot be interrupted."

Yates wanted to scream with frustration. "If anything happens to cause more American deaths before I get a chance to talk to the president, you'll be looking for a new job. Understand?"

A flicker of unease flashed in his eyes. "I'll do my best, sir."

"Good plan. Get me in to see him, sooner than later."

Yates forced himself to relax his fingers as he turned and walked away.

Several people tried to stop him, but he ignored them all as he left the White House. Politics always got in the way of doing what was right. When really, it should be the exact opposite.

Yeah, he was definitely too old for this.

JANUARY 31 – 9:18 a.m. – Beijing, China

Sam suppressed a sigh as he climbed onto the back of Jia's stolen motorbike. He looped his arms around her slim waist, the only perk of riding this way. She knew the city far better than he did, so it made sense for her to drive. Yet the way she zipped in and out of traffic had shaved a good ten years off his life.

He'd prayed the entire ride from Tianjin to Beijing and firmly believed the only way they'd gotten there in one piece was because of God's grace in watching over them. But how much longer could they survive like this?

Every time they passed an armed police officer or a soldier, he felt the muscles in Jia's body tense. She had every reason to fear the authorities. Chinese prisons were no joke. And while he may be an American, he didn't doubt that they'd kill him too. It wouldn't be difficult to make it look like a terrible accident.

Jia took a circular route to the designated meeting place. He knew they were running low on cash, especially since they still needed to purchase plane tickets. But Jia assured him they would be fine.

He admired her strength and her ingenuity. The intel she'd already gathered was valuable, but her blown identity within the Six Red Dragons would leave a gaping hole in their intelligence. It couldn't be helped, especially since Jia had given up everything dear to her to provide key information to the United States.

Wincing when his knee smacked against the side of a car, he made himself as small as possible. Jia took an abrupt right-hand turn, cutting off another vehicle, taking the bike up and over the edge of the road onto the sidewalk.

Leaning forward, he peered into the side mirror. There was nothing unusual, but he trusted Jia's instincts.

After several more turns, she pulled up in front of an open market. They ditched the motorbike and made their way through the crowds of people.

He followed Jia as she went deeper into the market. When she finally stopped, he realized they'd reached their destination.

Jia and her contact Hu Zhen spoke only briefly. She handed Sam's passport photo to the man and paid half the fee, the rest due upon completion of the document. He'd promised to have it completed in two hours or less.

Then they left as swiftly as they'd arrived.

Only, when they reached the spot where they'd left the motorbike, it wasn't there. Jia instantly shifted to the right, merging with a group of Chinese pedestrians.

"Keep your head down," she whispered as they continued moving through the crowd.

Sam did as she asked, knowing his height was a hindrance. Hunching his shoulders and lowering his head, he tried not to draw undue attention from those around them.

"I see them!" The shout was in Mandarin, and Sam swallowed a surge of panic. Escaping on foot wouldn't be easy.

Jia quickly turned in the opposite direction from where

the shout had originated. She ducked into one ramshackle dwelling, then another. When they emerged from the second structure, she broke into a run. He easily kept pace with her, desperately trying not to turn around to see who was following them.

Armed police or Chinese soldiers, what did it matter? Either way, if they were captured, they'd be killed.

Their deaths would not be quick, but slow and painful. Tortured until they told their captors everything they knew.

Sam grimly realized it would be better to kill themselves than to fall into the hands of the Chinese authorities, known for their horrific torture tactics. Remembering the deep and jagged scar on her arm made him shiver.

He silently vowed to keep Jia from being hurt again.

CHAPTER ELEVEN

January 31 – 9:36 a.m. – Arlington, VA

Boyd scrubbed his hands over his face. Sitting around wasn't helping to keep his exhaustion at bay. When he was in the service, they'd usually been on the move. He'd spent hours standing in front of closed doors, but sitting? Rarely.

He rose to his feet and paced the small length of the room.

"What's wrong?" Lina asked, watching him with a slight frown furrowed in her brow. "You look stressed."

"I'm fine." He must be losing his touch if she was able to read his emotions so easily. He'd left a message for Jordan about having the local authorities sit on Lina's grandparents but hadn't heard back. He reminded himself patience was a virtue. "Why don't you get some sleep? I'm sure we'll hear from Jordan if anything changes."

Lina stared at him for a moment, then nodded. She crawled into the bed fully dressed and closed her eyes. Satisfied, he returned to the computer. His vision blurred, but he blinked and focused.

Where had Lina seen the Six Red Dragons mural? He'd

tried every search option he could come up with but had only found the one mural located in Beijing.

Even though she couldn't remember anything about being taken overseas, Boyd knew it was possible that Lina had been to China. Had her mother taken her to visit family? Maybe the link to the Six Red Dragons was through Lina's maternal grandparents. Did she know her grandparents' names? He glanced over his shoulder, but she appeared to be sleeping.

Too bad the DNA information she'd uploaded had been wiped clean.

Shu Yan Chen had been identified as Lina's aunt. Her mother's sister. Thinking about that now, though, he realized how unusual that would have been, especially twenty-five years ago.

To prevent overpopulation, which frankly continued to be a huge problem, Chinese leaders only allowed a family to have one child.

How was it possible Lina's mother had been one of two children? Had Lina's grandparents been given special dispensation to have two children? Had they come from a powerful and influential family? He had to assume they were distressed to have given birth to another girl as boys were more highly sought after to continue the family lineage.

Had Lina's maternal grandparents been involved in the Six Red Dragons? He made sure Lina was still sleeping as he slid his phone from his pocket. Feeling a little foolish, he hid in the bathroom to call Jordan.

"Lina's grandparents are fine," Jordan assured him.

"Good to know, but I'm calling about her other set of grandparents. Her mother's parents."

"What about them?" Jordan's tone was wary.

"We should have realized earlier that Lina finding her mother's sister through DNA was unusual because people in China are only allowed to have one offspring not two."

There was a long silence as Jordan pondered that. "Maybe they escaped to America before the birth of their second child."

"That's possible, but we found the mural Lina remembered of the Six Red Dragons in Beijing, which makes me think Lina had been taken there, maybe to visit her mother's family."

Jordan let out a low whistle. "Does she remember going to China?"

"No, but as she was only four years old, that isn't unusual." The more Boyd considered the mural and the two siblings, the more convinced he was that Lina's grandparents had connections to the Six Red Dragons. "Don't you see, Jordan? They eliminated all the DNA evidence to cover their tracks."

"Okay, if we go with your theory, then why set her up to take the blame for the bombing? And why keep trying to kill her?"

"I don't have all the answers yet," Boyd admitted. "But I believe the link to her family is key. Maybe Lina's grandparents are no longer alive and the new head honcho wants to eliminate any potential trail back to the mafia. You know how paranoid some of them can be. It's why they listen in on the conversations of their citizens."

"How does the terrorist attack fit in?" Jordan asked. "I still have a bad feeling about what the ultimate plan is."

"I know." Boyd shared his apprehension. More so since he'd started fitting some of the puzzle pieces together. "But as someone who worked within the Secret Service, I can assure you that getting anywhere near the president will be impossible."

"Nothing is impossible," Jordan countered. "The previous terrorist attempts prove that."

"None of those took place within the White House," Boyd said firmly. Suspecting what Jordan would say next, he went on to explain, "I messed up when the First Lady and her daughter, Kali, were in New York City to attend a Broadway show. I had far less control over the environment there. Despite having the place fully vetted, some guy managed to get through, and I am still thankful that he was caught before he could do permanent harm."

"Exactly my point," Jordan said. "No one is safe."

"The difference here is that the White House is secure," Boyd insisted. "They've tightened security since the incident at last year's inauguration."

"I hope you're right," Jordan said wearily. "Because my gut is screaming at me that there's something bad going down."

Boyd grimaced. He hoped he was right too.

JANUARY 31 – 9:47 a.m. – Beijing, China

Jia took refuge in the back of a shanty, pulling Sam with her. She honestly wasn't sure how they'd managed to escape the Armed Police. Maybe Sam's prayers had helped because she felt certain they'd almost been caught.

More than once.

Paying a bribe allowed them to seek sanctuary. Jia knew they couldn't stay long, though, because the Chinese woman who'd allowed them to enter her shanty could just as easily take money from the Armed Police to turn them in.

That was just the way things worked in China.

"We'll need transportation to the airport," Sam whispered in her ear.

She nodded, trying not to show her despair. Stealing a car in the middle of the city was difficult, even at night. Beijing was twelve hours ahead of Washington, DC. If they could just get on the plane, she'd feel better.

The flight would get them to DC in roughly fourteen hours if they could go direct. Which was not common. She tried to quell a flash of panic. Even though they would be gaining those hours, it was cutting it close.

Her disposable phone vibrated. She quickly answered Hu Zhen's call. "Do you have it finished already?"

"Yes. Get here soon, though, as I'll need to relocate." Hu Zhen didn't sound happy.

"We'll be there in ten minutes." Thankfully, she hadn't gone too far from Hu Zhen's hideout, taking a circular route to get rid of the police who'd spotted them. She slid the phone into her tunic pocket and glanced at Sam. "It's ready."

"Good." Sam eyed her warily. "We're going on foot?"

"Yes." She didn't want to steal another car until after they had the replacement passport. Taking Sam's hand, she ducked out the back of the shanty. Merging with other Chinese, she managed to get them to Hu Zhen's place in less than five minutes.

The passport looked amazing. She paid his fee and handed the passport to Sam. She still had a passport under a name unknown to the Six Red Dragons. As they left, she saw Hu Zhen go in the opposite direction.

This time, they managed to avoid the police. When they were far enough from their previous location, she found an old car sitting off on a side street. It only took a minute for her to hot-wire the vehicle. She glanced at Sam who was squished into the passenger seat. "Next stop, the airport."

"Thank you, Lord Jesus," he murmured.

Despite her lack of faith, she found herself silently echoing his sentiment. There was no denying they needed all the help they could get.

Upon arriving at the airport, they ditched the car and hurried inside. Passing a shop, she paused long enough to purchase a suitcase and a few items of clothing. Not that she needed them but to avoid drawing undue attention.

She approached the ticket counter with Sam at her side. "What is the earliest flight to Washington, DC?"

The male attendant brought the information up on his computer. "There is a flight about to board in twenty minutes. You'll have a layover in Heathrow, but the total flight time is seventeen hours."

A flight leaving in twenty minutes? Seventeen hours of flying time? Maybe God was watching over them because she'd expected much worse. "Two tickets, please."

"I need your passports," he said. "And there will be an additional fee."

"I understand." Jia knew the fee would go into his pocket, but she didn't care. She held her breath as he entered their fake identification into the system. When she had their boarding passes in hand, she breathed easier. They'd made it over the first hurdle.

As they waited in line to get through security, she eyed the people around them. The Beijing airport was huge and crowded, unlike their previous flight. Maybe it was the lateness of the hour, but she was glad no one seemed to pay them any attention.

The second hurdle was getting through the security checkpoint. She didn't get a second glance, but the security officer spent a long time peering at Sam's passport. Finally, he handed it back and waved them through.

Jia kept her expression impassive despite the thrill of anticipation surging through her. When they reached the gate, the plane was just starting to board.

"Perfect timing," Sam whispered.

"Yes." She gripped his hand tightly, continuing to survey the people around them as they waited for their turn to board. Again, no one paid them any attention.

Because they'd booked late, their seats weren't near each other. It occurred to her that was probably a good thing. Better to not appear to be traveling together. When she took her middle seat, Jia allowed herself to relax. Their fake identities worked. Her scar was covered. They were on a flight that would ultimately get them to Washington, DC.

For the first time since losing her husband, she silently prayed. *Thank You, God!*

JANUARY 31 – 10:23 a.m. – Washington, DC

Yates was tired of waiting for the idiot chief of staff to get back to him. Normally he could get directly to the president, but today, with the Chinese leader in house, nothing was normal. Even he couldn't override the president's orders. The minutes crawled by, and while he knew there was still time to cancel the upcoming Chinese New Year celebration during Xi Jin Ping's visit, he'd feel better if he'd been given the chance to discuss his concerns with the president personally.

When his phone rang, he pounced, hoping it was the chief of staff. But it was Jordan Rashid. "What's wrong?"

"I heard from Boyd, he has an interesting theory about

Lina's link to the Six Red Dragons. Her maternal grandparents may have been involved."

Yates scowled. "How does that help me?"

"It doesn't yet, but you have resources we don't," Jordan pointed out. "Get us the information on Lina's maternal grandparents."

Yates stared out the small window of his office. "You need to stay with Mack and Sun doing that work because I don't know who to trust. Other than the president himself."

Jordan was silent for a long moment. "I can put Mack's hacking skills to work, but he's still trying to find out who had clearance to access my company's information. At this point, all trails lead back to the NSA."

"I know, I'm sorry." Yates didn't like how things were going.

First the leak, then the inability to get to the president.

"That doesn't bode well," Jordan said, interrupting his thoughts.

"Tell me something I don't know." Yates's scowl deepened. "I may have to break down and trust Doug Weatherby. I don't want to believe the head of the NSA is involved in this."

"Let's wait to see what Mack and Sun can dig up for us," Jordan said, avoiding the topic of whom he should trust.

"Let me know what you find out." Call him cynical, but he had more faith in Jordan's team than his own counterparts in the intelligence community.

He paced, trying to come up with a plan. He needed to head back to the White House. Staying in sight would make it more difficult for the president's chief of staff to ignore him.

He'd get his audience with the president if it was the last thing he did.

The thought was not reassuring. Because if something did happen to the president, he was finished.

They all were.

JANUARY 31 – 10:28 a.m. – Arlington, VA

Lina awoke with a start. The nap had helped, but she still felt guilty for sleeping when Boyd was still working. Then she felt cranky. Was the guy made of steel? Maybe he was like the tin man in the *Wizard of Oz*, born without a heart.

With a groan, she rolled into a sitting position. Boyd glanced at her from his spot in front of the computer. "How's your hip?"

"Fine." There was no reason to take her annoyance out on him. Swallowing a sigh, she slipped around the bed to head toward the bathroom.

Splashing cold water on her face helped, although she would have given anything for a toothbrush. The past fifteen hours felt more like fifteen days. At least they were safe here at this motel.

Physically safe, but not emotionally. Being in close confines with Boyd wasn't easy. She knew this dependence she had on him wasn't healthy. Yet she was all too aware of his every movement.

Giving herself a stern lecture, she straightened and left the bathroom. Boyd was hunched over the computer screen, and from here, she could tell he was fighting exhaustion.

"Time for you to get some sleep." The way he spun to face her only reinforced her opinion. "Before you fall over."

"No time." His bloodshot eyes pinned her with a narrow look. "We may need to move again."

Her heart sank. "So soon? We've only been here a couple of hours. Did something change?"

He shook his head. "Nothing has changed. I can't explain why, but I feel vulnerable here."

"In broad daylight?" She wondered if being weary was making him more paranoid. "I don't think men with guns can sneak up on us here."

He shrugged. "I can't help how I feel."

She crossed over to him and rested her hands on his shoulders. His body tensed for a moment, then slowly relaxed beneath her touch. "Please get some rest. I need your strength for the long haul."

To her surprise, he nodded. "Okay. I'll take a thirty-minute break."

That wasn't long enough, but she didn't argue. Once he fell asleep, he'd likely be down for the count.

When he stood and lurched toward the bed, she took his seat at the computer. Only when she heard his breathing deepen did she glance back at him.

Even asleep, Boyd looked strong and capable. She was grateful God had sent him to watch over her.

Curious about his stint with the Secret Service, she did a quick search on his name. The first article that came up made her jaw drop.

Secret Service Fails to Protect First Lady.

"Oh, Boyd," she whispered under her breath. He should have told her about what happened since it had occurred just two months ago. As she read on about how the First Lady was attacked going into the theater with her daughter on Broadway, in Manhattan, New York, she vaguely remembered hearing about the incident. At the time, she hadn't paid much attention because the First Lady wasn't hurt. The article mentioned Boyd Sinclair as the agent in charge of the First Lady's detail, and the journalist admitted that the knife only scratched her because Boyd had thrown himself at the guy. Still, that anyone had gotten close enough to her with a knife had been viewed as a failure. Boyd had resigned his position, clearly taking the blame for the incident.

Lina sat back, feeling bad for what Boyd must have gone through. Based on how well he'd reacted to the threats against her, she felt certain he'd done everything possible to keep the First Lady safe.

Learning the truth gave some clarity as to why he was always so serious in his determination to protect her. Clearly, he was trying to make amends for what had happened in the past.

She sat for several long moments, thinking about Boyd's dedication to safety. First as a marine, then as a member of the Secret Service. And now determined to protect her.

Hearing the solid thud of a car door slamming shut, she rose and peeked through the window. Boyd had kept the curtains closed, but she was able to see the parking lot out front through the narrow opening. Her heart squeezed when she saw two Chinese men wearing dark clothing walking away from a black truck, talking rapidly to each other as they entered the lobby.

Visitors, she assured herself. No doubt here to celebrate the visit of the Chinese leader, Xi Jin Ping and his second wife, Peng Li Yuan.

Still, she continued watching, waiting for the two men to come back from the lobby. They hadn't moved in a secretive fashion or carried weapons, so she didn't think they were members of the Six Red Dragons.

Yet seeing them had caused an instinctive fear. Ridiculous, really, as she was half Chinese and proud of her heritage.

Well, she had been until learning of the possible link to the Chinese mafia.

The men were gone for so long she started to think they were interrogating the manager for information on her. But then they came back outside and stood, staring directly at their motel room.

Ice coalesced at the base of her neck, and she quickly crossed over to wake Boyd. She put a hand on his shoulder, and he bolted upright so fast they almost knocked heads.

"Two Chinese men outside," she whispered.

Boyd shot off the bed and grabbed his weapon. He peered through the narrow opening. "Where?"

"Right in front!" She looked through the window. The two men were now standing outside the black truck. "By the Chevy."

Boyd gave a terse nod and grabbed the satellite computer. If he noticed the article about the First Lady's attack, he didn't let on. He threw the computer into the case and handed it to her. Then he grabbed his phone. "Jordan? We need to move."

She couldn't hear the other side of the conversation but assumed Jordan wasn't happy to hear they may have been found.

"I'll call you when we're safe." Boyd shoved the phone into his pocket and looked at her. "I gave you the computer so I can go first. Wait here until I've cleared the area."

"Maybe we should hold off, they might leave. I saw them go into the lobby, they may not be the bad guys, they could be simply waiting for their room."

His dark eyes narrowed as if she'd committed a cardinal sin by not telling him the second she'd seen them. But then he turned toward the door. He took a deep breath, opened the door just far enough to squeeze through.

The men let out excited shouts in Mandarin, then she heard the gunfire.

No! Boyd!

CHAPTER TWELVE

January 31 – 11:01 a.m. – Arlington, VA

Boyd tucked his head and rolled off to the side as the gunfire rang out. He smoothly came up into a crouch and shot twice at each Chinese man. They fell to the ground where they stood. This time, he rushed forward and searched for IDs and keys. No ID but the key fob was helpful. No more running around the city on foot.

"Lina!" he shouted. "Let's go! Hurry!"

She bolted from the motel room, her green eyes wide and frightened. She carried the satellite computer, drawing in a harsh breath when she saw the two Chinese men on the ground. He took her arm and steered her toward their black Chevy.

"Get in." Without waiting, he lifted her up and into the seat. Then he slammed the door and jogged to the driver's side. Seconds later, they were leaving the motel. The wail of sirens indicated someone had already called in the gunfire. In his rearview mirror, he could see people coming out of the motel, staring after them their mouths agape.

Witnesses. Just what they didn't need.

"I—don't understand. How did they find us?" Lina asked.

"I'm not sure." He mentally berated himself for taking a power nap. If he'd have noticed those guys earlier . . . but he hadn't. *Idiot*, he inwardly raged. He'd been stupid to believe they were safe.

Lina would never be safe. Not until they figured out who kept sending these mafia assassins after them.

If Lina hadn't mentioned the two men, they likely would have burst open the door and killed them both. The mere thought of Lina being killed made his stomach churn. He did his best to stick to the speed limit despite the sense of urgency that rode on his back like a monkey. They couldn't use this vehicle for long, one of the gapers may have gotten the license plate. Especially if the motel had any security cameras.

Boyd winced. If the cameras had caught him shooting and killing the two men, the authorities would be after him very soon.

As if they didn't have enough trouble dogging their heels.

"Where are we going?" Lina's voice trembled slightly. "Shouldn't we call Jordan?"

"Soon." He didn't want to call Jordan just yet. Not until they were safe. "The traffic in DC will be terrible, so I think we'll stay in the outskirts of the city. We'll stop somewhere in the Springfield area."

"Sounds good." She sounded steadier now, as if the initial rush of fear had abated. "I still don't understand how they found us."

Now that they'd put some distance between them and the

scene of the crime, he tried to focus. Jordan had dropped them off at the motel. The vehicle he'd used hadn't been linked to his name or the company. Granted, they'd stayed in Arlington, close to where the bombing of the Institute for Nanoscience had taken place. But there hadn't been enough time for anyone to search every local motel for them. And what name would they have used anyway? He'd paid in cash and used an alias.

Then it hit him. Lina had called her grandparents. He smacked his hand on the steering wheel with frustration. "I can't believe I didn't think of that! I'm so stupid."

"What?" Lina stared. "Why would you say that?"

"You called your grandparents from the motel." He shot her a grim look. "It's possible they had a trace on your grandparents' phone and somehow used that to track us to the motel."

"But—I thought disposable phones were untraceable?"

"There's new technology that allows those phones to be traced by law enforcement." *Or someone with high security clearance*, he added silently. Like the suspected leak inside the NSA. Something he should have thought of earlier. He dug his phone from his pocket and threw it out his window. "Toss yours too."

Lina did as he asked but then frowned. "Now that we don't have either phone, how will we call Jordan?"

"We'll figure something out." Calling Jordan wasn't as high on the list compared to getting out of there. He wasn't going to take any more chances. Not when they'd almost been killed for the fifth time.

The clock was ticking. There was no doubt the attempts to find them were escalating. Yet they were no closer to figuring out who wanted Lina dead and why.

Feeling grim, Boyd realized if they didn't get some

decent intel and soon, this case would be his first and last with Security Specialists, Inc.

Either because he'd be fired or because he'd be dead.

JANUARY 31 – 11:15 a.m. – Washington, DC

"We lost them."

The three words filled him with rage. How was it possible that two people couldn't be found and killed? "And where exactly do you think they are?" he asked in an ominous tone. "Still in Beijing?"

"We believe so, yes," his contact hastened to assure him. "An officer with the People's Armed Police saw them, but they escaped. We have yet to pick up their trail."

"How long ago?" he demanded.

There was a moment of silence before his contact admitted, "Ninety minutes."

He gripped the phone so tightly he heard the plastic crack. "They're probably out of the city by now."

"We have a flag on their passports and their known aliases," his contact said. "So far they have not been at the airport."

He knew that didn't mean anything. Someone with the skills of a CIA agent and a CIA asset would know how to get new untraceable passports. He felt certain they were already in the air on their way to the US.

"Your services are no longer required," he said. Ignoring the sputtering response, he disconnected the phone and dropped it onto the floor. Using the heel of his shoe, he ground the phone to bits.

He'd need a new untraceable device to contact Manchu. He didn't look forward to that conversation, although Manchu had provided the inept contacts in the first place. Two different men had been unable to get the job done.

Swearing under his breath, he glanced at the clock. If Sam King and Jia Ling Ling were in the air, they had time on their side. He needed to figure out what names they were traveling under and soon.

His best option of keeping them from interrupting his plans was to meet them at the airport.

Killing them the moment they stepped on US soil.

JANUARY 31 – 11:22 *a.m.* – *Richmond, VA*

Kali groaned and put a hand to her head. She blinked in the darkness, wondering how long she'd slept.

Too long.

A wave of hopelessness hit hard. Why were they keeping her here? If they were going to kill her, why not get it over with already?

She told herself no more eating anything they brought her. Whoever they were.

Where was the Secret Service? The FBI? Anyone?

She cried out for her mom and dad . . . despite knowing they wouldn't hear her.

Then fell asleep once again.

JANUARY 31 – 11:25 *a.m.* – *Somewhere over Asia*

Sam could see Jia from his middle seat along one side of the plane. She was in the center aisle. He didn't like being separated, but there was nothing he could do. It was a good sign that the plane hadn't exploded the moment they'd taken off. He was grateful to God for getting them out of Beijing, China, without being caught.

At least, so far.

He was under no illusions that they were home free. Bad guys who send the People's Liberation Army and Armed Police after them would not give up so easily. The fact that they'd gotten away would only make those in charge double their efforts to find them.

Jia edged out of her seat and stood stretching in the aisle. She offered a brief smile and whispered in English, "I believe God may have been watching over us."

Her words warmed his heart. "I know He has been guiding us, Jia. We are very blessed to be here."

"Yes." She stared at him for a long moment. She was so beautiful he ached to kiss her. "However, we will need to take great care when we reach London."

"I know." He understood her fear. They were safe for the moment, but the long flight provided plenty of time for those searching for them to find their new identities. "Thankfully, the layover isn't too long."

"Yes." She looked away as if there was more she wanted to say but couldn't. Not under these circumstances. He watched as she moved away, disappearing into the tiny bathroom, then eventually returning to her seat.

He wanted to tell her how much he appreciated her help. Sam knew he'd been more of a hindrance than providing help during their mad dash through China. But it would be his turn to return the favor once they reached the US.

China had been her area of expertise. When they were on his turf, he'd take the lead in guiding her through customs and out of the airport.

The realization made him smile. He'd felt like a hindrance until now, but not for much longer.

Maybe they did make a great team.

. . .

JANUARY 31 – 11:35 a.m. – Springfield, VA

Lina stared down at the satellite computer resting on the floor between her feet. Calling her grandparents had almost gotten Boyd killed.

She felt sick to her stomach due to the never-ending danger. She hated knowing how much Boyd was in harm's way just because he'd been kind enough to take on the dubious honor of protecting her.

Not that she wanted anyone else in danger either. She didn't know Jordan or the rest of the Security Specialists team very well, but no one should have to be given the impossible task of keeping her safe.

When would it stop?

Never.

The possibility filled her with despair.

"Don't, Lina." Boyd reached over to take her hand. "None of this is your fault."

"It feels like it is," she whispered.

"You saw those guys in time to prevent them from getting to us." Boyd's tone was likely meant to be reassuring. "I shouldn't have taken a nap. If anyone is at fault, it's me."

"You can't stay awake for days on end," she argued. "Sleep deprivation isn't healthy or smart. Don't they use sleep deprivation as a way of torturing people?"

"I've been trained to need minimal sleep," he responded evenly. "First through the marines, then through the Secret Service."

She shook her head in frustration. "Was that why the First Lady was nearly stabbed?"

He dropped her hand as if her skin burned him. The instant she'd said the words, she regretted them.

"I'm sorry. I shouldn't have said that." Maybe her own sleep deprivation was getting to her. "I know I'm only alive because of you."

He didn't say anything for a long minute. Finally, he pulled off at the side of the road, shut off the engine, and turned to face her. "No, that wasn't why the First Lady was nearly stabbed. Being in the service can be boring. Routine. Mundane. The theater had been thoroughly vetted, but that maniac still managed to slip past the perimeter. Two other agents besides me lost their jobs that day. But ultimately, it was my fault. Because protecting her was my responsibility."

"You're excellent at your job, Boyd," she said. "I shouldn't have let the stress get to me. Normally, I don't lash out at people."

"Normally, you don't have the Six Red Dragons sending men to kill you," Boyd countered. "None of this is your fault."

"It's not yours either," she said, but she could tell by the way he avoided her gaze that he was taking the blame. The same way he had with the incident involving the First Lady.

He turned back to stare out the windshield. "We'll need to ditch the truck soon. I know your hip is still sore, but we can't risk the possibility that the police have the license plate number."

"My hip is feeling much better." That wasn't entirely true, but no way was she going to hold them back. Especially since she had been resting it as much as possible considering they were running for their lives.

"I can always carry you if necessary." He turned the car on and continued driving. "I'm going to find a dead-end road. Hopefully, that will buy us some time. We'll walk from that point on."

"Sounds good." She forced herself to sound positive even though the thought of going to yet another motel room filled her with dread.

Lina closed her eyes and prayed. Yet for the first time since this nightmare began, she couldn't seem to feel God's reassuring presence.

A wave of hopelessness hit hard.

It was all just too much.

JANUARY 31 – 11:53 a.m. – Springfield, VA

"Would you like something to eat?" Boyd glanced at Lina, noting the brackets of pain deepening each side of her mouth. They'd only been walking for twenty minutes, and she was already favoring her left side.

"I guess it is lunchtime." She didn't sound very enthusiastic.

"Come on, we need to refuel. We'll try that café." He gestured toward the restaurant. It wasn't a new place; rather, it appeared run-down, as if it had been around for several decades. In his opinion, that meant the food must be decent. Otherwise, it would have gone out of business a long time ago.

"Okay." She turned toward it. He could tell she was trying hard not to limp.

He swept his gaze over the area. So far, they hadn't seen a single cop. Avoiding the interstate by taking side roads had helped. But he felt certain that once they'd found the abandoned truck, they'd be swarming the place.

Maybe once they were inside the restaurant, he'd borrow someone's phone to call Jordan. He wanted to be in a different city before the truck was identified as being part of the crime scene in Arlington.

The restaurant was jam-packed, reinforcing his thoughts about the food. He spied a small table in the back corner and quickly snagged it. He dropped the computer bag at his feet as Lina slid across from him. The flat despair in her eyes worried him.

"Hey, we're going to be fine." He smiled reassuringly.

She shrugged. "For how long? Only until the next pair of gunmen find us."

He never should have allowed her to make the call to her grandparents. "We're not going to be found."

"I wish I could believe you."

He didn't respond as a harried server showed up with water and menus. "We have a meatloaf special. Can I get you something to drink?"

"Just water for me, thanks." He glanced at Lina. "What would you like?"

"Water is fine."

Five minutes later, they'd placed their orders. Meatloaf wasn't his thing, so he ordered a cheeseburger with the works while Lina ordered a grilled chicken sandwich.

Her morose expression was killing him. He reached across the table to take her hand. "Please don't give up hope, Lina."

"I'm trying not to." Her voice was so soft he barely heard her.

"What if we prayed?" The words came out of his mouth without his thinking them through. He didn't know if he truly believed in God, but Lina did.

Her gaze shot up to his. "You'd pray with me?"

"Yes." He smiled. "But I need you to show me how."

Lina nodded and tightened her fingers around his. "Dear Lord, we thank You for keeping us safe in Your care. Please continue guiding us to safety. Amen."

"Amen," he echoed.

Lina's bright smile made him feel good. Better than good. As if they might really be okay after all.

JANUARY 31 – 12:11 p.m. - Washington, DC

Jordan frowned when his second call to Boyd went unanswered. He'd heard about the gunfire outside the motel where he'd dropped Boyd and Lina earlier.

The two dead Chinese men must have been put down by Boyd. Jordan had already intervened with the local police, assuring them that Boyd was working under the direction of the FBI and that the two men were likely involved in the Chinese mafia. Meanwhile, he hoped they were both safe and on the move.

Yet why hadn't they called him? His gut was a churning mass of nerves. He had no idea how Boyd and Lina had been found at the motel. They should have been safe. He'd used a completely different alias to obtain the car. No way could it have been tracked back to him so quickly.

He stared out through the window of his office. Good thing his wife, Diana, was home with their young son and daughter. He didn't want her or Sloan's wife and daughter anywhere near the epicenter of danger. Still, he missed her reassuring presence. And her intelligence. Diana's thinking was less linear and more creative than his.

His phone rang. Seeing Mack's name on the screen, he quickly answered. "Tell me something good."

"Can't say it's good," Mack drawled. "Sun wanted me to tell you directly. It appears a sample is missing from the institute."

His gut clenched. "Like what?"

"*Strychnos nux vomica,*" Mack replied. "Better known as strychnine."

Strychnine? Jordan felt his knees go weak. "Didn't Lina assure us the institute didn't have any dangerous chemicals?" As soon as he asked the question, he remembered Boyd telling him she'd specifically said they didn't have high-level biological samples like smallpox and Ebola. Apparently, your average everyday poison didn't count.

"Yeah, well, this appears to be an anomaly. The sample came in a few days ago. And now it's gone."

He sagged against the wall. Dear Lord in heaven, this was bad. Very bad. "How much strychnine? Enough to kill someone?"

"I'm afraid so," Mack said somberly. "I'm still trying to hack into the security system to find out who tampered with it. The link seems to be someone within the NSA. If we can find that person, we'll likely find the strychnine."

"You better hurry," Jordan said grimly. "I have to let Yates know as soon as possible. Any threat has to be taken seriously, especially knowing the Six Red Dragons may be the very ones holding the strychnine in their hot little hands."

"Will do." Mack disconnected from the call.

Strychnine. Jordan found it difficult to wrap his mind around this latest development. A person would have to get very close to his or her target to use a poison like that. No easy task if the intended recipient was the president. The kitchen was watched like a hawk. Slipping poison into the president's food would be nearly impossible.

Still, he couldn't ignore the threat. He quickly called Yates, groaning when he reached his voice mail. "Call me," Jordan said tersely. "Poison is missing from the Institute for Nanoscience. The bomb was likely set as a diversion so there would be a delay in realizing what was taken. We need to talk."

He disconnected from the call, his thoughts whirling as he paced.

And prayed.

CHAPTER THIRTEEN

January 31 – 12:22 p.m. – Washington, DC

Yates hated visiting the White House. It took forever to get inside, the Secret Service took their sweet time checking everyone over and through the metal detectors, and then once you were inside, staffers rushed from one place to the next. As he entered the West Wing, he kept his gaze peeled for Steve Jones, the president's chief of staff.

This time, he wasn't leaving until he'd met with the president.

He nodded to the First Lady as she walked past. She returned his nod, then continued speaking to a female staffer saying something about the party that evening. He noticed her security detail following right behind her. Once that would have been Boyd Sinclair, but now some other guy was keeping Eloise safe while Boyd was doing the same with Lina Parker. Which was turning out to be no easy feat. Probably far more difficult than it had been to protect the president's wife.

He wondered where their daughter, Kali, was, then he realized she must be in school. He shifted from one foot to the other, trying not to look as impatient as he felt. When he caught a glimpse of Jones, he rushed forward.

"I need to see the president!" Yates drilled the guy with a steely gaze. "Now!"

"He's still meeting with Xi Jin Ping," the chief of staff informed him. "But I think I can get you in at two fifteen."

"That's almost two hours from now!"

"I'm doing my best," Jones snapped. "There's a lot going on here today."

Yates reined in his temper with an effort. "Listen, this is important." He handed Jones a sealed envelope. "Give this to the president. Once he reads it, I think he'll agree to see me right away."

Jones looked suspiciously at the envelope, but then nodded. "Fine. I'll be heading into the meeting in roughly twenty minutes. I'll give it to him, then. Now if you'll excuse me?" The annoyed chief of staff brushed past him.

Acid burned from his stomach up into the back of his throat. Yates idly rubbed the center of his chest, then turned to head to the vending machines located in the staffers' break room. Maybe food would help. Either way, he intended to stay here in the White House because he felt certain the president would meet with him once he read the letter.

After feeding dollar bills into the machine, he chose a protein bar. He'd have given anything for a cheeseburger, but the president was focused on improving the health of his staff. *Figured there wasn't a sweet roll or bag of chips in sight*, he thought sourly. Yates dropped into a chair, the pain in his chest persisting.

He tried to eat the stupid protein bar. It tasted awful, but he forced himself to take one bite and then another. He was about to pull out his phone to check his messages, since there wasn't any internet while waiting to get through the metal detector into the building, but he hesitated, feeling—off. Sweat popped out on his brow, giving him a twinge of worry. The pressure in his chest intensified.

Maybe this wasn't simple heartburn from being stressed.

A staffer came into the room. Yates looked at the young man, pressing his hand against the center of his chest. "I'm having chest pain. I—think I need a doctor."

The guy's eyes widened before he snapped to attention. "Stay here, I'll get someone right away!"

Yates blinked as the room spun. The pressure grew to astronomical proportions as if an elephant had plopped down on top of his chest.

Then he slumped from his chair and onto the floor as darkness claimed him.

JANUARY 31 – 12:48 p.m. – Springfield, VA

Lina ate her chicken sandwich with a renewed appetite. Despite the shabby interior of the restaurant, her meal tasted delicious. Maybe her appreciation came from within. She'd been touched by Boyd's willingness to pray with her. Her earlier despair faded, replaced by a sense of peace.

She was humbled by God's presence as they'd prayed together. And hoped this meant Boyd was learning to believe.

"I'm going to see if there's a pay phone near the restrooms in the back of the restaurant," Boyd said, breaking the silence.

"Pay phones?" She chuckled. "Not likely. I haven't seen one in years."

"This place has been here for years," he pointed out. "At least fifty, maybe more."

He had a point. "Even if they have one, it probably doesn't work."

"Can't hurt to try." He used his napkin to wipe his face. "And if not, I'll borrow one. Either way, we need to let Jordan know we're safe."

"Of course." She'd sensed he hadn't wanted to call Jordan, maybe because of how they'd been found at the motel in Arlington. Her hip had grown sore after walking several miles, but she was determined not to complain.

Yet she knew Boyd had noticed her limp. It was likely the reason he'd chosen to stop here for lunch. From what she could tell, he was much like an ironman, one who didn't need to do anything as mundane as to eat or sleep.

She sipped her water and glanced around the interior of the diner. Every stool at the counter was in use, and each table was occupied by at least two guests. She found that oddly reassuring, especially since no one paid any attention to her. There was certain anonymity in being part of a crowd.

She finished her meal and pushed her plate to the side. Boyd must have found a phone, or he'd have been back by now.

As if on cue, Boyd emerged from the short hallway and reached down for the satellite computer. "We have to go."

"What? Go where?" She jumped up from her seat, hiding a wince as her hip protested. "Wait, we didn't pay the tab."

"This will cover it." Boyd left two twenty-dollar bills on the table. "Follow me." He took her hand and led her toward the restrooms.

As Boyd had suspected, there was a pay phone hanging

on the wall. She wondered if it had worked, but Boyd led her past the phone toward a rear door. He paused, looking both ways, before leaving the building.

She silently followed his lead, holding back the questions that tumbled through her mind. Why were they on the run again? What had Boyd seen or heard that sent them through the back door?

Would this madness never end?

Lina sought solace in prayer as she and Boyd headed down one side street and then another. When they finally stopped in an alley, she leaned against the side of a brick building, pressing a hand to her hip.

"What's going on?" she whispered.

"Believe it or not, the pay phone worked. I was able to leave Jordan a message, but then I saw two police cruisers coming from where we'd left the Chevy." Boyd's expression was grim. "Maybe I'm just being paranoid, but when one of them turned the corner as if heading toward the restaurant, I figured it was time to bug out."

"I'll always trust your instincts," she said with a nod. "But I was hoping we'd get support from Jordan. If the police have found the truck, they're likely looking for us. Maybe they'll even assume we're walking around the area. They might double their efforts to find us."

"I know." Boyd peered around the corner, glancing up and down the street, then looked back down at her. To her surprise, he dropped a quick kiss on her lips, the gesture so brief she feared she'd imagined it. "We'll have to try to call Jordan again once we're out of this area."

Lina swallowed a protest. There was little choice but to keep moving on foot.

Dear Lord, give me strength!

. . .

JANUARY 31 – 12:59 *p.m.* – *Washington, DC*

Yates blinked up at the circle of faces staring down at him. There was something covering his nose and mouth, and he could feel air coming through the opening. An oxygen mask? He heard a beeping noise above the murmur of voices. It took a moment for him to realize he was being wheeled through the hall while lying on a gurney.

"Wait," he croaked. "I . . . need a minute . . . to talk to the president." He felt breathless even though the pain in his chest wasn't as bad as it had been earlier.

The people rushing him out of the building ignored him. Had they heard him? He could barely hear himself.

"Give him more nitro," someone shouted. "His blood pressure is sky high."

A hand pressed something against his bare chest. Wait a minute, where was his shirt? Was he really being wheeled out of the White House halfway naked?

"Stop! Wait!" He reached out to grab one of the men's hands. There was an IV catheter in his arm, dripping fluid into his veins.

"Give him something to calm down," someone snapped, "or we'll never make it to the hospital!"

"Try to relax, sir. We're getting you the care you need right away!" The cart moved faster, so much so that he couldn't see anyone's faces clearly. Then he noticed a syringe attached to a port on the IV tubing.

The darkness returned once again.

JANUARY 31 – 1:04 *p.m.* – *Washington, DC*

Jordan couldn't believe Yates hadn't called him back. He'd been trying to call the director of the FBI again when he'd gotten a call from an unknown number. He'd left Yates another message, then picked up the message. The call had been from Boyd, but when he'd tried the number back, the call was picked up by someone who worked in a diner located outside of Springfield, Virginia. He wasn't happy to have missed Boyd's call, even though it was nice to know his new recruit was still alive.

Unable to sit still, Jordan left his office to drive to Springfield. He needed to do something productive. This case was more frustrating than any of the others he'd worked on for the Feds, mostly because there were so few leads.

The Chinese mafia had too many members to count. Even if they could figure out who was in charge, he doubted that guy was here in DC. No, he felt certain the guy pulling the strings was back in China. Mack and Sun hadn't found any links to Lina's maternal grandparents either.

No surprise to learn of the Chinese men Boyd had taken out had fingerprints in the system. They'd put a request in for a DNA match but hadn't heard back yet. Jordan didn't plan on holding his breath. He didn't believe any of these guys were known to the US government.

He doubted they were US citizens. Any passport they may have used to enter the country was likely burned to ashes.

Disturbing to realize these men had come here to kill Boyd and Lina while fully prepared to die in order to accomplish their mission. Granted, US soldiers entered the military with the same philosophy. So had he, Diana, Sloan, Natalia, Mack, and Sun. There was a huge difference, though, in that they were sworn to fight the enemy in pursuit of freedom.

Not to be a personal assassin.

He merged into the awful DC traffic with only one

thought. To find Boyd and Lina before another pair of Chinese mafia members did.

JANUARY 31 – 1:16 p.m. – Washington, DC

"He's having an acute MI, get him to the cath lab, stat!"

Yates heard the voice as if the person speaking was off in the distance. At the end of a really long tunnel. It took a minute for the meaning to sink in.

MI? As in a heart attack? What exactly was the cath lab? Were they going to crack his chest open to perform surgery?

No! This couldn't be happening. He didn't have time for a medical emergency. He needed to talk to the president!

"Make sure the cardiac surgeon is on standby," the voice continued. "He may need a trip to the OR."

More faces popped in and out of his line of vision. But when he tried to talk, he couldn't. It was as if they'd paralyzed him, although he could lift his arm.

Barely.

It must be the drugs they'd given through his IV to keep him calm. With every ounce of strength he possessed, he lifted his hand, grabbed the side rail, and shook it.

Nothing. It was as if they didn't realize he was awake. That he had important business to discuss with the president that couldn't wait.

He felt cold fluid on the inside of his groin. Mortified to realize he was completely naked now. Then a sharp poke.

"Put him under, I'm accessing the femoral artery."

Noooo! But it was too late.

This time when the darkness came, Yates knew there would be no waking up until this was over.

If he survived at all.

JANUARY 31 – 1:22 *p.m.* – *Somewhere over Asia*

Sam had just fallen asleep when his elbow was jostled by the flight attendant. He blinked and looked up at the man. "May I see your passport, please?" he asked first in Mandarin, then in English.

He swallowed hard and patted his pockets, buying time. He sensed Jia's concerned gaze on him from her location a few rows away. Why were they asking to see his identification? They were already in the air and had been for several hours.

"Is there a problem, sir?" he asked politely.

"No problem," the flight attendant said. Although his expression remained impassive. "This is just a routine check."

"Of course, I have it right here." He began to slowly pull the passport out when there was a ruckus from the other side of the plane. Two people were arguing in Mandarin over a pillow and blanket.

The flight attendant turned to deal with the unruly passengers. Fearing this was nothing more than a temporary reprieve, Sam glanced at Jia. He mouthed the words, "Do they know who we are?"

She shrugged and shook her head, indicating she wasn't sure. He couldn't help but think the Six Red Dragons had some way to access the flight manifest.

Sam sat back, trying not to consider the possibility that they may have someone waiting for them in London.

The authorities could detain them on the plane until everyone else was off. And if that happened, he wasn't sure how they'd escape.

Jia caught his gaze and sent a reassuring smile. He tried to respond in kind, but his features felt tight, as if they might crack under the pressure.

Once the passengers had been dealt with, the flight attendant moved on to other duties.

Yet Sam knew he'd be back. They had hours of flight time left.

And no way to escape.

JANUARY 31 – 1:29 p.m. – Richmond, VA

"Mayleen, your lunch has been served."

Kali blinked, wondering if she'd imagined the voice in the darkness. "My name isn't Mayleen, it's Kali."

"Eat your lunch," the voice said sternly.

"Why don't you let me out?" Kali shouted.

The only answer was the sound of a door closing and a deadbolt being shot home.

Kali rose from the cot, feeling along the floor for the tray. After being drugged at breakfast, she had no intention of eating whatever slop they'd provided for lunch. But her mouth was so dry she desperately wanted to try the water. Maybe, just maybe the water hadn't been tampered with the way the food had been.

She had to stretch all the way out, the steel band around her ankle digging into her skin to reach the edge of the tray. When she pulled it close, the tantalizing scent of a grilled cheese sandwich made her stomach rumble.

Don't eat! Kali screamed the words in the back of her mind, but her fingers touched the sandwich, feeling the warm gooey cheese.

No. She would be strong, the way her parents would expect her to be. Kali forced herself to bypass the sandwich to reach for the glass of water. Drinking it slowly, she hoped and prayed it wouldn't make her throw up. Or go back to sleep.

Then again, what else was there to do in here? Nothing. Absolutely nothing.

Except to cry over why she was being held against her will and worry that the Secret Service and FBI would never find her.

Leaving the grilled cheese on the tray wasn't easy, but she managed to find the strength to turn away. Except it didn't matter as she soon felt the same dizziness she'd experienced after breakfast.

They'd drugged the water. Tears slipped from her eyes, running freely down her cheeks as the realization hit hard.

No matter what she did, they planned to starve her to death or drug her.

Why? What was the purpose of keeping her here? She balled up her fists and pounded the mattress until her strength began to fade.

As she drifted off, she couldn't help but wonder who Mayleen was.

JANUARY 31 – 1:35 p.m. – North Springfield, VA

Boyd wrapped his arm around Lina's waist. "Just a little farther."

"That's what you said ten minutes ago."

"I know." He needed to borrow a phone, sooner than later. Lina had been a trooper through all of this, but her limp was attracting too much attention.

They'd made it to the shopping center in North Springfield. When he saw a woman pushing a stroller, he turned toward her.

"Miss? Could you help us?"

The woman eyed them warily. Boyd didn't blame her for not trusting them. He offered a sincere smile, hoping to put her at ease.

"I don't want to scare you, but my wife fell and hurt herself. Would you be so kind as to allow me to borrow your phone to call for a ride? My buddy isn't too far away."

"Please," Lina added. "We mean you no harm. I've been praying God would send us someone to help, and here you are."

The woman hesitated, taking note of how Lina leaned against him. "Stay here," she finally said. "I'm going to put Tommy in the car."

"Of course, that's not a problem. I don't blame you for being careful." Boyd was glad Lina was leaning against the side of his body where his weapon was located. If this woman saw the gun, she'd take off faster than a rocket.

After she buckled her son into the car seat, she held the keys in one hand and held out her phone with the other. "One call. I'll hit the alarm if you try anything."

"I understand." Boyd took the phone and quickly dialed Jordan. He inwardly sighed in relief when Jordan quickly answered. "It's Boyd. I'm using a kind woman's phone."

"I figured. Where are you?" Jordan asked. "Still in Springfield?"

"North Springfield at the shopping center," Boyd said, smiling at the woman who was clearly listening. "Lina hurt herself, so we could use a ride."

"I'll be there as soon as I can, but you know the traffic in DC is terrible."

"Thanks, Jordan, we'll be waiting." He disconnected from the call and handed the phone back. "Thank you, ma'am."

"You're welcome." She quickly took the phone and jumped into the car. Then she took off as if anxious to put distance between them.

Boyd led Lina over to the closest store. It happened to be a large appliance and furniture store. Through the window, he could see breaking news flashing on one of the large screen TVs.

Clarence Yates, Director of the FBI, is currently undergoing an emergency cardiac catheterization to treat a sudden heart attack. In his absence, Senior Assistant Director Randal Stone will take over his duties.

Boyd stared in horror. Their FBI contact was out of commission, indefinitely. What did that mean for them? What if Stone was the inside leak?

Jordan couldn't get there to pick them up soon enough.

CHAPTER FOURTEEN

January 31 – 1:47 p.m. – Washington, DC
Things were finally going his way. Learning of the director's heart attack had him smiling for the first time since he'd learned the two CIA agents had managed to escape capture in Beijing. He had a plan in place to watch both Dulles and Reagan airports, but he knew they could fly in through Baltimore or even Richmond. And without their current aliases to track, it wasn't likely he'd succeed in finding them.

Yet it was better than doing nothing. Which is what those incompetent idiots had done in Beijing.

Well, they weren't doing anything any longer. He'd taken care of that.

The woman here in the US was still a problem, but he'd sent men to take care of her too.

He stared at his phone, wondering how much longer he could put off calling Bo Dung Manchu. China was twelve hours ahead of the East Coast, so it was the middle of the night there. Not that he'd normally let that stop him. No, the crux of the matter was that Manchu would not be happy to hear of their dual failures, of which there were many. None were his fault, but Manchu wouldn't care.

The man was brutally ruthless. A trait he could appreciate and identify with as long as Manchu's anger wasn't taken out on *him*.

Leaving the phone on his desk, he turned and stared out the window. He'd wait a few more hours before calling. Maybe he'd have better news to share by then.

In the meantime, he'd relish the fact that one problem had resolved itself. Only seven more hours to go before the festivities began.

The smile on his face broadened. Soon, very soon he'd get what he deserved. This night would go down in the history books.

An evening the country would never forget.

JANUARY 31 – 1:49 p.m. – North Springfield, VA

Lina could tell something was wrong. Boyd's expression had grown even more grim than usual, and that was saying a lot. Reading his face had become second nature. Her attraction to Boyd Sinclair wasn't healthy, but she couldn't seem to convince her heart to ignore the chemistry between them.

"This way." He ushered her into a nearby coffee shop, choosing a table away from the other patrons.

She sat across from him and leaned forward. "What is it?" she asked in a hushed whisper. "What's going on?"

He shook his head and gestured to the counter. "Do you want something?"

She resisted the urge to roll her eyes. As if that mattered. Clearly, he didn't want to talk about it. "Coffee with cream and sugar, please. And I need to use the restroom."

"Go now, and I'll hold our table."

Ignoring the pain in her hip, she went into the restroom. After using the facilities, she looked at her hip in the mirror. Oh yeah, the skin over her left hip was turning a magnificent purple hue. Lovely.

The area was tender and walking hurt, but she didn't think anything was broken.

When she returned to the table, Boyd was talking on what must have been another borrowed phone. "We're at the Coffee Clutch, north of the shopping area." He paused, then said, "Get here soon."

"Was that Jordan?" She didn't know who else he'd be chatting with.

"Yes, he's out of the worst of the traffic and should be here within the next few minutes." Boyd rose and went over to hand the phone back to the young man seated nearby. Then he murmured, "Stay put, I'll get our coffees."

Lina didn't appreciate being kept in the dark. She was in the center of this mess, in more ways than one. Whatever bad news he'd learned likely impacted her. Five minutes later, he returned with their drinks, sliding one cup across the table to her.

"Thank you." She curled her hands around the cup, basking in the warmth. "I wish you'd clue me in."

"There's a lot to discuss, but not here." Boyd's steely gaze bored into hers. "We'll talk when Jordan picks us up."

"Fine." She looked out the window, relieved she didn't have to keep walking. Yet the grim expression on Boyd's face weighed on her.

How much more bad news could she take?

She tried to focus on the small bit of good news. They hadn't been shot at for a couple of hours now. Maybe that was an indication that they'd shaken off the stupid Six Red Dragons mafia.

The minutes ticked by slowly, an uneasy silence hanging between them. When a black SUV pulled up, Boyd rose and held out his hand. "That's Jordan. Let's go."

She gratefully took his hand. Jordan was parked right in front of the door with the motor running.

"Thanks for the lift," Boyd said when they were seated. She was once again the back, not that she minded. She subtly rubbed her bruised hip. "I'm afraid I have bad news."

"Me too," Jordan said, pulling away from the café.

"I'm sure it's the same news. What do you know about Stone?" Boyd asked.

"Stone?" Jordan shot him a surprised look. "What are you talking about?"

"Yates is in the hospital, which means Randal Stone is in charge." Boyd scowled. "What are you talking about?"

Jordan yanked the steering wheel hard to the right, stopping abruptly at the side of the road. He hit the brakes so hard the vehicle bounced. "How did you hear Yates is in the hospital?"

"It's all over the news stations." Boyd grimaced. "You really didn't know? According to what they're reporting, he's currently undergoing a cardiac catheterization to treat his heart attack."

"Heart attack?" Jordan closed his eyes and dropped his chin to his chest. "No wonder he didn't return my calls."

Lina glanced between the two men who appeared equally devastated. "Yates is our contact with the FBI, right? Are we able to trust his replacement? Does this Randal Stone even know about us?"

Jordan lifted his head and turned in his seat to face her. "I don't think Stone knows about us, which is a good thing since I have no idea if he's trustworthy or not. Yates also mentioned potentially reaching out to Doug Weatherby, the head of the NSA, although I convinced him to hold off on that for now. I'm not sure if we can trust him either. Regardless, this isn't good. I was trying to get in touch with Yates to let him know about the strychnine."

"What strychnine?" Lina asked. Then she remembered. "You mean the strychnine at the institute? It's missing? Is that why they bombed it?"

"Yeah, that's why," Jordan agreed. "You knew there was poison there?"

"I—didn't think of it as poison. It's something we're using for a biological research study. It's not unusual to use chemicals that are harmful to humans, although this is the first time we've used strychnine. A shipment came in late last week." She couldn't believe what she was hearing. "Are you sure it's gone?"

"Oh yeah, it's gone, and it was taken by whoever used your access to get into the building."

Boyd muttered something harsh under his breath. She couldn't blame him. Here she'd been thinking things were looking up because they hadn't been shot at recently. The joke was on her. "What are they going to use it for?"

Jordan stared at her. "I need you to tell me. How much strychnine would it take to kill someone? Or a group of people?"

Her mouth went dry. There wasn't a doubt in her mind it could be used as a weapon. "The two vials we had are enough to kill two people, one vial per person. It's not exactly a weapon of mass destruction, so it can't be used to kill a group of people. Yet it is a very powerful and rapid-acting poison."

"Okay, hold on a minute," Boyd said. "Let's take a step

back here. To use something like strychnine, you'd need to get up close and personal to the person you intend to kill. Or have access to his or her food and drink. Which begs the question, who is the ultimate target? I mean, it's not going to be easy to slip a vial of strychnine into the White House. Especially not all the way into the kitchen. And from there, it would be impossible to know which meal is intended for the president or anyone else in attendance." He lifted his hands. "Maybe there's another target we're not aware of?"

"Got any ideas?" Jordan's tone held a barely refrained sarcasm. "I'm open for suggestions. The timing of all this is a huge concern. Especially since Xi Jin Ping is visiting from China. The president is hosting a Chinese New Year celebration tonight in his honor. It feels like the perfect storm."

"Do you think he's the target instead of the president?" Lina asked. "It wouldn't look good for us to have the current leader of China poisoned to death while visiting with the President of the United States."

"No kidding," Jordan said wryly. "But again, how is that going to be possible? Boyd is right about the security at the White House." He turned and put the SUV in gear. "We need to get back to DC ASAP."

"What's our next move now that Yates is out of the picture?" Boyd asked.

Jordan shook his head, looking weary. "I honestly don't know. We may have to consider trusting Stone or Weatherby. Although, really, I'd rather talk to the president himself."

Lina sat back in her seat, her mind whirling. Strychnine had been stolen from the research lab using her credentials. As if the bombing wasn't bad enough. What if the poison was used against someone important? Her stomach knotted painfully.

If they didn't figure out who the mastermind was behind all of this, she'd be arrested and tossed in federal prison for the high crime of treason.

And there wouldn't be anything anyone could do to help her.

JANUARY 31 – 2:05 p.m. – Somewhere Over Asia

Glancing subtly around the other passengers on the plane, Jia noticed the flight attendant was back to checking passports.

She drew in a breath and tried to relax. Maybe they were checking passenger IDs for another reason. Why? She couldn't fathom. Nothing like this had been done on her previous trips, but the last one had been several years ago.

Turning in her seat, she glanced at Sam. A flicker of alarm crossed his features, and she understood his concern.

She hoped the Six Red Dragons weren't looking for them. She was glad they had separate seats, but anyone looking closely at the records would note that she and Sam had purchased their tickets at the same time.

She swallowed hard and turned to face forward. The less attention she paid to Sam the better. Shifting in her seat, she tried not to think about the possibility that the authorities would be waiting for them in London.

For all she knew, the Six Red Dragons may wield enough power to force them to land at the next closest airport. Jia's area of expertise was escaping tight spots, fighting off attackers, disappearing into crowds.

But this? This interminable waiting was killing her.

As the flight attendant stepped up beside Sam, he abruptly stood and shouted, "I'm going to throw up!"

The flight attendant instinctively stepped back,

unwilling to be puked on. Jia watched in amazement as Sam covered his mouth and rushed toward the closest lavatory. There was a stunned moment of silence before the passengers went back to their movies, music, or chatting.

"Weak stomach," someone said in Mandarin.

Jia avoided the flight attendant's gaze, hoping and praying he'd simply move on.

Sam's antics had given them a brief reprieve, but he couldn't stay in the bathroom for the entire flight.

How long would they be safe?

She glanced out the window at the dark sky.

Not long enough.

JANUARY 31 – 2:13 *p.m.* – *Washington, DC*

The traffic wasn't bad until they grew closer to the metro DC area. Boyd tried not to show his frustration, but it wasn't easy.

Losing Yates as their FBI contact was a big problem. He could tell Jordan was upset about what had happened, making Boyd wonder if the guy's heart attack was natural. Or if Yates had been slipped something, not strychnine but some other medication that had caused it.

He opened the satellite computer and pulled up Randal Stone's image. The guy looked vaguely familiar, maybe he'd seen him once or twice during his stint as the First Lady's security detail. He did the same with Doug Weatherby. Weatherby looked familiar too.

"I don't know if we can trust either of them or not," Jordan said, noticing the face on the screen.

"I'm leaning toward not," Boyd admitted. "Although with Yates out of touch, we'll need to figure out who we can trust and soon."

"Yeah." Jordan paused, then added, "Or we could attempt to meet with the president himself."

Boyd scoffed. "Not likely. Unless you know him on a personal level?"

"I've only met him twice, after we found the nuclear bomb at the inauguration last year." Jordan sighed. "That's when I met you, remember?"

"Yeah. The president is smart, he'll probably remember you," Boyd said. "And after the way you saved his life, I'm sure he'll listen to you."

Jordan glanced at him. "Actually, I think you should try to meet with him. The president knows you, Boyd, far better than he knows me. You worked in the White House for several years, spending the last full year guarding the First Lady."

His frown deepened. "After the debacle in New York, I highly doubt the president holds me in high regard. You saved countless lives by finding that nuke. I almost got his wife stabbed by a zealot."

"Don't cut yourself down, Boyd. Besides, it's worth a shot. Maybe the two of us together can make that happen."

Boyd swallowed a groan and shook his head. "Fine. We can try, but don't get your hopes up on my presence helping you reach this goal. I'm more of a liability, Jordan."

"I doubt the First Lady truly blames you for what happened," Lina said. "As you said, the guy who tried to stab her was a zealot. I think they deemed him mentally incompetent to stand trial."

He winced, remembering how Lina had looked up and read all about his failure. Why that bothered him, he had no clue. "Regardless, I can assure you the First Lady was not happy with my performance." Or lack thereof.

"Boyd, you're being too hard on yourself," Lina insisted.

"You need to try to get access to the president. You know the White House better than we do."

He knew the White House all right, inside and out. After all, he'd practically lived there for the past six years.

But he didn't share their confidence in his ability to obtain an audience with the president. Especially not with short notice. The president's schedule was booked well ahead of time, every minute of every day allotted for important issues.

Then again, the missing strychnine was a pretty important issue.

"I'll try," he agreed. "But maybe we should split up our efforts, Jordan. You should see if you can visit with Yates in the hospital. Once he's finished with his procedure, he might be able to talk to you. We need him to give us some idea on whether or not to trust Randal Stone or Doug Weatherby."

"I was thinking about that," Jordan admitted. "From what I know about cardiac cath procedures, they don't take that long, just an hour or so. Unless, of course, they find something so serious they end up doing open heart surgery."

"We all need to pray that Yates doesn't need open heart surgery," Lina murmured. "By the way, what is his first name? It seems disrespectful to call him by his last name."

"Clarence," Jordan supplied. "But he often refers to himself as Yates."

"Good idea, we should pray for him." Boyd was more than willing to add his prayers, too, for what they were worth. He couldn't deny that he'd felt a sense of peace after he and Lina had prayed together, what seemed like days ago rather than a few hours.

Lina clasped her hands together in her lap and bowed her head. "Dear Lord, we ask You to keep Clarence Yates safe from harm and to provide him quick healing from his medical issues. In Jesus's name, Amen."

"Amen," Boyd and Jordan replied at the same time.

The traffic grew snarly the closer they got to the city. Boyd tried to think of a way to approach the president. Or rather Steve Jones, the president's chief of staff. Because getting past the bulldog in charge of the president's schedule would be the most difficult part of the task before him.

Boyd hated failing, and his stint with the Secret Service was a blatant reminder of his biggest screwup yet.

But if there was even the most remote possibility the president, Xi Jin Ping, or anyone else in the White House was poisoned with the missing strychnine, he'd do whatever was humanly possible to get inside the Oval Office.

He just hoped he didn't get arrested before he completed his mission.

JANUARY 31 – 2:32 *p.m. – Washington, DC*

The scent of antiseptic pierced his consciousness. Yates tried to open his eyes, but they felt as if they were glued shut. It had been many years since he'd been a field operative, too many to count, but some finely honed skills remained.

He held himself still, straining to listen. Had he been captured? About to be tortured? There was a stabbing pain in his groin, but the rest of him seemed unaffected.

Maybe his captors had just gotten started. For a moment, panic hit hard. He wasn't a young man anymore. He was very much afraid he wouldn't be strong enough to keep from spilling secrets.

"Good thing he came in when he did," a deep male

voice said. "If he'd have waited any longer, he'd be dead."

"Yeah, surviving the widow-maker isn't easy, especially when it's nearly one hundred percent blocked," a woman agreed.

Widow-maker? He didn't understand what they were saying. He was a widower, his wife having passed away from breast cancer over a decade ago. Her being gone was one of the reasons he lived and breathed all things FBI.

"Well, good thing is that he'll recover quickly," the male said. "Thankfully, he only needed two stents placed rather than needing to go to the OR."

"It's a very good thing. Oh, you better head down to talk to the press," the woman said. "They've been camped outside the hospital for the past hour waiting for an update."

"Vultures," the man said disdainfully. "They're not getting much other than the director of the FBI is in stable condition."

Slowly, the pieces fell into place. Yates remembered the massive chest pain, the trip to the hospital via an ambulance. When he'd been in the emergency department, they'd said something about going to the cath lab.

Rather than being tortured, the medical team had raced against the clock to fix his heart. The way they'd mentioned stents made him realize they must have put catheters into the arteries of his heart to keep the blood flowing. He still didn't get the widow-maker reference but sensed it didn't matter.

He was alive, that's what counted. Yates grew restless as his mind went back over the events preceding the chest pain. He rattled the side rail to get someone's attention. He had work to do! There was no time to waste.

He needed to talk to the president ASAP.

CHAPTER FIFTEEN

January 31 – 2:45 p.m. – Washington, DC

As Jordan expertly navigated the gnarly traffic, Lina tried to think of a way to help Boyd get through to the president. She suspected that Boyd was being way harder on himself about what happened, especially since the article she'd read indicated he'd resigned from his position.

Not fired, the way he'd made it sound.

Yet she understood that as a former Secret Service agent, he wasn't going to be able to waltz into the White House and demand a meeting. Maybe if they used Clarence Yates's name, letting the president's staff know they've been working closely with him, they'd get more traction.

"I think Yates is our key to get inside," she said. "We can say that we have a message from him to give directly to the president."

"We can try, but keep in mind that there might be guards outside of Yates's room," Jordan said. "He's a powerful man in Washington. No way will they risk anyone trying to get to him when he's at his most vulnerable."

"Great," Boyd muttered. "Both of our missions may prove to be impossible."

"Stay positive," Lina said with a frown. "Expecting the worst isn't going to help."

Boyd glanced at her but didn't respond. She sensed that he was more apprehensive about his role of getting inside to see the president than he was about Jordan's ability to see Yates.

Despite having lived in DC for the past several years, she'd never once been inside the White House. Not even back when they'd allowed tours, a practice that had been discontinued indefinitely. The building was impressive, even from a distance.

Jordan's phone rang. He answered it using the hands-free function. "Rashid."

"Boss, it's Mack and Sun. First, Lina's maternal grandparents are dead, so they're not involved. But we did find the source of the information leak. A guy by the name of Don Tillman who works for the NSA is the one who accessed the information."

"Good work," Jordan praised.

"The access was Tillman's, but you should know that if someone above him managed to finagle access to his password, they could have used it to get in," Mack pointed out. "My research on Tillman doesn't give any indication he's a bad guy. I'm sending Sun to pay him a visit, but my gut is telling me someone is using him as a decoy."

Boyd sighed. "Guess that means we shouldn't trust Weatherby."

"Okay, we'll take it from here," Jordan said. "Thanks for the info. Tell Sun to stay safe but to keep searching for information on the Six Red Dragons."

"Will do." Mack and Sun disconnected from the line.

There was a long silence in the car as they inched along. Lina's thoughts whirled. A leak within the NSA was not good.

"Guess we stick with our plan to go to the president directly," Boyd finally said. "We can probably walk from here. It will be quicker than driving through this mess." Then he glanced at her. "If you're up to it, Lina."

"Of course."

"We need to find a place to meet," Jordan said. "I'll head over to the hospital to see Yates, but we need to stay in touch."

"I ditched our phones," Boyd said. "I could try to bring the sat computer, but I doubt they'll let me take it through security."

"They won't." Jordan scowled. "I'll contact Sloan and have him meet you outside the White House with a new set of phones."

"We can't wait, that will take too long," Lina protested.

"Okay, then you need to call Sloan by borrowing a phone if you need him," Jordan clarified.

"Oh, we'll need him," Boyd said darkly. "I don't want you to get your hopes up that this meeting with the president will actually happen."

"I'll pray you are given the chance," Jordan replied, seemingly unconcerned. "In the meantime, I'm also praying Yates is doing well and will be able to talk to me when I get there."

Lina was more than willing to add her prayers to the mix.

"Ready?" Boyd asked.

"Leave your weapon too," Jordan cautioned. "No way will they let you take that inside."

Boyd slipped the gun and holster off and tucked them inside the computer bag.

"I'm ready when you are," she said.

They waited until Jordan was stopped near an intersection, then quickly got out of the car. Several drivers honked their horns, but she ignored them. It wasn't as if they were causing a traffic jam; the cars weren't going anywhere.

Boyd took her hand and set out at a brisk pace. They were out in the open in the middle of the city, but she wasn't afraid. The Capitol Police were everywhere, and as they came closer to the White House, she could see the Secret Service patrolling the perimeter. The guards looked at them curiously as they approached the gate.

Oddly enough, she felt they were probably safer here than anywhere else. If they were able to get inside. Normally, requests needed to be made far in advance to have security checks performed on anyone wanting to get inside.

Would they let Boyd in but refuse to allow her to accompany him? She ignored the niggle of worry. Just because she'd been next to Boyd for nearly a full day didn't mean she couldn't survive without him for a short time.

The January wind was brisk, but inside her quilted jacket, she was sweating. The fear of being separated was causing her to panic.

No matter how crazy it sounded, she was afraid that once she and Boyd were separated, she'd never see him again.

And that men from the Six Red Dragons faction of the Chinese mafia would find and kill her.

JANUARY 31 – 2:58 p.m. – Somewhere over Europe

Sam spent as long in the bathroom as possible. When he emerged, he tried to look shaky and sick, moving with an unsteady gait to his seat.

It wasn't long, though, before the flight attendant returned. "Are you feeling better?" he asked the question first in Mandarin, then again in English.

"Yes, thank you," Sam replied in Mandarin, giving the attendant a tiny bow of his head. There was nothing he could do about his American features, but he fully intended to speak and act like he'd spent most of his life in China. "I am sorry for causing distress."

"Please don't be concerned. Not everyone enjoys air travel." The Chinese prided themselves on being polite, even when they were about to shove the tip of a blade between your ribs. "May I see your passport, please?"

"Oh, yes. Of course." Sam didn't think another performance would do anything but cause more suspicion. He pulled the passport from his pocket and handed it over.

The flight attendant stared at it. "What is your address?"

Sam quickly rattled off the address listed on the document. Good thing he'd taken the time to memorize it. He hoped the attendant didn't notice the sweat forming along his temples, or if he did, that he'd chalk it up to being ill. Sam kept his expression bland as if he didn't have a care in the world.

"You are an American citizen, yes?" The flight attendant looked at Sam, then down at the passport photo.

"I have dual citizenship," he lied. "I was born in America, but my mother is from Beijing. Are you familiar with the Haidian District? She works in a restaurant there." He named the place, hoping the additional details alleviated the man's concerns.

"Yes, they have good food." The flight attendant stared at him for a long moment before handing the passport back. "Enjoy your flight."

"I will try, thank you." Sam slid his passport back into his pocket. The flight attendant moved on, asking the next passenger for his passport. He wasn't reassured to know they were checking everyone's information.

How many Americans were on this flight? He hadn't seen many. Which likely made his presence even more noticeable.

Jia caught his gaze and flashed a reassuring smile. He nodded back at her, wishing they were seated next to each other so he could cuddle her close, breathe in her unique scent, and share her strength and courage.

If the plane made an emergency landing, he hoped and prayed Jia would be able to escape even if he was detained.

One of them getting through was better than nothing.

Closing his eyes, he tried to rest, knowing he'd need his strength for whatever awaited them in London.

JANUARY 31 – 3:08 p.m. – Washington, DC

Boyd eyed the Secret Service agents on guard as he and Lina approached the White House's gated entrance. He recognized Theo Burns and John Thompson. "Theo, John. How are you?"

"Fine, but what are you doing here, Sinclair?" Theo asked. "You don't work here anymore."

No kidding. Boyd kept his expression neutral. "Theo, it's critical that we get in to talk to the president's chief of staff." He'd decided that asking to talk to the president himself would only hurt their chances of getting access. "I know Jones is tied up, but this is important. I wouldn't ask if it wasn't."

Theo and John exchanged a look. "We'd like to help, but you're not on the list."

"Theo, you know me well enough to know that despite what happened two months ago, I'm still dedicated to our national security. I'm working for the FBI on a highly classified case. We have information that is critically important. I'm only asking for a brief conversation with Jones."

"Who's the woman?" John asked.

"She's with me." Boyd knew this part would be tricky. "Lina Parker, she's involved in this case too."

He was secretly shocked they didn't seem to recognize her name. The bombing had happened several hours ago, but the intel must be slow in making its way through the service. He knew from experience that despite their role of protecting the White House and those inside, information didn't always flow down to the front lines.

One small point in his favor.

"We can let you in, but I'm not sure about Ms. Parker," Theo finally said. "Not unless she has security clearance."

"I do," Lina said quickly. "However, it's fine if you'd like me to wait outside." She glanced at Boyd. "I can wait for Sloan, if one of these fine men would allow me to borrow their phone to call him."

He appreciated her attempt to help, but he didn't like the idea of leaving her behind, even for a moment. "Theo, I'll take full responsibility for Ms. Parker. We are both working for Clarence Yates. Since he's in the hospital, we really need to talk to Jones as soon as possible."

He could tell using Yates's name swayed them.

"Fine. We'll let you pass," Theo agreed reluctantly.

"But don't be surprised if they turn you away once you get inside."

"I understand." Boyd knew full well this was just the first layer of security they'd have to get through.

One small hoop and several more to jump through before they were allowed to the inner sanctum.

He hoped Jordan had better luck at the hospital in his quest to talk to Yates. Because he truly didn't see how anyone would let him and Lina inside the inner sanctuary of the White House.

And if they did, the service agents who allowed them to enter should technically all be fired for their breach in protocol.

He tried to ignore the heavy cloak of guilt, telling himself the risk was worth it.

If the president died tonight, it wouldn't matter anyway.

The entire world would erupt into chaos.

JANUARY 31 – 3:22 p.m. – Washington, DC

Jordan decided to follow Boyd's lead and head the rest of the way on foot after he found a place to park.

Parking was ridiculously expensive, but he didn't care. He needed to move. And sitting in traffic was driving him crazy.

Despite his encouraging words to Boyd and Lina, he wasn't sure they'd get anywhere near the president. Still, they had to try. What else could they do? Sitting around and wringing their hands wasn't going to cut it.

The leak within the NSA was troubling. Missing strychnine was also a big deal. And while the threat was small, targeted at one or two people, the very idea of that stuff getting anywhere close to the White House made him feel sick to his stomach.

It was worse, really, than the previous threats he and his team had worked. Even though the previous threats had endangered hundreds of innocent lives, he felt certain this targeted attack could have even worse implications. They had no idea who had the strychnine or who might be the intended target.

He wanted to believe Boyd's theory that getting to the president or Xi Jin Ping was impossible. But the bad feeling that plagued him the moment he'd learned of the shooting of Shu Yan Chen was growing worse by the second.

There wasn't a doubt in his mind that they were running out of time.

When he was able to park his SUV, Jordan took off running. The George Washington University Hospital wasn't far.

But as he approached the facility, his spirits sank. There were dozens of news reporters outside and a slew of security and police keeping people out. He pushed his way through the crowd, determined to find a way inside.

"My wife is having a baby!" He shouted the words at the top of his lungs. "I need to see her!"

The truth was that Diana had recently given birth to a baby boy they'd named Benjamin Joseph Rashid. But she wasn't in labor again now.

Miraculously, the crowd parted to let him through. Jordan didn't have to work hard to look harried and wild-eyed at the possibility of missing his baby's birth. The thought of not getting to Yates was enough to make him feel panicked.

He burst into the hospital lobby, then quickly ran over to the front desk. "Where is the maternity ward?" He decided he'd have a better chance of continuing the charade rather than asking for Yates directly.

"Sixth floor," the woman replied. "You need to get a visitor pass, though."

"Thanks." Jordan turned toward the line waiting for a visitor pass, then spied the restrooms. He diverted from the line and ducked inside.

What he needed was a pair of scrubs or maybe a lab coat. He wouldn't be allowed a visitor pass without giving the name of the person he was going up to see. Something he'd had to do last year when Ben had been born.

He used the facilities, then bided his time. Hanging out in the restroom wasn't high on his list of fun things to do, but when a young man came in wearing scrubs, a lab coat, and a name tag identifying him as a lab tech, Jordan made his move. He grabbed the guy and held pressure against his carotid arteries until he passed out. Then he quickly changed clothes with him. When that was finished, he placed him in a locked stall.

The switch wouldn't last for long, so he quickly emerged from the bathroom and made his way to the closest elevator. He remembered the cardiac unit was on the fourth floor, only because he'd accidentally gotten off there during a visit to see Diana and Ben.

From there, he'd need to find Yates's room. Hopefully, he could get inside to talk to Yates under the pretense of needing to draw his blood before anyone found the real lab tech tied up in the bathroom downstairs.

Jordan needed to talk to Yates and escape from the hospital before his butt was tossed in jail for assault and battery.

And impersonating a hospital employee.

. . .

JANUARY 31 – 3:31 *p.m.* – *Washington, DC*

Lina knew she was holding Boyd back. "I still think you should have let me stay outside to wait for Sloan."

"You've never met Sloan, how will you know who he is?" Boyd asked, his gaze focused on the Secret Service agents bracketing either side of the metal detector. "Besides, that may still happen depending on how this goes."

"You'll get in easier without me." Lina had decided this mission was more important than her fears of losing Boyd. She highly doubted anyone from the Six Red Dragons would try to hurt her while she was standing near 1600 Pennsylvania Avenue near cameras and cops.

Her pulse quickened as she followed Boyd toward the staff entrance of the building. Being this close to the most famous building in the nation was humbling. Granted, the president, his family, and those who worked for him were as human as the rest of them, but still, she couldn't contain her sense of awe.

Even if she didn't get all the way inside, she'd never forget this moment. She was in a place where most people weren't allowed.

If they didn't figure out who had the strychnine and what it was going to be used for, Lina felt certain the memory of the past twenty-four hours would be all she'd have as she sat in federal prison awaiting her trial.

Think positive, she chided as they approached the metal detector. *God is watching over us.*

The Secret Service agent standing there eyed Boyd. "Haven't seen you lately, Sinclair."

"I know. But this is important. We have information from Clarence Yates that needs to get to Jones."

"Yates?" A flicker of uncertainty darkened the guy's

eyes. "He's in the hospital. He fell unconscious near the vending machines."

"I know, and that's the only reason we're here." Boyd subtly urged her to step up beside him. "Please, Tim. I know this is asking a lot, but I just need a few minutes."

"You're not on the list," Tim argued.

"I'm aware. Please believe me when I tell you that Yates would have put me on the list if he wasn't in the hospital fighting for his life."

Tim's expression was full of doubt. "You, maybe, but the woman?"

"I'll wait outside," Lina offered quickly.

"Lina knows more than I do," Boyd said, ignoring her comment. "She must be included."

Tim was clearly torn by indecision. "Why don't you two wait over there? I'll get Jones to come here and talk to you."

"We're happy to wait, but you should probably put us through the metal detector first, just to be safe," Boyd said.

Tim flushed at his comment even though Boyd had been polite about pointing out his lapse in security.

Their getting into the White House unannounced and not on the list would be a much bigger lapse. She felt certain Tim was thinking the same thing.

"I'll take full responsibility if Adams finds out," Boyd said.

"Yeah, like that will matter," Tim muttered darkly. "You don't work for Adams anymore."

Lina was about to turn away when Tim waved her forward. "Come on, let's get you through the scanner."

She removed her jacket as Boyd did the same. They were scanned and their jackets examined closely before they were cleared.

"Stay right there," Tim said, gesturing to a small alcove

to the right. He used his earpiece and lifted his wrist to his mouth. "Steve Jones, I have Boyd Sinclair here on behalf of Clarence Yates asking you to come speak with him."

Lina felt certain the request would be denied, but Tim nodded. "Thank you. He'll be here in five to ten minutes."

"Thanks."

Lina gazed around with frank curiosity. Did all the employees have to go through this process every single day? She imagined they would. Otherwise, what was to prevent one of them from sneaking in a weapon?

Funny, she'd always felt like security hoops she had to go through to get into the institute were annoying. The thought was sobering.

That part of her life was over. She doubted they'd let her back, even if she was cleared of wrongdoing.

"Boyd Sinclair? Is that you?" A female voice interrupted her thoughts.

"Ma'am," Boyd said, nodding his head in greeting. "I hope you've been well."

"I'm surprised to see you here." Lina almost dropped her jaw when she recognized the woman, who was none other than Ms. Eloise Copeland. The First Lady of the White House.

"I have important information to share with President Copeland," Boyd said, his gaze drilling into her. "We're waiting for his chief of staff, but if there's anything you can do to help get word to the president about my need to talk to him, I'd appreciate it."

"This is a really busy day for Trevor," Eloise said with a frown. "I'm not sure that's possible."

"Ma'am, please, I wouldn't be here if this wasn't a matter of national security." Boyd smiled at her in a way that caused an irrational flash of jealousy. Especially when his voice softened. "Eloise, you know I would do anything to protect you and the president."

"I'll, uh, see what I can do." The First Lady gave a tiny nod of acknowledgment toward Lina before turning and hurrying away.

"I told you she didn't blame you," Lina whispered.

"She should have," Boyd countered. "But at this point, all that matters is that she's able to help us get to the president before it's too late."

CHAPTER SIXTEEN

January 31 – 3:48 p.m. – Washington, DC

Yates fought off the weary exhaustion that plagued him. It wasn't easy; whatever they'd given him had hit him hard. He put a hand to his chest, feeling the spongy patches attached to cables on his chest.

At least he hadn't been cut open. Something to be thankful for. But the doc who'd just left had informed him that the widow-maker was the main artery in the heart. And that when that gets blocked, many people die.

Cheery guy, the doc. He'd smiled and informed Yates how lucky he was to be alive.

And he was grateful for that, but when he'd told the doc he had work to do, the guy had gotten cranky. Informed him that his working too hard had contributed to his being there in the first place.

That and his crummy diet, lack of exercise, and not taking his blood pressure meds.

After the doc had left, Yates stared at the ceiling, trying to think of a way to contact Jordan. He was told he needed to lie flat or the artery in his groin could open up, causing him to bleed to death.

Yates figured he hadn't come this far to bleed to death now. Turning his head, he could see a phone, but it was too far out of reach.

His door opened, and a man in scrubs and a white lab coat pushed a cart into the room. Yates couldn't see him clearly until he approached the bed.

"Rashid?" He couldn't help but wonder if the drugs were playing tricks with his mind. "Is that you?"

"Yeah, it's me. And we don't have much time. I left the real lab tech in the restroom off the lobby." Rashid's expression was grim. "I need your help to get to the president."

Yates grimaced. "Yeah, well, I'm not going anywhere soon. They have me on strict bed rest for the next four hours."

"I know, I'm sorry to hear about your heart attack. And I was surprised there wasn't someone standing outside your door." Jordan gripped his hand. "Listen, we learned strychnine is missing from the research lab. We're concerned the president or the Chinese leader are potential targets."

"Strychnine!" Yates couldn't believe what he was hearing. "I didn't even have time to fill the president in on the fact that Lina was set up for the bombing. Stupid heart attack got in the way."

"Any ideas on how to get through to the president?" Jordan shot a concerned look over his shoulder, then added, "They put Randal Stone in charge while you're out on medical leave. Can we trust him? You should know Mack and Sun traced the leak about my company to a guy named Tillman within the NSA, so I'm not sure we should trust Doug Weatherby."

"I don't trust anyone," Yates admitted. He tried to think

of a way to help Jordan and Boyd get through to the president. "I told Steve Jones that I had an important security update to tell the president. I even gave him a note to give to the president. He was going to get me in at two thirty."

"It's past that now. Do you have anything I can use to make sure the president knows I'm speaking on your behalf?"

Yates sighed. "Yeah, you can use my codename, Falcon. But that will only work once you are actually talking to the president or the head of the Secret Service. I'm not sure how to help you get past his guard dog, Jones."

"Okay, thanks. I have to go before they find the real lab tech. Take care of yourself, Yates. You should ask for someone to be on guard outside your door."

"You too." By the time he'd responded, Jordan was already gone.

He fought the rising panic. He wasn't worried about his own safety, there was no reason for anyone to come after him. The president was the likely target. If anyone had the ability to get through to the president, it was Rashid and his Security Specialists, Inc. team. They'd managed far more dangerous tasks.

Yates closed his eyes and hoped it wouldn't be too late.

JANUARY 31 – 3:53 p.m. – London, England

As they stood to disembark from the plane, Jia swept a keen eye over the group of passengers. The six-hour flight had proved uneventful other than the flight attendants checking everyone's passport. She shot a glance at Sam, who looked apprehensive.

She didn't blame him. If anything were to happen, it would be the moment they stepped off the plane and into the airport. Visions of being surrounded by security and hustled off to a tiny cell caused a shiver of fear to ripple down her spine.

Maybe the passport checking wasn't related to their fake IDs. How would the authorities figure out that she and Sam were the ones they wanted instead of the other American men and Chinese women?

Jia was ahead of Sam. She turned, gesturing for the passenger behind her to skip ahead, but there wasn't enough room. The crowd surged forward, taking her with it.

Now she couldn't see Sam anymore. Jia decided the best thing she could do was to keep moving. Getting off the plane first would give her a few minutes to potentially warn Sam of trouble.

If airport security members were waiting for them.

Jia found herself silently praying no one would be there. Or at customs. Or at the international gate they'd have to go through to catch their next flight to DC.

After what seemed like forever, Jia found herself in the terminal. Nobody paid any attention to her. Still, that didn't mean Sam wasn't a target, so she stepped over to the wall and waited.

Sam's height gave him away. She watched as he followed the passengers off the plane. Like her, he looked around, expecting to be accosted. His gaze clashed with hers, and his eyes widened, a smile tugging on the sides of his mouth. She gave him a small nod of encouragement, thankful that no one seemed to pay any attention to him either.

Then she turned and began walking toward customs. Better that she and Sam didn't look as if they were traveling together. She headed for one line, then gestured for him to take a different one.

This would be the ultimate test. She held her breath as the line slowly moved forward inch by inch. When she reached the window, she kept her gaze down as most Chinese women did. "Good day, sir," she said politely. They'd lost six hours since leaving Beijing, but her exhausted mind couldn't come up with the current time.

Was it her imagination or did he stare at her passport for a moment too long? Finally, he stamped the page and shoved the passport back to her.

"Next," he said, indicating the person behind her.

Jia continued into the main terminal, her gaze instinctively searching for the gate from which their next flight would depart. Then she turned partway and pretended to look at her watch, her gaze tracking Sam's progress.

The knot in her stomach tightened as he approached the customs agent. She had to give him credit, he smiled and made small talk as if there was nothing to fear. Forcing herself to turn her back and continue forward wasn't easy.

A few minutes later, Sam came up beside her. "I—uh, think I need to head to gate twenty-eight." He showed her his ticket as if she were a stranger. "Is that right?"

"Yes, that is correct." She allowed herself to look into his eyes and somehow managed to hold back a warm smile. Just in case anyone was watching. "Gate twenty-eight will be where you'll get your connecting flight to Washington, DC."

He flashed a reassuring smile. "Great, thank you."

Jia wanted to throw herself into his arms but didn't. Instead, she walked ahead of him toward their designated gate.

Hard to believe they hadn't been stopped or arrested. Hope filled her heart.

So close. Another eight hours from now, they should land in DC.

When she'd learned the Six Red Dragons had someone high up in the government doing their will, she'd leaked the information to Sam, who forwarded it on to the higher-ups. Then her cover had been blown, and she'd been unwilling to trust anyone.

Except Sam.

The threat against the US government was very real. She could only hope and pray they arrived in time to prevent anything bad from happening to the President of the United States of America.

JANUARY 31 – 4:19 p.m. – Washington, DC

Once he'd been a patient man. But Boyd shifted from one foot to the next with barely restrained annoyance. Eloise Copeland had left what seemed like hours ago and hadn't returned.

Finally, he saw Steve Jones walking swiftly toward them. The chief of staff's expression was one of disapproval.

"Jones." He gave him a nod. "It's been a while."

"Just a couple of months, right?" Jones flicked a glance at Lina. "Who is she?"

"Ms. Parker. Listen, let's get straight to the point. Yates has sent me to talk to the president about an urgent matter involving his security."

Jones lifted an arrogant brow. "Then why not discuss the issue with Sean Adams?"

Boyd knew Jones's reference to the head of the Secret Service was a jab. Adams had never liked him much, and the fiasco with the First Lady had sealed the deal. Boyd knew that if he tried to go through Adams, he'd be tossed out of the White House before he could blink.

"Yates instructed me to go directly to the president." Jordan had called to let him know that he'd spoken to Yates and that the director had tried to get through Jones earlier to no avail. And lastly, he'd been instructed to use the code name Falcon when speaking with Copeland. "You didn't let Yates see the president earlier, tried to hold him off until two thirty, didn't you? Even after Yates gave you a letter to give to the president. Did you even bother to do that? Or did you forget about it once the poor guy had a heart attack while waiting for you to do your job?" He pinned the man with a narrow glare. "You better make up for that, starting right now."

Jones looked surprised at the fact that Boyd knew about the earlier meeting and the letter. His expression turned uncertain. "Okay, give me a few minutes. I may be able to get you in before five."

"You had better," Boyd said ominously. "If anything happens to the president, we will hold you personally responsible."

"The Secret Service is in charge of the president's security, not me," Jones snapped. But Boyd noticed a flicker of fear in the man's eyes. "I'll see what I can do. Stay here, I'll let you know what the president says."

"You do that." Boyd watched as the staffer hurried off. He relaxed his shoulder muscles, feeling pretty good that this time the jerk would let them in.

"Nice," Lina murmured. "You scared him."

"Not enough to take us to the president right away," Boyd said. He managed to smile at her. "But it does sound as if we'll get in to see him soon."

"The First Lady's doing?" Lina asked.

He shrugged. "Doesn't matter as long as we get what we came for." Sweeping another gaze around the entryway to the West Wing, he found himself hoping Jones didn't go back on his word and decide to send Adams to talk to them instead.

Failing to speak to the president was not an option.

JANUARY 31 – 4:29 p.m. – Richmond, VA

Kali woke again, fighting a wave of despair when she saw nothing but darkness. This was pure torture, although obviously whoever was holding her didn't care.

Her mouth was dry, and her stomach rolled. No more eating or drinking anything they brought her. If she continued taking the drugs, she feared she may not wake up.

Where was the Secret Service? The FBI? Her father? They should be breaking down the door to rescue her.

But they weren't. Why? Why hadn't anyone found her?

"Mayleen, you will soon be traveling away from this place."

The voice was distorted, seeming to echo off the walls of her jail cell. For all she knew that's where she was.

"My name is Kali," she croaked. Her dry throat made it difficult to speak, but she gathered all her strength. "My name is Kali! Not Mayleen."

"Soon, Mayleen. You will be away from this place, very soon."

"Who are you? What do you want?" Kali turned her head from side to side, desperate to see something, anything in the blackness.

There was no response to her questions. Only the interminable silence.

She thumped the thin mattress with her fist. Kali didn't know who Mayleen was, but that didn't even matter as much as the threat to move her.

Take her where? As much as she desperately wanted nothing more than to be out of this place, she couldn't help a shiver of fear that had her wondering if the new place they were taking her was even worse than this.

Here, she was alone. Relatively unharmed, other than being drugged and chained to the bed.

But what awaited her outside of here?

Kali shivered, a terrible sense of dread washing over her. She wasn't sure she wanted to know.

JANUARY 31 – 1:33 p.m. – Washington, DC

Lina could tell Boyd was getting annoyed with the ongoing delay in getting to see the president. In her mind, they were doing okay so far, at least they were still inside the building.

"Oh, that figures," Boyd muttered.

"What's wrong?" The moment the question left her mouth, she saw a shorter man striding purposefully toward them.

"Jones is going to pay for this," Boyd said in a low tone. Lina realized that Jones had in fact gone to the head of the Secret Service rather than arranging for them to meet with the president. She couldn't blame Boyd for being angry. The guy hadn't listened or maybe he just didn't care what Boyd had to say. Boyd stepped forward. "Adams."

"Sinclair." She stepped forward too, ready to jump in as needed. The two men eyed each other like two large gorillas about to fight over the lone banana. "Why are you here? You don't work for me anymore."

That dig was far from subtle. She sensed Boyd was struggling not to lose his temper, but his tone remained even. "I have information the president needs to hear."

Adams crossed his arms over his chest. "I'm the one in charge of the president's security detail."

"And I'm the one here on behalf of Clarence Yates, Director of the FBI, appointed by Copeland himself." Lina could almost see the testosterone sparks bursting in the air between the two men.

"So you say," Adams said with a snort of derision. "As far as I can tell, we only have your word for that."

There was a long pause as the two men stared each other down. "Yates is in the hospital. Did you know he was trying to get an audience with the president before he suffered his heart attack? That he even gave Jones a note that he probably didn't bother to pass on?"

Adams shrugged. "It's not my job to keep track of the director's schedule. And again, that's your story. Doesn't mean anything to me."

Another long tense moment passed as the two men stared at each other. Lina wished they would bring the anger and resentment down a few notches. At this rate, they'd never be granted an audience with the president.

Finally, Boyd broke the prolonged silence. "Let me ask you something, Adams. Does the code name Falcon mean anything to you?"

Adams scowled. "Where did you hear that?"

"Where do you think? From Yates himself." Boyd scowled and waved a hand. "I'm done with you, Adams. You want something bad to happen to the president on your watch? Fine with me. You'll be out on your butt so fast your head will spin. Don't say I didn't try to warn you." Boyd turned to leave.

"Hold on, Sinclair." The shorter, stockier Adams reached out to grip his arm. "If you know something that threatens the security of the White House and the president himself, you are obligated to tell me."

"I don't work for you, remember?" Boyd glanced pointedly at the hand on his arm. Adams hastily removed it. "I work for Yates. Just remember this moment when the cow dung hits the fan. It won't be pretty."

Adams muttered a curse. "Jones says you can meet with the president at quarter after five."

Lina wanted to smack the guy herself. Honestly, what was the point of all this posturing if they had been granted a time to see the president?

"Great. Smart move on your part." Boyd gestured to her. "Ms. Parker has an injured hip. You need to take us somewhere she can sit down for a bit. We've been standing here for the past hour."

Adams looked as if he wanted to argue, then abruptly turned. "This way."

Boyd offered his arm, and she gratefully leaned on his strength as Adams led them down a narrow hallway. She couldn't help gaping around curiously. The house where the president lived was both bigger and smaller than she'd imagined. The rooms were tall, but the hallways were narrow.

"I'll come and get you when it's time to meet with the president," Adams said stiffly. Then without waiting for a response, he left, closing the door sharply behind him.

"Jerk," Boyd muttered.

"Why does he hate you so much?" Lina asked. "I mean, you resigned your position, right? And the First Lady wasn't harmed. Why does he care?"

Boyd shrugged. "I think it's mostly because I made him

look bad. You know how the big boss always takes the heat when something goes wrong. Although the agent that let the guy slip through was one that Sean Adams personally handpicked for the First Lady's detail. I think that stuck in his craw."

"Idiot," she said. "He should be glad you're here to let the president know about a potential security breach."

"The only reason we've gotten this far is because no one wants to ignore something that could come back to bite them in the butt." Boyd rubbed the back of his neck. "And I have just enough credibility that they're not willing to take the risk."

He looked so discouraged she reached out to take his hand, soaking up his warmth. "Hey, we're going to convince the president to listen. I'm sure that once he hears what you have to say, he'll gladly call off the Chinese New Year celebration tonight."

"Yeah." Boyd didn't look convinced. "There's only one small problem with that plan."

"What's that?"

He slowly lifted his gaze to hers. "What if the strychnine is already here inside the White House? It was stolen hours ago. For all we know, the poison has already been handed off and smuggled inside."

"Not easily," she argued. Considering the hoops they'd had to jump through, it was impossible to imagine how it would have gotten in. "I'm sure someone would have noticed and asked about them."

"The vials could be changed to look like insulin or some other medication." The way Boyd's mind worked was impressive. She had to admit she wouldn't have considered that option. "Besides, that's not the point. I keep wondering if the threat against the president will remain even if the stupid party is canceled at the last minute. How will we manage to mitigate that threat?"

She blinked and sat back in her seat. "I—guess we'll need the Secret Service to search the entire place to make sure the strychnine isn't here. There can't be that many places to hide two small vials, even if they are disguised to look like a prescription medication."

"Oh, there's plenty of places to hide something that small." Boyd sighed deeply. "Especially if they're being hidden by someone the president trusts."

CHAPTER SEVENTEEN

January 31 – 4:45 p.m. – Somewhere over the Atlantic Ocean

Sam could just barely see Jia's head on the other side of the plane. Despite their fears, they'd been able to get through security and board their flight to Washington, DC, without a problem. They were on the last leg of their journey to the US.

Yet he didn't think their troubles were over. Not by a long shot.

The way their passports had been double-checked after leaving Beijing wasn't normal. It had been done for a purpose. Most likely to put their names on some sort of list. He'd watched carefully but hadn't noticed anyone paying attention to him or Jia as they'd gone through the Heathrow airport.

Yet the sick feeling that they were heading straight into a trap wouldn't leave him alone.

Sam stared at the phone embedded in the seat in front of him. Should he attempt to call the head of the CIA? Would Gerald Woodland even take his call? Since Sam had missed several check-ins with his immediate supervisor thanks to his and Jia's mad dash out of China, he couldn't bank on it.

It was difficult to know whom he could trust. Jia certainly hadn't wanted him to call anyone within the agency. And he couldn't blame her. This all started hours ago when she'd called in a panic to let him know she was in trouble. Then he'd learned her true identity had been uncovered. But how? That was the key question. There were only a handful of people who'd known she was a CIA asset. He and his direct supervisor, maybe one more guy up the chain of command.

He didn't like it. Not one bit.

Regardless of who'd blown her cover, they needed a plan. They wouldn't get anywhere near the White House without help.

What they needed was assistance from someone high enough in the agency willing to at least listen to their story.

Sam closed his eyes and tried to logically decide who within the agency he could trust. The plane abruptly shook and shimmied as they hit a pocket of wind.

"This is your captain speaking, we are experiencing some turbulence, so please remain in your seats as we attempt to fly above the storm."

Turning, he tried to meet Jia's gaze, but she was too far away. He missed having her close.

The plane jerked up and down again. Sam wasn't afraid of flying or even of dying. He looked forward to being welcomed into heaven, should that be God's will.

Yet he couldn't die now. Not when he desperately wanted to make sure the president was safe from harm.

And maybe he was selfish enough to wish for some

personal time with Jia once the danger was over. He wanted her to know how much he cared for her.

How much he loved her. Had grown to love her over the years they'd worked together.

Yet they'd been on the run from danger for so long he couldn't help but think the danger that followed them at every turn might never be over.

JANUARY 31 – 4:48 p.m. – Washington, DC

Jordan managed to escape the hospital without being caught, but he scowled when he realized he'd picked up a tail.

Had someone tracked him leaving the hospital? Maybe his stunt with the lab tech had been discovered, and now the NSA was aware of how he'd gotten in to see Yates.

Pushing the phone button on the steering wheel, he called Sloan. "Where are you?"

"I'm close to 1600 Pennsylvania Avenue, just in case Boyd gets tossed out on his butt, why? Do you need me?"

Jordan smiled grimly. Sloan was always about the action. "I have a bogey on my six, a black SUV, two car lengths behind me. Traffic is a nightmare, so losing him won't be easy."

"Where are you now?" Sloan's tone turned serious. "I'll meet you halfway."

"No, I want you to stay where you are." The black SUV moved into the next lane, edging closer. Jordan didn't like it, then again, it wasn't as if there was anywhere to go. The guys in the SUV wouldn't make a serious attempt to get him, they'd be dead in the water stuck in the middle of traffic.

Unless they didn't plan to survive the attack.

The thought filled him with dread. As far as he knew, the Chinese mafia wasn't known to operate the way suicide bombers did in the Middle East. They didn't normally volunteer to kill themselves while taking others down with them.

Yet he wasn't willing to put anything past these guys.

Not now when the Chinese New Year celebration was scheduled to kick off in roughly three hours.

Three hours. He prayed Boyd and Lina would find a way to convince the president to cancel the party.

"Jordan, Diana will kill me if something happens to you. Standing here isn't doing anyone any good." He could tell Sloan had broken into a run, no doubt heading to wherever he'd left his vehicle. "Where are you?"

Jordan gave him the coordinates. "If this guy gets close enough, maybe I'll catch his license plate."

"Call me if you do. I'm on my way." Sloan abruptly disconnected from the line.

Jordan kept one eye on the black SUV as he navigated the mess of traffic up ahead. While he appreciated Sloan's willingness to back him up, he hoped his partner's leaving the White House wasn't a mistake.

Nothing was more important than keeping their country safe.

Crack!

Both his passenger side window and his driver's side windows shattered beneath the impact of a bullet. He'd instinctively reared backward at the sound of gunfire, but he had felt the force of the bullet whiz right past his face. So close the sharp scent of cordite stung his nostrils.

Car horns blared, brake lights flashed, and he heard people screaming. Tightening his grip on the steering wheel, he glanced to the right. The black SUV was beside him, the driver's side window was open just an inch.

The windows were tinted, making it impossible to make out the features of the person behind the wheel.

In a heartbeat, the small round barrel of a gun became visible in the inch-wide opening.

No! Not again!

By the grace of God, the traffic thinned, probably because the sound of gunfire had caused several cars to make a rapid exit off the interstate. Braced for more gunfire, Jordan hit the gas and jerked the wheel, shoehorning his way into the other lane. The move helped as the gap he'd left behind in the previous lane was quickly filled with another vehicle.

Still, that wasn't enough. He didn't trust the shooter not to take out innocent lives to get to him.

It wasn't easy to keep his eye on the traffic and the shooter inside the black car, but he did his best. He needed to outmaneuver the driver of the black SUV.

Had anyone witnessed the open window with the gun barrel in the opening? He'd barely saw it himself; the shooter had gone to great pains to make sure the barrel didn't protrude from the window. The lack of police sirens wasn't reassuring, it likely meant no one knew where the gunfire had originated.

He wrenched the wheel again, going out onto the shoulder. Then he passed several cars, ignoring the loud honks from annoyed drivers. After passing several cars, he forced his way back into traffic just in time to take the next exit. More horns blasted loudly as he cut off two drivers in the process.

Right now, he didn't care if he caught the attention of the state police. He needed to get away before the next bullet hit its mark.

Taking him out, permanently.

JANUARY 31 – 4:53 p.m. – Washington, DC

He paced back and forth, his gut knotted with tension. As if his call with Manchu hadn't been bad enough. This latest news was even worse.

Why was former Secret Service Agent Boyd Sinclair here at the White House? To see the president? Highly likely. He could not, *would not* allow that to happen. From the moment he'd learned the news about Sinclair, he'd been trying to come up with a plan to eliminate him and that woman with him, who should have been dead hours ago.

Obviously, Manchu's men hadn't fulfilled their obligation to this joint venture either. The man was just as incompetent as the many men he'd hired to perform the fairly simple task of killing two people.

Two targets here in the US and two targets in China.

Both missions had been botched beyond belief. The assassins who should have been the best had failed too many times to count.

Maybe it was time to pull the trigger to silence Manchu. After all, that was his ultimate plan. One that wasn't supposed to happen yet. However, his alliance with the leader of the Six Red Dragons was proving useless. At this point, what good was he? Oh sure, Manchu had sent as many men as he'd requested, but they'd proven just as lame as those working on their own soil.

He felt certain the two CIA operatives had escaped Beijing and were currently en route to DC. He had men stationed at both international airports, armed with a grainy image of Sam King. Unfortunately, he didn't have a decent picture of King's asset, just a blurry one provided by Manchu that had been captured via one of the many cameras in China. He told himself the pair would likely be together, so getting them both shouldn't be a problem.

Yet now he'd learned Sinclair was in the West Wing. No doubt determined to meet with the president. Appalling that a disgraced Secret Service agent could get inside the hallowed grounds so easily.

The only positive note to date was that Yates should be dead very soon. One problem solved.

But there were still too many loose ends for his peace of mind.

He thumped his fist on the top of his desk, reining in his temper with an effort. He couldn't afford to lose his cool now. Not when he was so close. This plan had to work. Too much time and money had been used to allow it to fail now.

Calmer now, he approached the problem as analytically as possible.

First, he needed to dispose of Sinclair, then the rest.

All of them. He wouldn't be satisfied until all of them were dead.

Especially the current President of the United States.

JANUARY 31 – 5:04 p.m. – Washington, DC

Yates drifted in and out of sleep, satisfied that Jordan would finish the task of alerting the president to the threat. He told himself that stress wasn't good for his heart. The pain he'd experienced while sitting at the White House had been so bad that he had no intention of going through that ever again.

Which meant making changes he'd resisted up until now. Rest, diet, exercise, and no salt, exactly as his doctor had recommended. Once he would have said there was no point to living if you couldn't eat what you wanted.

Now he knew better. Being on the brink of death had illustrated the precious gift of life. Maybe he'd lost his wife and didn't have children or grandchildren to spoil, but that didn't mean he couldn't enjoy what little time he had left on earth.

The snick of his door opening caught his attention. Normally, the doctors and nurses knocked at the door before coming in. But not this time. Jordan? No, he felt certain Rashid was far away by now.

He pretended to be asleep, his senses on full alert.

The squeak of a sole against the linoleum was like a gunshot. He instinctively reared upright, the pain in his groin an unwelcome reminder that he was supposed to be on strict bed rest. He swung his fist toward the man standing there while simultaneously yanking the call light from the wall.

His fist connected with flesh, but not with the force he'd hoped for. Yates rolled off the hospital bed as the call light alarm rang loudly.

The intruder hissed a curse, whirled, and left, giving him just a glimpse of the hospital scrubs he wore. When Yates peeked up over the edge of the bedframe, he saw the knife embedded in the mattress up to the hilt, in the exact spot where he'd been a few seconds earlier.

He stared at the weapon in horror. What was going on? Why would someone try to kill him? He was out of commission being in the hospital and not on duty. It didn't make any sense.

Unless whoever was behind all this had decided he still posed a threat.

A warm gush of blood ran down his leg from his groin

site. Two nurses bolted into the room, staring open-mouthed at the knife in the bed.

"I broke open my groin site," he said, rising to his feet. The blood ran freely down his leg now, making him feel light-headed. "You'd better call the doctor. I'm bleeding a lot. Oh, and you should get me a new room, along with calling the police. That man who was just in here tried to stab me."

The medical staff jumped into action. Since lying on the bed wasn't an option, Yates pressed his hand against his groin, hoping to stanch the worst of the bleeding. Unfortunately, it didn't seem to help.

As he watched the blood spreading around the floor at his feet, it occurred to him that this recent attempt to kill him may succeed if the medical team couldn't get the bleeding stopped in time. Hadn't they drilled that into his head? How important it was for him to stay flat so he didn't bleed to death?

Well, he hadn't stayed flat. And now he was bleeding to death.

His hearing became distorted; the people coming toward him looked fuzzy. The nurse said something he couldn't understand. Yates wondered if this was it. If his time on this earth was over.

Then he collapsed into the chair behind him, succumbing once again to the darkness.

JANUARY 31 – 5:10 p.m. – Washington, DC

"Something's wrong." Boyd paced the length of the conference room he and Lina had been sitting in for close to thirty minutes. "They should have been here by now."

"I'm sure the president is allowed to be late for a meeting," Lina said with a lopsided smile. "Who would call him out on it?"

"I still don't like it." The back of his neck tingled in warning, the same way it had moments before the knife-wielding man had lunged toward the First Lady. For weeks, those moments had replayed over and over in his mind as if he could change what had happened by will alone.

Allan Zilky was currently still in prison for his attempt to assassinate Eloise Copeland. Granted, the tip of his knife had only scratched her because Boyd had thrown himself at him in the nick of time. Still, his intent had been clear. The guy was also undergoing a multitude of psych evals as he was completely obsessed with the First Lady.

Boyd hated to admit that since taking on the job of guarding Lina, those painful reminders of his failures hadn't happened. For the first time in weeks, he'd thought solely of the task at hand. Usually it took pushing himself to his physical limits—doing fifty push-ups, fifty pull-ups, and running ten miles—to banish the memories.

Then again, guarding Lina and keeping her safe had taken him to the edge of his mental and physical limits, too, albeit in a different way.

"There're still a few minutes to go," Lina said consolingly. "Try to be patient just a little longer."

He'd spent a good ten years of his life being patient, first deployed overseas, then working for the White House. That's what being in the service was all about.

Maybe he'd used up all his patience because he couldn't stand staying in this room a moment longer. "Stay here, I'm just going to find Jones. Or Eloise."

Lina glanced from him to the door and back again. "Okay. I'm sure I'm safe enough waiting for you here."

He paused in the act of reaching for the door. He'd

promised Jordan he'd keep Lina safe. Leaving her alone, even in the middle of the White House, wasn't an option. He turned and held out his hand toward her. Then he surprised himself by drawing her into his arms and kissing her.

Lina melted against him, eagerly returning his kiss. He wished more than anything they weren't in a White House conference room, up to their eyeballs in danger.

Boyd forced himself to lift his head. "I'm not apologizing this time," he said roughly.

"Good. Me either." Lina's smile lit up her face, and it took all his willpower not to kiss her again.

No way could he leave her. He cleared his throat. "I want you to come with me. This will probably prove futile. I'm sure it won't take long for the security detail to herd us back in here. I'm hoping to cause enough of a ruckus that they'll get the president here to see us."

She nodded. "I like your plan. Let's do it."

It wasn't much of a plan, but it was all he could come up with. He stepped away from her, opened the door, and looked around. Despite being past five, there were still plenty of staffers running around. They would remain until they felt certain the president wouldn't need them any longer.

Boyd knew from experience that those who chose to work here pretty much gave up any chance at a private life to do so. A quick glance at Lina made him acutely aware of just how much he'd given up.

And how much of a normal life he secretly longed to have.

He pulled himself together with an effort, scanning the hallway for signs of Steve Jones, Eloise, or even his former boss, Sean Adams.

Since no one seemed to be paying attention, he moved cautiously down the hallway that would eventually lead to the Oval Office. Adams would have several agents standing guard, so it wasn't as if there would be an opportunity to burst inside unannounced.

When he caught a glimpse of Eloise, he stopped, causing Lina to lightly bump into him from behind.

He glanced at her over his shoulder. "Sorry about that."

"I'm fine." She frowned when she saw the First Lady.

"Oh, Boyd, there you are." Eloise smiled and came toward him. Kali, their daughter, trailed in her wake, looking bored in the way teenagers perfected. Kali was still wearing her school uniform, and he nodded at the security detail hovering a few steps behind them.

"Hi, Kali," Boyd greeted the girl. "How's school?"

"The usual." The girl shrugged.

There seemed to be something off about Kali. Granted, he'd been gone for two months and hadn't been assigned to protect the girl, but still, he'd been around Kali often enough over the past year that he'd gotten to know her pretty well.

"Boyd, I spoke with Trevor, he's going to make time to see you," Eloise interjected.

"He's already late for that," Boyd drawled, glancing at his watch.

"Thank you, we appreciate it," Lina added, no doubt trying to smooth over his clear impatience.

Before he could say anything more, there was a loud blaring sound. Red lights flashed, and the loud sounds continued, making it impossible to hear.

The fire alarm! Boyd instinctively put himself in front of Eloise but then belatedly remembered his job was to protect Lina.

"Let's go!" Secret Service agents shouted over the incessant alarm.

"No! I have to see the president!" Boyd tried to push past them, but it was no use. The agents surrounded Eloise and Kali, hustling them off to a secure exit while the rest of the staff swarmed toward the exit, carrying him and Lina along with them.

Failure hit him with the force of a boulder. He'd failed to warn the President of the United States.

And now it may very well be too late.

CHAPTER EIGHTEEN

January 31 – 5:22 p.m. – Washington, DC

The fire alarm had worked. He smiled with grim satisfaction as the West Wing staff scattered like rats fleeing a sinking ship.

It was a temporary measure at best, but he'd take it. All he needed was a few more hours. Once he'd succeeded in pulling this off, he'd be the most powerful person in the world. Far better than that idiot Copeland.

Glancing at his watch, he scowled as he realized the two CIA operatives would be landing soon. The fact that they were traveling from east to west meant they gained time. There were two flights in particular that he had his men watching, each originating from different international airports in Beijing. One that had left Beijing Capital International Airport with a layover in Heathrow, London, before coming to DC and another flight that left Beijing Nanyuan Airport with a layover in Paris, France, before continuing to DC. The first flight was scheduled to land in less than twenty minutes. The second an hour from now.

He needed his men to come through for him. Once he

had taken care of the CIA operatives, he could focus his attention on Security Specialists, Inc.

The failed attempt against Jordan Rashid had ticked him off. It had been a rash, desperate move to make a play for him during rush hour. That was not what he'd paid them for.

Imbeciles, every one of them. If he continued to experience these failures, he'd have little choice but to take care of things himself. It wasn't optimal, but better than dealing with a pack of idiots who couldn't figure out how to take care of a simple problem.

Or two.

Despite the bad news, his smile widened. Soon, very soon he'd have everything he wanted, and more.

No one could stop him now.

JANUARY 31 – 5:25 p.m. – Washington, DC

Lina gasped as Boyd ducked into a meeting room, dragging her along with him. It was a different room than they'd been in earlier, but she didn't bother to look around. She had to raise her voice to be heard over the earsplitting shriek. "What are you doing? We need to get out of here."

"It's a false alarm, designed to keep us from talking to the president." Boyd lunged for the phone on the long conference room table. "I need to call Jordan."

"How do you know it's a false alarm?" she demanded.

"The timing is suspicious. Besides, no sprinklers have gone off yet, which means there isn't any smoke to trigger them." Boyd punched in a series of numbers on the phone, then frowned and replaced the receiver. "Nothing but a busy signal. The phone lines must be jammed with people calling out because of the alarm."

"Where do the president and the First Lady go in this situation?"

Boyd glanced at her. "Likely the situation room, it's in the East Wing."

"Not outside the building?"

"No, the sit room is essentially a bunker. Besides, there's also an escape route through an underground tunnel if needed. Either way, the first family will be kept safe. It's our inability to talk to the president at all that concerns me." He paused, then added, "There has to be a way to get through to him."

Lina understood his frustration even as she secretly marveled at the resources available to keep the president and his family safe. It was why it was so insane to think about the fact that strychnine could be a real threat. "I'm sure they escaped, as you suggested. I can't believe they would stick around inside the White House, at least not until it's been determined the fire was a false alarm." She frowned. "They'll figure out who triggered the alarm, right? I mean, there are cameras everywhere."

"They will, eventually. But we can't wait, there's no time to waste." He picked up the phone and tried again, only to slam it down in frustration.

"Hey, we'll get through to the president." Lina crossed over to rest her hand on his arm. "I have faith that God will give us the strength and courage we need."

Boyd's muscles were tense beneath her hand, but she felt him slowly relax. "Okay, you're right about one thing. We need to stay focused on the positive. We're still inside the building, one that I know very well."

Lina stared up at him, realizing he knew exactly where the situation room was located and that secret tunnel exit too. "Even you can't follow the president wherever they decide to take him for safety; the agents assigned to him will prevent you from getting too close. And if that happens, we'll for sure be tossed out on our butts without any opportunity to return."

He nodded and covered her hand with his. The warmth of his fingers seemed to reach all the way inside to surround her heart. The way he'd kissed her had filled her with hope. "True, but at some point, we'll need to take the leap. It's that or let the president move forward with his Chinese New Year celebration and very likely die of strychnine poisoning."

A horrible thought hit hard. "Two vials."

"What?" Boyd asked, raising his voice.

"Two vials. What if there are two targets?" She tightened her grip on Boyd's arm. "What if there's a plan for both the president and Xi Jin Ping to be taken out at the same time?"

Boyd frowned. "All the more reason we need to talk to him."

"How? Do you have another plan?"

"Not yet, but I'm working on one." He reached for the phone again when the alarm abruptly shut off.

The resulting silence felt surreal, and she couldn't help being impressed that they'd investigated the source of the alarm so quickly. Then again, one expected this sort of thing to go smoothly in a place like the White House. Before she could say anything, Boyd glanced around warily.

"They silenced the alarm faster than I expected," he muttered darkly. "The moment we're discovered, they'll try to get us out of here."

Lina watched as he tried the phone one more time. This time, his expression indicated he'd gotten through. "Jordan? We have a problem. A fire alarm was pulled, which means the president has been pulled someplace safe before I was given the chance to talk to him."

Hearing the truth stated so bluntly made her realize the magnitude of their failure. Two targets. She shivered, then lifted her heart and her mind to God.

Please, Lord, show us the way!

JANUARY 31 – 5:42 p.m. – Washington, DC

Jia tried to catch Sam's eye as their plane pulled into the gate. They'd arrived a few minutes early, although she knew they still needed to clear customs. But they needed a plan. A way to disguise themselves.

It would be easier for her to blend into the crowds, but Sam was tall and broad-shouldered. Granted, his hair was now dyed black, which may help. Yet she knew his tall body and broad shoulders would easily be noticed by anyone searching for them.

And she truly believed Bo Dung Manchu had requested passports to be checked to find her.

Sam finally caught her gaze, smiling at the fact that their long journey was nearly over. She returned his smile, but then tapped her watch, indicating he should wait for her once they were off the plane. He nodded in understanding before following his fellow passengers down the aisle.

Jia wanted to push her way through to the front but knew that attracting attention would not help their cause. She kept a sharp eye out for anything suspicious while keeping her expression demure and calm. Her scar was suitably covered, which was good.

Once she was off the plane, she saw Sam off to the side, pretending to rummage through what she knew was an empty bag while he waited for her.

"Customs first, then we'll head over to pick up a taxi," he said in a low tone.

"Customs first, but we need a disguise to get out of here. I'm going to find a cleaning lady, to use her uniform and ID tag." She eyed him critically. "I'm not sure if that same approach will work for you."

"Cleaning lady?" He looked surprised, then thoughtful. "I'll try to come up with something similar to use as a disguise. A hat, maybe a sweatshirt."

"A hat is most important," she said. "You lost the one you were wearing in the river. You're too tall to take over most uniforms, but a hat is essential to keep your face partially covered."

"Okay. So we'll eventually meet at the taxi line?"

She nodded. "Yes. I'm sure I can find it."

"Let's do this." Sam zippered the bag as she moved forward, heading toward the customs windows.

She found herself praying that God would watch over them so they could escape the airport without being caught.

Although the next leg of their journey would be just as perilous, if not more so. Jia drew in a deep breath and let it out slowly.

She and Sam had gotten this far against seemingly insurmountable odds.

Exhaustion weighed on her. Sleeping on a plane was impossible with everything going through her mind. Just a few hours to go. Soon they'd be able to rest, satisfied in the knowledge that they'd prevented a terrible global-wide tragedy.

The alternative was unthinkable. If they didn't succeed in their mission, the only reason she'd accept was that they were dead.

They could not allow anything to stop them.

. . .

JANUARY 31 – 5:51 p.m. – Washington, DC

After telling Jordan about his failure to speak to the president, Boyd had learned about Jordan's near miss on the highway and then about the attack against Yates. He tried not to let the news interfere with his concentration. But it wasn't easy. The way their plans were thwarted at every turn only reinforced they were close to uncovering the truth.

"What was that about the hospital?" Lina asked.

"There was a botched attempt to kill Yates in his hospital room," Boyd told her. "He's currently in surgery to repair a bleeding artery."

"They stabbed him?" Lina's eyes widened in horror.

"No, but something happened to the site where they entered his bloodstream to do the cardiac cath procedure." Boyd shook his head. "Although the result is much the same, isn't it? Either way, Yates is indefinitely out of commission for the foreseeable future."

If the older man survived at all.

"Come on, we need to move." Boyd crossed over to the door. He opened it a crack and peeked out. The hallway was still relatively empty, no doubt because everyone that left the building during the fire alarm would need to go back through security before returning to work. And maybe, at this hour, some of them had just decided to call it a day.

Well, except for people like Steve Jones, the president's chief of staff. And the Secret Service agents.

"All clear, let's go." He caught Lina's hand and slipped through the doorway.

"Go where?" she asked.

It was a good question. She was right about the fact that

Sean Adams and his detail protecting Copeland would make it impossible for him to barge into the situation room. Besides, his palm print wouldn't gain him access into the hallowed space.

Which left only one alternative that he could think of. They needed to slip into the Oval Office before anyone had a chance to see them, so they could wait for the president to return.

He could only hope and pray the security detail watching the cameras didn't pay close enough attention in time to send the Secret Service dogs after them.

JANUARY 31 – 6:00 p.m. – Washington, DC

Lina couldn't stop staring around the inside of the Oval Office. The White House was impressive in and of itself, but this? She was shocked Boyd had managed to get them inside the president's inner sanctuary at all.

Yet they'd been waiting for several minutes without any sign of the president or the First Lady.

"How long do we stick around?" she asked in a whisper. There was no question they were trespassing. And if they were found, they'd be tossed out. Or maybe even put in jail.

"I'm not sure." Boyd didn't seem nearly as uncomfortable as she was. Then again, he'd worked here. "I'm hoping soon."

She trusted Boyd's instincts, but even replaying their most recent kiss didn't keep her from feeling like they were in big trouble. "Okay, but what if the president doesn't come back here? I mean, he was taken to the situation room, maybe he's in their private quarters getting ready for the party?"

Boyd shrugged. "Let's give it a little more time. I think

he'll come back here, especially since he'd been forced to leave in a hurry."

Lina shifted on the sofa, reminding herself that Boyd had gotten them this far. No reason to give up on her faith in his abilities now.

In fact, she was beginning to wonder how she'd manage to go back to her old life, one without Boyd, once this was over. She'd miss him.

Far too much.

JANUARY 31 – 6:02 p.m. – Washington, DC

Jia was shocked at how quickly she made it through customs. Maybe God was guiding them. It would explain how things seemed to be going their way.

At least, for now.

Upon heading into the airport, Jia immediately searched for a restroom. She didn't see anyone cleaning at the first two she'd stopped at and wondered if it was too late in the evening for the staff to be doing that task. For a moment, her stomach clenched. What if she didn't find anyone? She could purchase a hat with some of the American cash she'd exchanged for a ridiculously high rate at the window located just outside of customs, but that wasn't the same as impersonating an employee.

Don't panic, she inwardly warned. Surely, there would be a second shift in an airport as large as this.

She continued walking, keeping her head down even as she searched for cleaning personnel. When she saw a cart parked outside a women's restroom, she breathed a tiny sigh of relief and angled toward it.

Unfortunately, the woman who should be using the cart was nowhere in sight. Had she gone off on break? Maybe she was sitting nearby using her phone? Jia looked around the immediate area but didn't see anyone who appeared to be wearing a uniform. Swallowing a sigh of frustration, she turned back and began looking through the cart.

Oddly enough, there were head coverings, face masks, gloves, and booties on the cart. Possibly for really bad messes? She'd rather not know. For now, she'd take what they had. Jia quickly pulled on the booties, gloves, and face mask. Then she tucked her long dark hair into the poufy hat. Pushing the cart in front of her, she continued walking through the concourse, pretending that she worked there.

As she wasn't wearing a uniform of any kind nor had an ID, she expected airport security to accost her. At one point, she noticed a tall man standing off to the side, looking from his phone screen, then at the passengers walking by. Had he been sent to find her and Sam? She held her breath as she walked past with the cart. He glanced at her but quickly dismissed her. She hid her surge of satisfaction. People were so easily fooled. No one paid any attention to the bathroom cleaning staff. Jia kept her pace sedate, as if she had all day, as she made her way to the baggage claim area. Because of the cart, she had to take the elevator, but that only worked to her advantage.

When she reached the crowded baggage claim area, she pushed her cart toward the closest restroom. She swiftly ditched the hat, mask, and booties. Leaving the cart behind, she followed the signs to the taxi service.

Outside, the cold winter air stole her breath. She hoped her lack of warm clothing wouldn't draw attention as she scanned the area for Sam. He was already in line, wearing a baseball hat from a local sports team pulled low on his brow and a bulky sports team sweatshirt over his dingy white shirt.

She eased up alongside him. "We made it."

"We did." He flashed a smile and pulled her close, hugging her. "Let's get out of here."

Standing out in the open was unnerving, but in a few minutes, it was their turn to obtain a taxi. Sam held the door for her, and soon they were pulling away from the curb, leaving Reagan International Airport behind.

"Where to?" the cabbie driver asked.

"The White House," Sam said without hesitation.

The driver eyed them warily in the rearview mirror. "That's going to take a while in traffic."

Jia's spirits sank. "Please get us there as soon as possible."

"It's your money," the driver said as he took the nearest on-ramp for the interstate.

Money was the least of their worries. She sank back against the torn seat cushions, taking several deep breaths.

They'd made it this far, but they still had a ways to go in order to prevent Manchu from following through with his evil plan. She could only hope they weren't too late.

JANUARY 31 – 6:21 p.m. – Washington, DC

Boyd was quickly losing his patience. He couldn't deny that Lina might be right about the president heading to their private quarters to get ready for the Chinese New Year celebration.

He was loath to leave the Oval Office, knowing they risked being picked up on camera by the Secret Service. They may have been distracted by the fire alarm, but now they'd be on high alert with the party going on. They were safe here as there were no security cameras inside the Oval Office or the president's private quarters.

Maybe he should have risked going all the way to the second floor to enter their private residence. He glanced at his watch and grimaced. At this rate, he may as well try to get them into the East Room, which was the largest reception hall in the entire building. It was also the most logical place to hold the evening's festivities.

Boyd abruptly stood and held his hand out to Lina. "Come on, we may as well try to find the president."

"Are you sure?" Lina had looked distinctly uncomfortable when they'd come inside the Oval Office. He could understand her feeling overwhelmed, but to him it was just another room in the building.

"Yeah. We've waited long enough." She took his hand and stood. He was far too aware of her dainty hand in his callused one. Before they could take two steps, though, the Oval Office door swung open.

"Boyd?" The president stared at him in shock. "What are you doing here?"

"That's it, you've gone too far." Joseph Danby, the senior agent from the Secret Service assigned to the president's detail nailed him with a narrow glare. Danby lifted his hand to his earpiece, no doubt to call for backup.

"Wait! Please, sir, I need to talk to you," Boyd said quickly. "It's important, or I wouldn't have dared to come in here to wait for you. Falcon sent us."

"I'm sorry, sir," Danby rudely interrupted. "I know you don't have time for this. We'll have Sinclair and his companion removed immediately."

"Wait, please, don't haul us out," Lina spoke up. "We've tried to go through proper channels, but then the fire alarm went off as a way to prevent us from meeting with you. Did you get the note Yates gave to Jones? This is really important."

"Lina is right," Boyd said, cutting a narrow glance at Danby. "In fact, your team should already know by now who triggered the false alarm."

"How dare you," Danby sputtered.

"Enough!" President Copeland's sharp tone brought a stunned silence. The president looked at Boyd. "Adams and Eloise did mention your request to talk. And you said Falcon sent you?"

"Yes, sir." Boyd nodded.

"I'd like to hear what you have to say," Copeland said.

"At the very least, we need to involve Adams and Randal Stone, the acting Director of the FBI," Danby said. "And Weatherby too."

"No." Boyd's tone cut quickly. "This has to be a small meeting. Someone inside the White House has turned traitor."

"That's ridiculous," Danby snapped.

"Let's hear what he has to say," Copeland repeated.

"Thank you, sir." Boyd swallowed a smile at the frustrated expression on Danby's face. "If you would please sit down? This may take a while."

CHAPTER NINETEEN

January 31 – 6:25 p.m. – Washington, DC

Boyd had barely begun to explain the recent events when the door burst open and a man strode in. Lina knew Danby must have gotten a message out for others to come despite Boyd's request to keep the meeting small. Trailing behind the stranger was Sean Adams, the head of the Secret Service.

Lina's spirits sank. She had a bad feeling about this.

"Mr. President, I understand you're being alerted about a possible threat?" The stranger was older than Copeland, maybe in his late fifties. "I can assure you that while I'm happy to keep an open mind, the recent threats related to tonight's celebration have been thoroughly vetted and have been deemed a nonissue."

"I understand, Randal, but since Mr. Sinclair and his companion have gone to great lengths to bring me their concerns, I feel the need to give them a few minutes."

Ah, so this was Randal Stone, the man who'd taken Yates's place as being in charge of the FBI. Lina felt Boyd tense beside her as he had the same reaction to Stone's presence.

Did they dare trust him?

Lina knew they probably didn't have a choice. It was time to lay out their concerns, regardless of who might be in the room. But when the door opened again, she couldn't hide her low groan.

"Mr. President—oh, I didn't realize you had a meeting." The scowl on Steve Jones's face indicated there shouldn't be a meeting without his being aware of it.

"Thank you, Steve, but I won't need you for the rest of the day," Copeland said. "It's well past time for you to get home."

"As you wish." Jones stabbed Boyd a look of annoyance but then left.

"We are aware of a very *credible* threat from the Six Red Dragons," Boyd said bluntly. "The recent bomb blast at the Institute for Nanoscience was done in an attempt to cover up two stolen vials of strychnine."

Randal Stone abruptly turned toward her. "You're Lina Parker, the person responsible for the bomb and the missing strychnine."

Strong arms grabbed her shoulders from behind. She winced as Danby's fingers dug into her skin. "Lina Parker, you're under arrest."

"Get your hands off her," Boyd said firmly. "Lina has an alibi for the time frame of the bombing and for when the strychnine was accessed. Yates is fully aware that Lina is being set up by the Six Red Dragons."

"Let her go," Copeland said, a frown furrowing his brow. "Boyd, you know better than anyone that sneaking poison into the White House is nearly impossible."

"Normally, yes, but not if there's someone working with

the Six Red Dragons on the inside," Boyd insisted. "Think about it, sir. Two small vials could be disguised as a medication like insulin, and no one would be the wiser."

Danby let her go and came around to face her, his face mottled with anger. "Are you insinuating that someone has actually already gotten these vials past the Secret Service agents on duty?"

"I think there's a very good chance of that, yes," Lina spoke up. "The better question here is whether you're willing to risk the president's life, or that of Xi Jin Ping, by not taking this threat seriously?"

"We can search the premises for these vials," Stone said. "But in our review of the Six Red Dragons, they are long on manpower and short on follow-through. Both the NSA director Weatherby and the CIA director Woodland feel the same way. No reason to suspect they have the ability to get inside the White House."

"What exactly does this celebration entail?" Boyd asked, his gaze centered on Copeland. "I assume you have performers coming in?"

"Yes, but they have been fully vetted," the president said.

"How many?" Boyd pressed.

President Copeland glanced at Stone. "You know the exact number better than I do."

"Twenty-four performers will be here tonight, dressed in costume, including those doing the dragon dance," Stone said. "And they have been fully vetted. We can have them searched for vials, but it isn't as if they will be allowed anywhere near the president or Xi Jin Ping."

"You said credible threat," Copeland said. "Who is your source?"

Lina exchanged a glance with Boyd. Having Yates with

them would be really helpful about now. "Mr. President, we don't know this for certain, but it's possible one source was my mother's sister, Shu Yan Chen, who was murdered before she could meet with me last evening."

"I've heard enough," Stone muttered. "There was no evidence of a murder taking place at Turtle Park. No dead body, no sign of a crime at all." The acting director turned to the president. "We will gladly search the performers for the missing vials, but the rest of this is just a bunch of talk with no proof."

"The Chinese mafia have made several attempts to kill Lina Parker," Boyd said firmly, his attention centered on the president. "They also stole Lina's identity to access the institute and grab the strychnine. Not to mention the very untimely fire alarm going off right before our scheduled meeting with you, sir."

"That alarm was triggered by accident by one of the cleaning staff," Danby interjected. "No big mystery there."

"At the same time we were supposed to meet with the president?" Boyd shot back. "No way."

"What exactly do you expect me to do?" President Copeland asked, looking between her and Boyd. "Call off the celebration?"

"Yes, for starters," Boyd said.

"And search for the poison," Lina added. She was impressed the president was taking their concerns seriously, despite the lack of support from Joseph Danby and Randal Stone. She found it odd that they were so determined to minimize the threat.

"We can do the search," Danby reiterated. "That's not a problem." He spoke into his microphone, issuing the order to search the performers first, then the entire East Room reception space.

"Sir, calling off the celebration at this point would be a slap in the face to Xi Jin Ping, especially as the talks so far have not been as helpful as anticipated," Stone argued. "You spent hours with him this afternoon, calling off this celebration would eliminate all the ground you've gained with him."

"I have faith in our kitchen staff," Danby added. "No way would they allow poison to come near the president's food."

"Agree." President Copeland stood. "Thank you, Boyd, for your concern. I do appreciate you bringing the information forward about the strychnine. I think the FBI and Secret Service can take it from here."

Lina's heart dropped. He wasn't going to cancel.

"Wait, I have one more favor to ask." Boyd jumped to his feet.

"Favor?" Danby scoffed. "The only favor you're getting is the ability to leave here under your own power. By all rights, you should both be tossed in jail."

"Enough," Copeland said. "I understand your concern, Joe, but Boyd once worked for the service. And he came here out of concern for my safety."

"Would you please allow us to stay and watch the celebration?" Boyd pressed. "Two additional pairs of eyes watching for a threat can't hurt."

"Unless you're the threat," Danby said harshly. "We have plenty of Secret Service on staff tonight, no need for either of you to stick around."

"Please, sir." Boyd had ignored Danby, his gaze locked with President Copeland. "I wouldn't ask if I wasn't truly worried about your welfare and that of Xi Jin Ping."

"Fine with me," Copeland said.

"Sir, I strongly advise against this . . ." Danby said, but the president cut him off.

"Boyd is no threat, and as he said, more eyes keeping watch can't hurt." The president glanced at his watch. "Now if you'll excuse me, I have another phone call to make before I head up to get dressed. This little visit along with the fire alarm has put me behind schedule."

"Thank you, sir," Lina said, reaching out to grasp Boyd's hand. "You won't regret this."

"We'll see about that," Danby said snidely.

Lina and Boyd followed Stone out of the Oval Office where more Secret Service agents waited.

She squeezed Boyd's hand. "Now what?" she whispered.

"We pray," Boyd whispered back.

JANUARY 31 – 6:52 p.m. – Washington, DC

"What is the plan once we get to the White House?" Sam asked in a whisper. The impressive building was brightly lit with red and orange hues, no doubt in honor of the Chinese Leader Xi Jin Ping's attendance.

"I don't have a good one," Jia admitted. "I'm hoping to use my relationship to Xi Jin Ping's former wife to get his attention."

Sam knew about Jia's relationship to Ke Ling Ling, Xi Jin Ping's ex-wife who harbored a serious resentment toward Xi Jin Ping. Knowing the details of the animosity had helped her infiltrate Manchu's organization. "And if that doesn't work?"

Jia simply shook her head.

"I'll call the head of the CIA again," Sam offered. "I left Gerald Woodland a message, keeping it vague in case it was intercepted. But he might listen to us now, especially after everything we've gone through to get out of China."

"Can we trust him?" Jia asked. "I told you Manchu has someone high in the American government working for him."

Sam let out a sigh. "I don't know who we can trust. But if we can't get anyone at the White House to listen, then we may not have any choice but to take the risk."

Their taxi slowed as several brake lights flashed up ahead. Sam chaffed at the delay. He took Jia's hand. "We may be able to cover the distance quicker on foot."

"I think so too," Jia agreed.

"We're getting out here," Sam told the taxi driver. He handed over their fare, plus a substantial tip. "Thanks."

He and Jia slipped out of the taxi before the driver could say anything more. They had to snake between several stopped cars before they managed to get off the main highway to one of the side streets. It had been several years since Sam had been back, but he still knew the city well enough to find his way.

"We must hurry," Jia said, breaking into a run.

Sam increased his pace so he was jogging alongside her. There was no questioning the sense of urgency that plagued them.

As they approached the White House, he silently prayed that God might continue blessing them with the strength and ability to succeed in their mission.

JANUARY 31 – 6:59 p.m. – Richmond, VA

"Mayleen, you will change into these items." The mysterious voice woke Kali from her nap. She blinked but couldn't see anything through the persistent darkness.

"I can't. I'm chained to the wall." Even as Kali said the words, she moved her cuffed ankle. When she realized the metal chain was gone, she bolted upright and touched the chaffed skin around her ankle.

The soreness proved she hadn't imagined the metal cuff and chain. It had been there. When had they removed it?

"You will change your clothes," the voice repeated.

Kali wanted to argue, but fear of being chained up again stopped her. Unable to see, she used her hands to explore the area around her cot. When she felt the soft bundle of clothing, she pulled them toward her.

The items were simple from what she could tell. A Chinese tunic-like top made of satin and simple cotton pants. Her school uniform was beyond wrinkled and likely horribly stained, so she decided to go ahead and strip them off to don the clean clothes.

It occurred to her that the tunic resembled items she'd seen in pictures of China. Kali had done a report on China last year. She'd been adopted by the Copelands seventeen years ago when she was just a baby, but she'd always been curious about her heritage.

Not that she'd mentioned that curiosity to her parents. They had given her everything, and she knew how fortunate she was to have been adopted by a junior congressman who quickly climbed the ladder until he'd actually been voted in as the current President of the United States.

Although being drugged and kidnapped was not good. Kali still didn't know who Mayleen was and why the Secret Service hadn't found her yet.

Once she was dressed, she explored the room with her hands. Without the chain encumbering her movements, she was able to reach the door. Only to find it locked.

"Okay, I'm dressed," Kali said loudly. She was apprehensive about where they were taking her, but the dark room was doing funny things to her mind to the point she wondered if their goal was to drive her insane.

She desperately wanted to believe that getting out of there would provide an opportunity to escape.

Kali refused to consider the alternative. That, indeed, her fate could potentially be worse.

Much worse.

JANUARY 31 – 7:12 p.m. – Washington, DC

Boyd did his best to ignore Ash Otto and Nick Howell, the two Secret Service agents assigned to keep an eye on him and Lina. He knew them both and could tell they were not happy to be reallocated to babysitting detail. Although they would also be expected to keep an eye on the celebration too.

"We're not dressed for a party," Lina pointed out.

As they were both dressed in dark clothing, it wasn't as if they'd stand out too badly. "That doesn't matter, we're not going to be in the thick of things. What's more important is coming up with a plan."

"Your plan is to stand by and watch," Otto said. "Nothing more."

Boyd swallowed a sigh. "Have you ever known me to take a threat lightly?"

Otto and Howell looked at each other and shrugged. "You don't work here anymore," Howell pointed out. "And your performance was far from stellar when you did."

Otto snickered in agreement.

Boyd always knew he'd be judged by his one failure rather than all the successes he'd had during his six-year stint with the agency. He'd been so good at spotting bad actors that he'd been moved up to the First Lady's detail after the election.

Only to fall flat on his face when the knife guy managed to get past his team.

"Ignore them, Boyd," Lina said loudly. "You've kept me safe during four different attacks orchestrated by the Chinese mafia. I trust you more than any of these guys." She waved a dismissive hand at the two men.

It was all Boyd could do not to sweep her into his arms and kiss her again. A desire that was growing more and more difficult to ignore. Mostly because he didn't want to ignore it. He told himself to stay focused. Lina's loyalty was sweet and touching, but it wasn't going to sway the jaded opinions of the Secret Service.

"They'll know the truth soon enough," Boyd said. "Let's head to the East Room. I want to be there as they're setting up."

"They're already finished," Otto said in a derisive tone. "The cocktail party started at seven."

Boyd gnashed his teeth together. "Then why are we standing around doing nothing? Let's go."

Otto and Howell clearly didn't want to leave the conference room. Would they really defy orders?

"The president and the First Lady are expecting us," Lina said. "They will notice if we're not there."

That reminder was enough to have Howell open the door. Howell flanked Boyd while Otto stayed close to Lina.

Boyd knew the way, so when Howell tried to continue straight instead of going to the right, he purposefully slammed into the guy. "Oh, sorry, I thought you knew the East Room was this way?"

Howell shot him a withering look but didn't say anything in response.

Upon reaching the East Room, Boyd could see the party had begun. Thankfully, there weren't many people there yet, but there were some well-dressed guests milling about.

Soon the room would be packed, and then what? How on earth would he and Lina figure out who might attack the president?

He glanced at Lina whose expression was equally grim. He hadn't been kidding when he'd told her they needed to pray. He'd never felt so helpless in his entire life as he did at this moment.

Why the acting Director of the FBI and Sean Adams weren't taking this seriously was a mystery. Unless one of them was being paid by the bad guy?

If so, who? Boyd was afraid that much like the incident with the First Lady two months ago, the attack would happen right under his nose.

Only this time, he'd be seconds too late to stop it.

"We're going to do this," Lina whispered as if reading his thoughts. "Have faith, Boyd. God is guiding us."

"I'm doing my best to believe that," he murmured. A quick glance at Otto and Howell confirmed the two men were speaking into their mics and earpieces. He tugged Lina closer and dropped his head to kiss her.

She leaned into his embrace, kissing him back in a way that made him want to whisk her away from there. But, of course, that wasn't an option.

"That was nice," she murmured with a smile.

"Depending on what happens tonight, I want you to know you're the most beautiful and courageous woman I know." There was more, so much more that Boyd wanted to say, but Otto took that moment to step toward them.

"See something?" he asked in a dry tone.

"Not yet. We'll let you know when we do," Boyd responded evenly.

"Yeah, you do that." Otto turned away.

He'd never been a violent man, even during his deployment overseas he'd tried diplomacy over brute strength. But the strong desire to punch Otto and Howell in their smug noses was difficult to ignore.

"When do you think the president and First Lady will arrive?" Lina asked.

"Anytime now," Boyd answered. "They usually like to be early for these things."

"They must like to party," Lina said.

"Not really, they tend to leave early too." Boyd shrugged. "At least, they used to." He straightened and glanced over to the doorway. "Here they come now."

The president, First Lady, Kali, and Xi Jin Ping along with his current wife, Peng Li Yuan, entered the hall, smiling at their guests. There was another Chinese man beside Xi Jin Ping, but Boyd didn't know who he was.

He watched Kali standing near her parents. Earlier, he'd sensed something was off about her. Kali was wearing a long gown, similar to that of her mother's. This time the bored expression on her face was replaced with one full of anticipation.

He continued watching the teenager, trying to pinpoint what it was that bothered him. She looked the same as he remembered, and her interactions with her mother were the same, too, but there was something. He continued watching her as she followed in her parents' wake.

Kali's gaze met his, but she moved on as if she didn't recognize him.

The tiny hairs on the back of his neck lifted in warning. That was wrong. Kali knew him very well from the last year he'd been assigned to her mother. In fact, Eloise had joked that Kali had a crush on him.

Maybe the teenager had gotten over her crush. For all he knew, she had a boyfriend now.

Still, he couldn't shake the fear that he was missing something. Ignoring Otto and Howell, he took Lina's arm and steered her toward the teenager.

It was time to have a chat with Kali Copeland.

CHAPTER TWENTY

January 31 – 7:36 p.m. – Richmond, VA

After being in the dark for so long, Kali had to shield her eyes from the bright lights as she was pulled through a doorway and down a narrow hallway. Strong hands held her tightly on either side, making it impossible for her to make a run for it.

"Outside, Mayleen. Now!"

She stumbled as the rough hands dragged her through some sort of house. The cold air hit hard when the door opened, but the darkness of the outdoors was welcome. She breathed in the fresh air, hoping it would clear the drug-induced fog from her mind.

"This way." The woman had long, sharp fingernails that dug painfully into her skin as she pulled on her arm. Hunger gnawed at her stomach, and she would have given just about anything for a glass of drug-free water. Her captors, the Chinese man with an abundance of dragon tattoos and an equally mean-looking woman, did not seem inclined to feed or hydrate her. They shoved her toward a vehicle and muscled her inside. The man slid in beside her while the woman took the wheel.

"Put on your seatbelt," the woman said. With her hands on the steering wheel, Kali could see all ten pointy fingernails.

Fearing she'd be stabbed by them, she reluctantly did what they instructed. With only one captor beside her, Kali tried to assess her ability to escape. But when the door locks clicked into place, she knew that plan was useless.

The Chinese man next to her tightened his grip on her wrist. He was holding her so tight she winced at the pain. "Don't do anything stupid. We can always just kill you now and not bother with the rest."

The rest of what? "I won't." Her throat was hoarse from the drugs and lack of fluids. "Where are we going?"

The hand tightened with such force that she cried out. "Silence!"

Blinking her eyes against the urge to cry, Kali turned to look out the window. The area didn't look the least bit familiar. The only thing she knew for certain was that they were not in Washington, DC. Very soon, though, she saw a sign indicating they were heading toward the Richmond Airport.

She was in Richmond, Virginia, at least for now. As the driver of the car stayed in the airport lane, a fresh wave of panic crawled up her throat.

Were they really planning to fly her out of the country?

Glancing at her Chinese attire, she had a bad feeling that was exactly what this couple was doing. For what purpose? She was deeply afraid they intended to sell her into prostitution.

Battling the paralyzing fear wasn't easy, but Kali tried to

stay focused. Once they were in the airport, amongst the crowds, there would likely be an opportunity to escape.

She just had to remain patient and vigilant. Because leaving the US would not be a good thing for her.

No, she felt certain that if she ended up on a plane, the FBI and Secret Service would never find her.

JANUARY 31 – 7:41 p.m. – Washington, DC

"Kali, it's been a while, how are you?"

"Didn't you ask me that already? I'm good, thanks." Lina watched as Kali flicked a disdainful glance over Boyd, then turned to her. "Hello, I don't believe we've formally met."

"I'm Lina Parker." She took Kali's hand, surprised at the strength in the girl's grasp. "It's an honour to be here."

"I'm not sure you're actual guests, though, right?" Kali held a wine glass filled to the halfway point with a blush-colored liquid. Lina didn't believe Kali's parents would allow her to drink wine, but then again, maybe they did. Who would call them out on it? Absolutely no one. "I overheard my parents talking about a possible threat. I'm glad you're both here to help out." This time, Kali's gaze included Boyd.

"That's true." Boyd's frown indicated he wasn't happy with how this conversation was going. "You used to love school, what's changed?"

"Nothing has changed," Kali protested. "I still enjoy my classes, but honestly, I'm looking forward to spring break."

"Do you have plans to go somewhere fun?" Lina asked.

"Not yet, but I'm working on it." Kali turned and nodded at someone. "If you'll please excuse me? I need to speak with Pamela." Without waiting for them to respond,

Kali moved away from them to approach the vice president and his wife.

"Her parents let her drink alcohol?" Lina asked when they were alone.

"It's a nonalcoholic wine. It's actually what the president and First Lady drink as well. Trevor Copeland's father is a recovering alcoholic, so he's made a pledge to abstain. A vow his family supports."

"I didn't realize that," Lina admitted.

"They don't make a big deal out of it, but there is always a nonalcoholic brand of wine available wherever they go." His scowl deepened. "There's something off about Kali. She's not acting normal."

"She's what, seventeen?" Lina offered a wry smile. "Teenagers are rarely normal. And living in the White House over the past year has probably only made a bigger impact on the girl."

"It's not that." Boyd shook his head in frustration. "I wish I could pinpoint what exactly is troubling me."

"I'm surprised she's of Chinese descent," Lina said. "I'm wondering if her ethnicity was a primary factor in President Copeland's decision to have this celebration."

"The Copelands adopted Kali as a baby, so she's as much of an American as you are," he said, his gaze laser-focused on Kali's conversation with the vice president's wife.

"I wasn't adopted, I was born here," she pointed out. "But I see your point."

"Copeland is a politician," Boyd said. "A decent guy, but still a politician. All of this is motivated by improving foreign relationships."

Lina swept her gaze over the room that had become

crowded with guests. So many people, how on earth would they be able to figure out who might have the poison?

She wanted to believe the Secret Service's search, which so far had come up empty, proved the strychnine wasn't inside the White House.

But that would be too easy. No, she felt certain the threat was still there, poised and ready to strike.

Leaving her little choice but to hope and pray they'd figure out who was behind this before the lethal poison reached the president or Xi Jin Ping.

A seemingly insurmountable task.

JANUARY 31 – 7:45 p.m. – Washington, DC

He was not happy to see Sinclair and Lina Parker in the East Room. Even less so to watch them chatting with Kali. He'd fully expected the fire alarm would have gotten them both out of the building.

Unfortunately, he'd underestimated Sinclair's knowledge of the place. And the slack attitude of the Secret Service. That would be something he'd have to take care of once he was in charge. He would not tolerate such sloppiness.

Sipping his wine, not the fake stuff the president preferred but the real thing, he tried to come up with a way to get rid of them without causing a scene. The last thing he wanted was to draw any undue attention to himself. Not after he'd gotten this far.

It was beyond infuriating that the idiot had kowtowed to the president's wishes.

He took a deep breath and let it out slowly. He refused to let their presence here derail his plan. In fact, he'd decided to move the timeline up a bit. Why wait until midnight when he could simply take action sooner?

Hiding his satisfied smile behind his wineglass, he turned and found his contact. Making small talk as he went, he crossed over to smile at the contact. "We need to move up the timeline."

"Any particular time?"

"Sooner than later, but it needs to look natural."

"Of course. I will take care of it." His contact nodded and moved away.

He could barely contain his excitement. The significance of the stroke of midnight would be missed, but he was growing impatient anyway. There wasn't a moment to waste.

Soon, very soon he'd be exactly where he belonged. The most powerful man in the country. A position he deserved so much more than Copeland.

And the brilliance of his plan was such that no one would ever be able to point the finger at him.

No one.

JANUARY 31 – 7:52 p.m. – Richmond, VA

As they parked the car in the airport parking lot, Kali did her best to remain focused. She felt certain there would be an opportunity to escape. Already she was envisioning different scenarios.

Her captors would have to go through security, the same as everyone else, which meant they wouldn't be able to use a gun or a knife to keep her in line. What else could they threaten her with? She was feeling confident that they wouldn't have anything to use against her, until a thought hit hard.

Drugs.

The same drugs they'd used in her food and water.

And she couldn't forget the daggerlike fingernails on the woman either.

Okay, maybe they did have a weapon to use against her. But they hadn't drugged her yet. Most likely because it would be harder to drag a drugged teenager onto a plane. The thought was somewhat reassuring. The woman couldn't use the fingernails without drawing blood, right?

Right.

Kali swallowed and glanced around, taking in her surroundings. During the drive, her eyes had adjusted to the dim light. However, the brightly lit parking garage was enough to blind her again. Wishing she had a pair of sunglasses, she kept her head down and tried to use her peripheral vision to track the passengers who were walking briskly toward the terminals.

Unfortunately, none of them paid any attention to her and the Chinese couple. Her own Chinese heritage only added to the illusion. The woman grabbed a suitcase out of the trunk and came around to stand on Kali's right side. She had no doubt her kidnappers would pretend to be her parents.

"Walk and don't talk. You won't like the consequences, Mayleen."

Mayleen again. Kali had given up trying to figure out what game they were playing. She decided the name they called her wasn't important. The only thing that mattered was finding a way to escape.

What if she shouted out to one of the many strangers within earshot? Would anyone come to her rescue? Would they believe she was the president's daughter?

Kali was afraid to find out. Deep down, she feared she'd be looked at as a girl with psychiatric problems.

Okay, maybe focusing on the fact that she was really Kali Copeland wasn't the best idea. That didn't mean she couldn't find a way to escape. To claim these people were not her parents and that they'd taken her against her will.

All she needed was one person to believe her. Just one.

Kali hadn't been raised with religion, but she found herself praying anyway.

Please, God, help me escape!

JANUARY 31 – 8:01 *p.m.* – *Washington, DC*

Sloan had dropped Jordan off at the White House entrance, heading over to help Sun and Mack with the dead NSA agent named Tillman at the same time as a petite older Chinese woman and tall American man did. When he heard the guy explain he was Sam King with the CIA, and that Jia Ling Ling was his asset and that they needed to talk to the president, he turned to them. "I'm Jordan Rashid with Security Specialists, Inc. What do you want with the president?"

"It doesn't matter, none of you are getting in," the Secret Service agent said firmly.

"Director Clarence Yates sent me," Jordan told the agent. "You can call the president to verify that." Then he turned to Sam King and Jia Ling Ling. "What's going on?"

The pair looked at each other, then faced him. "I'm Sam King with the CIA," the tall man with dark hair said.

"And I am Jia Ling Ling. We have traveled from Beijing to alert the president about an attempt to harm him," Jia said. "I infiltrated the Six Red Dragons mafia group, but my cover was recently blown. Bo Dung Manchu is working with someone high in the Chinese government and high up within the American government. I fear the worst is about to happen."

Jordan didn't trust easily. After all, he and his team had been burned by corrupt FBI agents in the past. Yet his instinct was to believe them. "Do you have any proof of this?"

Again, the two exchanged a meaningful glance. "Only what I overheard," Jia admitted. "I also leaked that information to the CIA as a warning to the president. And lastly, there is also the family connection."

He lifted a brow. "What kind of family connection?"

"Shu Yan Chen. I know she has been murdered, yet that crime has been covered up."

Jordan whistled under his breath. For her to know those things made him lean toward believing her. He glared at the agent in their way. "You need to let us inside now."

"Can't do that," the agent drawled.

"Do you realize there was an attempt to kill Yates in his hospital room? And that he's right now fighting for his life in the ICU?" Jordan leaned in. "Yates hired me and my team to investigate a possible terrorist attack from the Chinese mafia. The three of us"—he indicated Sam King, Jia Ling Ling, and himself—"need to talk to the president. Before it's too late."

The agent called his boss, who in turn must have agreed. Jordan, Sam, and Jia were checked for weapons and sent through the scanner.

"Where is the celebration?" King asked.

"The East Room. Follow me." Jordan led the way, with Sam, Jia, and two Secret Service agents following behind. When they reached the doorway, he gestured to the pair to wait. "Stay here. I have a guy inside who is helping me. I want to talk to him first."

Sam and Jia nodded, their expressions tense.

Jordan went inside, casting his gaze around the room to find Boyd, hoping and praying he hadn't made a mistake in allowing the two to accompany him.

JANUARY 31 – 8:09 p.m. – Richmond, VA

"You will not cause trouble," the Chinese woman hissed. "We will drug you if necessary. The vial will say insulin, but it will work very differently." The woman stabbed her side with a pointy fingernail honed to a point. Kali could feel the blood seeping from the puncture mark. "You remember, yes?"

Kali managed a nod even though she didn't believe for one minute they were anxious to have her doped up. Having a teenager who could barely walk or talk would draw unwanted attention.

Now that her eyes were adjusting to the lights illuminating the inside of the airport, she continued searching for someone to trust. Someone who would take her allegations seriously.

Kali tried to relax her tense muscles, fearing the Chinese couple would sense her intent. She sensed she'd only have one chance to escape.

The man and woman spoke to each other in Chinese, no doubt deciding the best way to get her through security. Obviously getting through on a commercial flight was nothing compared to flying in Air Force One.

Wait a minute.

Security!

Kali thought about the TSA agents they'd have to get

past. There would be a moment when her captors would have to let her go so she could stand in the scanner with her hands over her head.

Her heart thumped with anticipation, although she did her best to keep herself lax under their grip. The more these two believed her to be scared and cowed, the better. So far, she'd done everything they'd asked of her.

But not for long.

Hope fluttered in her chest. Getting through the last security checkpoint would be her best opportunity to escape.

One she planned to make the most of.

JANUARY 31 – 8:15 p.m. – Washington, DC

Boyd tensed. Several of the guests were making their way toward the round tables set up along the west side of the room. There was a wide-open section of the room where he assumed the dragon dance would be performed.

The president, First Lady, and Kali were slowly, ever so slowly, making their way to the head table to join Xi Jin Ping and his wife, Peng Li Yuan. The lights were lowered, just a bit, in preparation for the upcoming performance.

This was it. He could feel it in his bones.

"Stay alert," he whispered to Lina.

The president's attempt to cross the room was hampered by several guests stepping forward to chat. No doubt making one last political play before the fun part of the evening was to begin.

In his role of guarding the First Lady, Boyd had been spared some of the political nonsense. Although he'd seen enough to know that everyone had an angle and wasn't above using whatever means necessary to work it.

For the first time since the debacle two months ago, he found himself glad to be out of the political arena. Well, he was still involved, but from a different perspective.

He watched as yet another congressman stepped up to take the president's arm. Boyd watched as Kali turned and swept her gaze over the room.

She was different tonight. Maybe it was just that she'd gotten over her crush on him, but his instincts told him otherwise.

Instincts that had failed in him the past, he silently acknowledged. After all, Kali had been spending time with her parents. If something was off about her, surely, they'd have noticed.

Kali stood a little off to the side, holding her glass filled with what he presumed was nonalcoholic wine.

He frowned and tried to think back. Had she taken a sip from the glass? Did it matter? She wasn't the target, of that he felt certain.

There was nothing to be gained by harming the president's daughter.

The president broke free of the congressman and took Eloise's hand. Kali joined them, and they crossed over to sit beside Xi Jin Ping and his wife. Vice President Eric Turner and his wife, Pamela, were already seated next to the president's spot, with Xi Jin Ping and his Chinese buddy on the other side.

Kali was the last to sit; in fact, she went over to speak to her father. Boyd watched as Kali set her glass down on the table before she whispered something in his ear.

Then she stood and reached for her glass. Only it wasn't her glass. It was the president's glass.

In that moment he knew. Kali was complicit in this.

The president reached for the glass that Kali had left

behind. At the same moment, Xi Jin Ping raised his glass of beer. The two world leaders lifted their glasses in a toast.

"No!" Boyd shouted as he made a mad dash across the room. "Don't drink it!"

Eloise looked over at him, her brow furrowed with concern.

Time seemed to stand still as the president lifted the glass to his lips.

CHAPTER TWENTY-ONE

January 31 – 8:20 p.m. – Washington, DC

Lina watched in horror as several Secret Service agents jumped forward to grab Boyd. She quickly darted around them, her gaze focused on the president and Xi Jin Ping.

Eloise abruptly smacked the wine from the president's hand. The glass fell onto the table and broke, the liquid contents soaking into the linen tablecloth.

Lina darted around the agents struggling to hold Boyd in time to snatch the beer glass from Xi Jin Ping's hand. The contents sloshed over the rim, but she managed to save some. She thrust the glass to Adams, who'd come over to intervene in the commotion. "Get this tested for strychnine as soon as possible."

Adams glanced over to where a circle of Secret Service agents surrounded the president and First Lady. Another set of agents had now surrounded the Chinese leader and his wife as well.

Boyd was still being held by Danby and another man. "Good job, Eloise," Boyd called out.

Lina breathed a tiny sigh of relief. They would know

soon enough whether the two leaders' drinks had been tampered with.

Then she narrowed her gaze as Kali was making her way out of the room. Two Secret Service agents were accompanying the teen, but that didn't deter Lina.

She quickly wove through the crowd. Most of the guests were seated or standing at their respective tables gaping at the commotion in the center of the room.

"Kali, wait!" Lina called.

The girl glanced over her shoulder, and Lina glimpsed the flash of fear that darkened her eyes.

"Stop right there," one of the agents said, pulling his gun. "You are not allowed to get any closer to the first family."

"Ah, but she is not Kali Copeland," a female voice said from the doorway. "She is Mayleen Chen."

Mayleen Chen? Lina stared at the woman, then back at Kali. The teenager crossed her arms over her chest.

"I'm Kali Copeland, and I—want to get away from here." The girl's eyes filled with tears, and her voice began to quaver. "Something bad almost happened to my parents, and I'm worried I'm next!"

"You are Mayleen, born to Shu Yan Chen seventeen years ago," the Chinese woman said. "Shu Yan bore female twins, one of which was given up to adoption. The other kept in China and raised within the Six Red Dragons faction of the Chinese mafia. Hui Genghis Chen raised you to hate the Americans and to study film of Kali with one purpose, to take her place."

What? Lina stared at the woman in shock. "How do you know this?"

The woman locked eyes with her. "Do you remember me, Li Na?"

The way she spoke her name in the Chinese way of using two syllables brought a long-buried memory to the surface. Her mother, reading her a story about a beautiful Chinese girl named Li Na, one whom she was named after.

Only it couldn't be. Her mother died twenty-five years ago.

"Take me away from here," the fake Kali shrieked. "I'm afraid these people want to hurt me!"

"Are you my mother?" Lina asked.

The woman smiled. "Yes, Li Na, I am your mother. And you must believe me when I say this girl is Mayleen, not Kali."

Kali, or rather, Mayleen roughly pushed at one of the Secret Service agents. "I'm going to be sick, please take me to my room."

"Right away," the agent promised.

"Hold on, no one is going anywhere," a deep voice said from behind them.

Still shaken by the news that her mother wasn't dead, Lina looked over to where Boyd was standing with Sean Adams. Both men stared at Kali with suspicion.

"I witnessed Kali exchange wine glasses with her father," Boyd said firmly. "She must remain under guard until we can test the contents of the glass for strychnine. The tablecloth soaked with spilled wine is being taken to the FBI lab as we speak. Along with the glass of Chinese beer removed from Xi Jin Ping." Boyd smiled darkly, pinning the teenager with a narrow look. "You didn't fool me, Mayleen. I knew you weren't the real Kali. And even better, your little assassination plan didn't work. I doubt those who brainwashed you to do this awful thing didn't bother to tell you that the penalty for your attempt to assassinate the president is life in a federal prison without the opportunity for parole. Then again, as a Chinese citizen, we may agree to have you serve your time in a prison located within your homeland, which I believe will be far worse."

Mayleen said nothing, but there was a flicker of uncertainty in the girl's dark eyes. Lina didn't know anything about the conditions of a Chinese prison, but she suspected Boyd was right in that they would be far worse than what the teenager would experience here in the US.

"How did she get the strychnine into the building?" Adams asked.

"I didn't do anything," Mayleen protested. "I'm Kali Copeland!"

"No, you're not." Lina noticed the girl was wearing a lot of makeup. "Did anyone check the contents of her cosmetic bag? She could have hidden the vials in something that looked like makeup."

The girl glanced away as if Lina had guessed correctly.

"Check her makeup stuff," Boyd said. Then he pinned the girl with a narrow glare. "You may want to consider telling us who else was involved," he added. "If you cooperate, you'll likely be allowed to serve your time here, in America. From what I hear, the death rate in Chinese prisons is very high. And especially brutal for young women."

The girl didn't respond, but Lina sensed she was weighing her options.

Lina was proud of Boyd's instincts. He'd known from the first moment he'd met Kali that something was off. Without Boyd watching the girl so closely, they'd never have saved the president in time.

Then she frowned. "If this girl is Mayleen, where is Kali Copeland?"

Adams glanced at the agents holding Mayleen's arms,

his expression grim. "We need to get the acting director of the FBI and Woodland with the CIA involved as soon as possible. If Kali is missing, we must find her."

Lina watched as one agent turned away to use his microphone and earpiece to make the call. She swallowed hard at the thought of Kali Copeland being held by members of the Six Red Dragons.

The satisfied smirk on Mayleen's face was not the least bit reassuring.

JANUARY 31 – 8:47 p.m. – Richmond, VA

Kali was held in a firm grip by the Chinese woman all the way to the TSA agent checking their boarding passes and passports. The Chinese woman dug her pointy nails into her side as they stood before the agent. Kali was shocked to see her picture on the passport under the name of Mayleen Chen. There was no doubt the picture was of her, same hair length, same clothing, same facial features.

Same everything.

How had they gotten her photograph? Granted, being the president's daughter meant her face was all over the newspapers and social media sites, but to make that picture into a passport photo? It didn't seem possible.

She told herself that the passport wasn't important. What mattered was getting through the security scanner, then trying to escape. She'd been a member of the cheerleading squad this past fall during the football season. She was young, fit, and healthy on a good day, but without food or water, she wasn't in the best shape. Her entire body felt weak from being held for hours in that jail cell of a room. She wished now she'd pushed herself to do some physical activity while being stuck in that tiny room, to keep herself conditioned.

Eyeing the narrow space between the scanner itself and the conveyor belt where personal belongings were checked, she could tell it wasn't enough for her to get much, if any, momentum.

Too bad. No way was she giving up. This was her best chance to escape, and she intended to make the most of it.

No matter what the Chinese couple did to her, she had to try.

The Chinese man with the dragon tattoo went through the scanner first. He stood right behind the TSA agent, watching her with his beady stare. The Chinese woman pressed her pointy nails into Kali's side, then gave her a shove. "Go on, Mayleen. It's your turn."

Kali stood for a moment until the TSA agent waved her forward. She stood in the center of the scanner with her arms up and over her head. Time seemed to slow down as the plexiglass window spun around her.

"Step forward, please," the TSA agent said.

This was it. Kali avoided looking at the Chinese man, her gaze was on the narrow opening between the agent and the conveyor belt. She took a step forward, then grabbed the edge of the scanner and used all the strength she could muster to vault over it, kicking out with her foot when the TSA agent tried to grab her.

She stumbled but managed to stay upright. She ran straight toward a round motherly type of woman wearing a TSA uniform. It was the agent she'd figured would be the most likely to believe her. "Help me!" she shouted at the top of her lungs. "They're going to sell me as a sex slave!"

Dozens of TSA agents swarmed toward her, but Kali didn't mind. She grasped the female agent's uniform and stared up into her eyes. "Please, help me," she whimpered. "They kidnapped me and drugged me. They're taking me to China to make me a sex slave!"

"Let's get her into the holding room," one of the TSA agents said.

"Yes, and call the sheriff's deputy too," the female agent said with a frown. "They'll need to investigate her claim of being a victim of sex trafficking."

Kali darted a glance over her shoulder toward where she'd left the Chinese couple, but they were gone.

Gone! She wanted to weep with relief.

She'd done it. She'd managed to escape.

Thank You, God!

JANUARY 31 – 9:02 *p.m.* – *Washington, DC*

No! This couldn't be happening!

He stared in horror as the president, the Chinese leader, and their respective wives were whisked out of the East Room without drinking the poison. He rose and allowed the Secret Service agents to usher him off as well, even as he inwardly railed at the botched attempt.

First the CIA agents had slipped past his man in Reagan International Airport, now this! So much time and effort wasted in the blink of an eye. A brilliant plan sixteen years in the making should have worked without a hitch. So much time and money poured into the Copeland campaign should have gotten them what they'd wanted.

But it hadn't.

They'd failed!

He wanted to pull the Secret Service agent's gun and start shooting, but of course, he would only die if he'd tried something so foolish.

He reined in his anger and frustration with an effort.

The plan hadn't worked, but that only meant damage control was desperately needed. He kept a serious expression of concern on his face, even as his mind spun with possibilities.

He could easily deny involvement, and there wasn't any proof that he could think of that would tie him to the assassination attempt.

The girl would have to die. It was the only way to shore up that connection.

He carefully slid the disposable phone from his pocket and sent a quick text message.

Erase target.

The response came very quickly. As he glanced down at the screen, he paled.

Target escaped.

Beads of sweat lined his brow. He read the message twice, unable to fathom how on earth the president's daughter had escaped.

As he moved through the room, he deftly removed a napkin off the table, wiped off the phone, and subtly dropped it in the garbage.

Damage control. He could survive this.

Still, his fingers shook as he wiped the sweat from his brow. This hadn't been part of the plan.

And even if he did survive the night, there was always the possibility Manchu would come after him at a moment he least expected it.

JANUARY 31 – 9:12 p.m. – Richmond, VA

Now that Kali had safely escaped the terrible Chinese couple, she needed to come up with a way to convince the

TSA agents and the sheriff's deputy that she was really Kali Copeland. So far, they were treating her as a psych patient.

Exactly as she'd feared.

"I need you to call the White House," she said. "I need you to ask for Sean Adams, he's the head of the Secret Service."

"Mayleen, you can trust us to help you," the motherly TSA agent said. "Just tell us the truth, okay?"

Kali suppressed a sigh. Having a fake passport was proving to be a real problem. She reached for the bottle of water they'd provided and took a grateful sip. It was nice to have something that wasn't drugged. She forced a smile. "I know this probably sounds crazy, but I am telling the truth. Will you lend me your phone? I'll make the call."

Her stomach growled loud enough for the woman to hear. "Would you like me to get you something to eat? A sandwich?"

"Yes, please." Kali smiled weakly. "The Chinese couple who kidnapped me put drugs in my food and water. I stopped eating what they brought so I could stay awake. I haven't eaten anything in hours.

"You poor thing," the woman said. "I can't imagine what you've been through. It must have been awful."

"It was," Kali agreed.

The deputy snorted. "Yeah, well, I'm not sure I'm buying this sob story. She's claiming to be the president's daughter. How is that even possible? There's been nothing on the news about a missing kid. The FBI would be all over something like this."

"Maybe they're keeping that information quiet," one of the other TSA agents said. "Waiting for a ransom or something."

"And maybe she's a nutcase. Until we know more, we'll

take Ms. Chen into custody at the Richmond jail. From there, we'll let Child Protective Services sort it out."

Kali ignored him, reaching forward to touch the female TSA agent's arm. "Please, I'm begging you. The passport with Mayleen Chen's name is fake, that's not me. Let me borrow your phone. I promise you won't regret it."

"Let me get you that sandwich first." The woman stood and left the room.

Kali bowed her head and tried not to groan. She tried to take heart in that she wasn't being taken out of the country against her wishes, but really? She just wanted to go home.

Even though she didn't really consider the White House to be her home, she still longed for the comfort of her parents. Even the Secret Service would be a welcome relief. She squeezed her eyes shut, vainly trying to prevent tears from leaking down her face.

If they really tossed her in jail, she'd have exchanged one prison cell for another. At least, this one wouldn't provide drugged food.

She sniffled and pulled herself together. Anything was better than being with the Chinese couple. *Anything.*

Even a long night in jail.

JANUARY 31 – 9:22 p.m. – Washington, DC

Boyd, Lina, Jordan, Sam King, and Jia Ling Ling were all placed in a conference room with two Secret Service agents inside. The entire White House had gone on lockdown so that no one could come in or leave.

"You must find Kali," Jia said to Jordan. "They may attempt to get her out of the country."

"We're waiting for Stone to come talk to us," Jordan

said. "He's the one who can make that happen. The FBI has jurisdiction in a kidnapping case."

"Time is of the essence," Jia persisted. "You must not let Manchu's men take her away!"

"I know, we're trying," Jordan said reassuringly. "I told them to flag Mayleen Chen's name in the system. Hopefully, they'll find something soon."

"Wait a minute," Lina said, stepping forward. "Are you saying that Kali and Mayleen are my cousins?"

Boyd hiked his eyebrow and shared a stunned glance with the two Secret Service agents standing at the door.

"Yes, Li Na, years ago, the Six Red Dragons tried to kill me and your father. Unfortunately, Tony died, but I managed to survive. But then I learned my sister aligned herself with Hui Genghis Chen, second-in-command to Bo Dung Manchu, the current leader of the Six Red Dragons." Jia placed a hand on Lina's arm, but she quickly shrugged it off and took a step away from the woman. Still, Jia pressed on. "We are related to Xi Jin Ping's first wife, who harbors a deep resentment toward him. Being in a position of power allowed our parents to have two children instead of the government-mandated one. My sister then had twins, one of which she was forced to give up for adoption. Years later, my sister managed to escape to America. Manchu was not pleased, and after I learned about Mayleen's training to take Kali's place, I called Sam. Unfortunately, Manchu discovered that I was spying on him and that Shu Yan was my younger sister." A shadow crossed Jia's features. "I had to kill Hui Genghis Chen to escape. The Six Red Dragons have tried several times to kill me and CIA Agent Sam King. I'm afraid they will not stop until they succeed."

This was all news to Boyd, and while he found it interesting, he hated seeing the pain on Lina's face. She looked so fragile he stepped up to wrap his arm around her waist. She leaned against him as if she were hanging on by a mere thread. It was incredible to realize Lina was seeing her mother for the first time in twenty-five years, especially after believing she had died in that terrible car crash years ago.

It was a whopper of a lie. And made him wonder how many more lies had Lina been told? He battled a wave of anger, hating knowing she was suffering. Her green gaze was awash in conflicting emotions—anger, fear, relief, and frustration.

He felt bad for her, but there were more pressing issues. Finding Kali Copeland and uncovering the true traitor that walked among them. Boyd didn't doubt for one second the traitor had been in the East Room that evening.

Then again, the guest list had topped out at one hundred and fifty.

The door burst open, and Randal Stone strode in, looking royally ticked. "I'm tired of you and your team, Rashid."

The feeling is mutual, Boyd thought but wisely held his tongue.

"I'm telling you, Kali Copeland is out there, somewhere," Jordan said. "You need to put every resource possible on this. When we find her, you'll know I've been right all along."

"And if there isn't anyone to find because Kali Copeland is safe here at the White House already, you'll be locked up for the rest of your life," Stone shot back. Boyd wondered if the guy was on edge because all of this happened under his watch. Not a great way to take over as acting director of the FBI. "We have no reason to believe Orchid was taken right under our noses."

"Yes, you do. We know Kali was adopted and she has an

identical twin sister. How easy would it be for one girl to slip into a crowd while the other is removed? Especially at school? You need to find her," Jordan said tersely.

"How long before the FBI lab sends over the results of the strychnine testing?" Boyd asked. "That will be all the proof you need."

Stone scowled. "Yeah, so you say."

Boyd could tell the guy was in way over his head. He wished Yates was there. They'd had little choice but to trust the guy, but he suspected things would be moving quicker if the more experienced Yates was in charge. And where was Doug Weatherby? Shouldn't the head of the NSA be here?

"Make a few calls and find out," Adams suggested. "The sooner we have some answers, the better."

His former boss's abrupt support was an unexpected relief.

Stone muttered a curse under his breath, then turned toward the phone. The moment his fingers gripped the receiver, it rang.

"Stone," he snapped.

The room fell silent as the eyes of the acting director of the FBI widened in shocked surprise. "Yes, put her through."

Her? Boyd glanced down at Lina.

"Kali, is that really you?" Stone asked. When it became clear from the one side of the conversation that the caller was indeed Kali Copeland, Boyd let out a pent-up sigh of relief.

The president's daughter was safe. At least for now.

Yet Boyd knew they would never be safe, not until they uncovered the traitor among them.

CHAPTER TWENTY-TWO

January 31 – 9:29 p.m. – Washington, DC

Keeping her composure wasn't easy. Lina couldn't take her gaze from her mother, and she was very thankful for Boyd's strong presence beside her. Boyd and Adams were working together now, deciding the next steps while the place was on lockdown.

As they discussed watching the security cameras, Lina wrestled with her emotions.

Her mother was alive, and by the way she and Sam looked at each other, it was clear there was more than friendship between them. Irrational as it sounded, Lina was irritated that her mother had moved on after her father's death.

Or was he alive too? She abruptly straightened. "Where is my father?"

Her mother's gaze was full of compassion. "I told you Tony died in the car crash that almost claimed my life too. That was not a lie. The goal was to kill us both, only I survived. Tony worked for the CIA too, and I believe that is why we were targeted that day. I'm sorry, Li Na. I know this is all a terrible shock. But I promise you, this was not a decision I made lightly."

"Oh, I'm sure it wasn't that difficult for you to walk away from your only child," Lina said, her tone full of disdain.

"Lina, you don't know all the facts," Sam said. "I understand you're upset, but there is much you don't know."

"Because I was left behind as an orphan to be raised by my grandparents," she shot back. "Not my choice."

"Yes, that is true," her mother said. "It was the only way I could protect you."

"From the Six Red Dragons?" Lina asked.

"Exactly." Her mother nodded. "When I survived the crash, I wanted justice for Tony's murder. Sam encouraged the US government to declare me dead, providing me the opportunity to go undercover to infiltrate the Chinese mafia. I wanted them to pay for their crimes, only I then discovered my own sister was part of the reason they came after us in the first place. From there I had little choice but to continue the charade, eventually convincing Shu Yan to escape."

"How does Sam figure in?" Boyd asked. "Why did he help you?"

"Sam and Tony worked together." Her mother's gaze was full of emotion. "Being declared dead also meant that you, Li Na, were no longer a threat to anyone within the Six Red Dragons. I can explain more later, but know this, I would have given up my life for you."

"She did give up her life for you," Sam said firmly. "Do you think she enjoyed infiltrating the Six Red Dragons? Trust me, she did not."

Lina had to look away from the condemnation in Sam's eyes. Maybe he was right and her mother hadn't made this decision lightly. Yet it was a lot to take in after all this time.

"Okay, we have a chopper heading out to pick up Kali Copeland from the airport in Richmond, Virginia," Stone said, interrupting their brief conversation. "Unfortunately, it appears her captors escaped, although we have TSA combing video surveillance to find them. Adams, you need your men to handcuff and isolate the girl pretending to be Kali."

"Her name is Mayleen," her mother said. "I know she is my sister's daughter."

Stone grimaced. "Yes, the real Kali has Mayleen's passport. Apparently, her captors tried to get her on a flight to Paris, continuing on to Beijing. We suspect their plan was to force Kali into prostitution. A decision that likely saved her life, considering they could have killed her outright."

Lina sucked in a quick breath. She was glad God had watched over the president's daughter. If not for Boyd keeping his eye on the impostor, the plan to get to the president may have worked. If he hadn't seen the fake Kali switching glasses with her father, she knew the president and possibly Xi Jin Ping would both be dead.

Assassinated within the White House. A feat that had never happened in the history of their country.

She tore her gaze away from her mother and Sam King to glance up at Boyd. "You saved the president's life."

"Technically, Eloise is the one who knocked the glass from his hand," Boyd said with a wry smile. "I'm glad she listened to me."

"We don't have proof of poison being in their glasses," Stone pointed out.

"And why not? Why is the lab taking so long? This is an issue of national security." Boyd gave her a hug, then moved away. "We really need to watch those security tapes. I'll show you the exact moment the fake Kali exchanged her glass with her father's."

Both Adams and Stone headed toward the door. Lina hurried to catch up with Boyd. "I'd like to come too."

Boyd glanced at her curiously, then over at Jordan, her mother, and Sam. Sam slowly nodded as if understanding Lina needed time to deal with all this. She could feel her mother's gaze boring into her back. Maybe she was avoiding the woman, but a little distance would help her put things in perspective.

Besides, the danger wasn't over yet. They had Mayleen in custody, but not the mastermind behind the assassination attempt.

She shivered at the idea that the person who'd boldly hatched this plan to kill the president was still within the White House.

If they didn't figure out who he was very soon, there was a very good chance he'd escape.

And if that happened, what was to prevent him or her from trying again?

JANUARY 31 – 9:34 p.m. – Washington, DC

Being on lockdown made sense, but he couldn't quite quell his panic. He subtly swiped away the sweat that continued to bead on his brow.

No one suspected him. They had no reason to.

Yet he also knew that time was not his friend. The longer the Secret Service dragged this out, the more likely they might actually come up with something. For one thing, he'd run for President twice and had not been elected. And there was also the possibility that idiot teenager had started talking.

He mentally reviewed the steps he'd taken in the East Room. Just the one meeting with his contact, brief enough to be considered nothing but a polite greeting.

Still, he mentally cursed Mayleen for failing to implement the plan. Despite her rigorous training, she must have given herself away as an impostor.

But really, it was Boyd Sinclair who was ultimately at fault. The man had alerted Eloise in time for her to knock the president's nonalcoholic wine out of his hand. And the woman, Lina, had taken Xi Jin Ping's glass from his hand too.

Not good. He needed a new plan.

But he couldn't come up with one that had him getting out of there alive.

He scowled. Fine. If he was going down, he would take as many others as possible down with him.

JANUARY 31 – 9:37 p.m. – Washington, DC

Boyd was far too aware of Lina beside him as he and Adams watched video of the party in the East Room. He knew he needed to stay focused, but knowing the danger was mostly contained meant his time with Lina was limited.

He wasn't ready to give her up. A sentiment he'd never experienced before.

"Slow it down," Boyd said when he saw the fake Kali making her way toward her parents. "She'll set down her glass, speak to her father, then pick up his glass."

Adams slowed the video. All eyes were glued to the screen as the fake Kali did exactly what Boyd had seen. The sleight of hand was impressive, she'd done it so smoothly that no one had noticed.

Except for him.

"You were right," Adams said grimly. "But what about Xi Jin Ping?"

"I didn't see anyone tampering with his glass," Boyd admitted. "But I had my gaze centered on the fake Kali."

"What made you suspicious of her?" Adams asked.

Boyd felt himself flush. "Kali had a crush on me when I was assigned to her mother's detail. When I saw Kali again today, she acted as if she couldn't have cared less about me. Granted, she's a teenager, so that type of mood swing isn't entirely unexpected, but there was something off about her." He shrugged. "Unfortunately, I couldn't put my finger on what was bothering me."

"If you hadn't been here tonight . . ." Adams didn't finish the thought.

"But I was." He tapped on the screen. "Let's back it up and see if we can pinpoint anyone tampering with Xi Jin Ping's drink."

"Mr. Stone? There's a call for you on line two," one of the agents said.

Boyd straightened and watched Stone as he answered the call. The man went pale as he listened. "Okay, thanks."

"They found strychnine in the samples?" Boyd guessed.

"Yes, both the tablecloth and Xi Jin Ping's glass showed high and deadly levels of strychnine." The man looked as if he might throw up. "I need to talk to the president."

You think? Boyd couldn't help but be glad he wasn't working for the service any longer. He could tell Stone feared his career was over. Adams looked just as grim. Both men now had to admit that the president had nearly been assassinated right under their respective noses.

And he'd thought his career had ended badly.

Maybe Lina was right about God's plan.

When Stone left the room to deliver the news, Boyd almost felt sorry for him.

"Boyd, do you see this man here?" Lina was pointing to a Chinese man on the screen. "Do you know who he is?"

He leaned closer for a better look. "No, although he's always been near Xi Jin Ping, so I assume he's a member of his security team."

"I believe his name is Tao Cho Nyan," Adams said. "He's the second-in-command behind Xi Jin Ping."

"Back the tape up again, please," Lina said.

Adams did as she asked.

A tense silence fell over the room as they all watched the man Lina had identified. "There," she said quickly. "He brings two glasses of beer to the table and sets one in front of Xi Jin Ping."

Tao Cho Nyan did in fact deliver the glass as he took his seat beside the leader. Boyd pursed his lips. "Looks suspicious, but there's no proof he knew the glass had been tampered with."

"Back it up again," Lina suggested. "You'll see that he stops for a moment at a small table. I can't really see what he's doing, though. See if you can capture more from another angle."

Adams pulled up two other cameras, but there were so many people it was nearly impossible to see what, if anything, the second-in-command to Xi Jin Ping did with the glasses of Chinese beer. Especially since he only paused there for twenty seconds.

Was that long enough to dump poison into a glass? Maybe.

"It's as if he knew where the cameras were located," Adams said grimly.

"If he's guilty, we know he had inside help," Boyd pointed out. "I think it's clear Mayleen must have sneaked the vials of strychnine into the White House using her makeup kit, but from there, she passed one of them on to someone else. Who helped her?"

"Who has the most to gain?" Lina asked. "The vice president?"

Boyd grimaced. "Eric Turner does have the most to gain, but again, we need proof."

"We saw Mayleen talking to Pamela," Lina reminded him. "They looked chummy."

"Talking isn't enough, especially since Pamela could be oblivious to whatever is going on." Boyd turned to Adams. "Let's say Turner is a suspect. Can you find him on the video and track his movements?"

"Yes." Adams seemed relieved to have a possible suspect. He went to the beginning of the gala and found Vice President Turner as he entered the room with his wife, Pamela, at his side.

For several moments they watched as absolutely nothing happened. Boyd tried to rein in his impatience.

He couldn't help thinking that if they didn't uncover the truth soon, they'd fail to find the traitor at all.

JANUARY 31 – 9:45 p.m. – Washington, DC

"We must find the mole," Jia whispered to Sam.

"Impossible." He glanced around the room. Jordan was on the phone speaking to someone he assumed was a wife or girlfriend. "We are locked in. They will not allow us to wander around in the middle of a crisis."

"We still have our brains. We must try to come up with a viable suspect." Jia tried to use the current situation to ignore the deep disappointment she felt by her daughter's response to learning the truth. Not that it was working.

What had she expected? That Lina would come rushing into her arms, embracing her long-lost mother?

No, but a little less antagonism would have been nice. Then again, she could understand her daughter's anger and confusion. Lies of this magnitude were difficult to overcome.

Her expression must have shown on her features because Sam gently squeezed her hand. Having him here with her had made all of this less intimidating. She owed him much for putting his life on the line for her.

"She'll get over her anger, Jia," Sam said reassuringly. "I pray God will lead her to the path of forgiveness."

Jia nodded slowly. That they'd made it there, relatively unscathed, seemed to indicate that God was indeed watching over them. Tony's parents practiced the Christian faith, did that mean Lina did as well? If so, maybe she would forgive Jia for what she'd done.

A spark of hope flickered in her heart.

Sam reached out to draw her close. "Jia, there's something important I need to tell you."

His expression was so serious her stomach clenched. "What is it?"

"I—I love you." He searched her gaze. "I know that we haven't spent a lot of time together until recently, but my feelings for you have grown stronger over the years."

She blinked in surprise. "Love?"

The corner of his mouth tipped up in a half smile. "Love. I love you with all my heart and soul. After every thing we've done for our country over the years, I think we deserve some time together when this is over. I beg you to grant me that much."

Jia's heart jumped at his words, but she held back. "Sam, you don't know the things I've had to do . . ."

"They don't matter," he swiftly interrupted. "Jia, I love you. Nothing can change that."

"Easy words to say," she murmured.

He lifted her scarred arm and pressed a kiss against the horrible, puckered skin. "I love you. All of you. I'm only asking for us to spend some time together," he said. "I plan to resign my position with the CIA, and we will get new identification for you so that Manchu or Chen cannot find you. We'll rent a place and see how things go."

Despite her misgivings, she nodded slowly. The normal life he described would be very nice. "Okay, I would like to take some time off together." Especially if Lina wasn't going to forgive her.

"Great. I can't tell you how happy that makes me." His smile lit up his entire face. It struck her how handsome he was and how much he'd helped her stay sane over the years. A lifeguard in a turbulent sea.

Before she could say anything more, he kissed her.

Jia's resistance melted. Despite her scars and everything she'd done, she wrapped her arms around his neck, held on tightly, and kissed him back.

JANUARY 31 – 9:51 p.m. – Washington, DC

Boyd watched the various video feeds with such intensity his vision blurred. From what he could see, the vice president didn't talk to anyone out of the ordinary. In fact, most of his conversations with other guests had been brief and seemingly superficial.

Turner spoke briefly to Tao Cho Nyan, the Chinese second-in-command. But then he did the same with Xi Jin Ping and many others.

Boyd carefully watched the serving staff. Especially the one woman who had given Tao Cho Nyan the two glasses of beer, one in which had been laced with strychnine. He didn't think she had poisoned the drink unless she had mentioned to Tao Cho Nyan which drink was the dangerous one.

That would indicate Tao Cho Nyan was involved in this scheme.

It wasn't unreasonable to consider Turner and Nyan were working together to overthrow their respective leaders. But in China, there was no guarantee that Tao Cho Nyan would take over as the new leader. They didn't function like a democracy, the appointment could go to anyone.

Then again, it was possible Nyan would be chosen.

Boyd kept feeling as if he was missing a key piece of information. He abruptly straightened. "I'd like to talk to Sam King and Jia Ling Ling."

Adams frowned. "I'm not sure I want them here in the control room."

"They risked their lives getting out of China to come here to warn the president of danger," Boyd pointed out. "I'm pretty sure we can trust them."

"Maybe, but I wasn't given the opportunity to properly vet them," Adams shot back. "I'm in enough trouble right now."

"Fine, then I'll go to them," Boyd said.

"I thought the surveillance tapes were the best way to find the traitor?" Adams demanded.

Boyd glanced at the screen. "There's a key piece of information missing. The video hasn't shown us who has tampered with the beer intended for Xi Jin Ping. We need to talk to Sam and Jia. *Now*."

"You really think they know something?" Lina asked.

"We never asked your mother what exactly she overheard related to Manchu's plans," he said. "She alluded to someone in charge within the Chinese government, but who? At this point, I don't have any other ideas on how to figure out who to arrest."

Adams huffed but opened the door to escort them back to the conference room.

The halls were eerily empty, and there weren't as many Secret Service agents standing on guard as he'd expected. Granted, there were probably a dozen agents guarding the president and First Lady, not to mention several others guarding Mayleen, but still.

"You've got people watching the hallway monitors, right?" he asked Adams.

"Yes, but as we're on lockdown, it's not as if they can get out." Adams waved a hand. "We're stretched here, Sinclair. My main goal is to protect the president. I've doubled his security and that of Jin Ping's and left strict orders that no one gets near either of them."

"Except for Randal Stone." A shiver ran down his spine. "Adams, you need to check with your team covering the president. What if Stone is our guy?"

Adams was already touching his earpiece talking to Joe Danby. "Is Stone in there? Keep him far away from the president."

There was a brief silence, and Boyd wished he was wired in to hear both sides of the conversation.

"Got it, thanks. No one gets in from this point forward, understand? Not anyone until you hear directly from me." Adams paused to listen, then said, "We're heading to the yellow conference room. Call if you need me." He turned to glance at Boyd with relief. "Stone was in, gave the news, then left. Woodland of the CIA was in and out too. The good news is that the president is fine."

He nodded. "That's one problem taken care of."

They continued down the hallway toward the yellow conference room. There was no one standing outside the door, but Boyd knew there were two agents standing guard inside. Adams opened the door, then gestured for him and Lina to go in.

"Sam, Jia, we need to talk." Boyd headed over to the couple standing arm in arm. "What exactly did Manchu say about the high-level person who was a threat to the president?"

Before either Sam or Jia could answer, Adams stumbled forward. Boyd turned, reaching for a weapon that wasn't there.

"Well, well. Just the group of people I was searching for."

Boyd froze when he saw Vice President Eric Turner standing just inside the doorway with a gun. He had the muzzle pressed to Randal Stone's head, which caused the other agents in the room to pause as well.

"Throw down your weapons, now!" Turner barked. "Take a shot at me and Stone dies, along with anyone else I happen to hit before I collapse. Get me out of here and Stone lives. Your choice, but make it fast." Turner's eyes hardened. "You have sixty seconds."

Boyd subtly edged Lina behind him, trying to think of a way out of this.

He'd vowed to give his life to save that of the president and the First Lady. If the choice was him or Stone, Boyd wouldn't hesitate to sacrifice himself.

CHAPTER TWENTY-THREE

January 31 – 10:03 p.m. – Washington, DC

"You're a smart man, Turner. You know there's no chance you'll leave the White House, alive," Boyd said in a calm voice. As he said the words, he kept his gaze on Turner. He'd learned in the Secret Service to read people's expressions and their body language. The guy was panicked, yet also resigned to his fate.

A dangerous combination.

Turner had run for President twice, without success. Was that why he'd gone down this terrible path of treason? "Yes, I will. Adams can make that happen." Turner tightened his grip on Stone. "Right, Adams?"

"Absolutely," Adams agreed. "No one will stop to question me if I escort you out of the building."

Boyd was familiar enough with Secret Service policies to know Adams would do no such thing. He'd arrange for one of his agents to take Turner out, even if that meant sacrificing himself and Stone, before he'd let the VP escape justice. The guy had a gun, which likely meant he'd taken it from his Secret Service detail, and then killed him. They hadn't heard a gunshot, but maybe he'd used a pillow as a silencer.

"You really had me fooled, Turner." Boyd hoped getting the guy to talk would stall him long enough for backup to arrive. It was also a distraction he used to creep closer. Too bad Jordan was well behind him and unable to help. "Using Kali's identical twin sister as a way to get to the president was brilliant. I can see how Mayleen was taught everything about the first family, even before Copeland was elected. Did the Chinese help finance his most recent election? Is that how he shot to the top so quickly?"

"Mayleen failed," Turner said tersely, avoiding his question about the president's campaign. The VP scowled at him. "She let herself be made because of you, Sinclair. It pains me to admit I failed in my goal to keep you away from the celebration tonight."

"Your hired guns almost killed us several times," Boyd said, taking another small step toward the vice president. "Unfortunately for you, I was better than they were."

"Don't come any closer," Turner barked. "I mean it. I'll start shooting and take at least a few of you with me."

He lifted his hands. "Okay, okay. I'm not coming any closer. But I am curious about one thing. Did you help the president adopt Kali seventeen years ago?"

"No. But once I learned Kali had a twin sister, the plan began to form. It was the perfect opportunity to infiltrate the White House in a way no one would ever suspect. Of course, I tried to get elected the old-fashioned way, but that didn't work. So this was my backup plan. And it would have succeeded if you hadn't intervened." Turner swept his gaze from Boyd to where Jia, Sam, and Jordan stood. "And the two of you were never supposed to make it out of Beijing.

The final execution of our plan has been nothing but a disaster."

"Time to give yourself up," Stone said as if there wasn't a gun pressed against his temple. "While watching the videotape, we saw you meet with Tao Cho Nyan. Easy enough to piece together that the two seconds-in-command plotted together to become the next leaders of their respective countries."

"Time to go," Turner said, ignoring his hostage's comment. "Adams, lead the way."

From the corner of his eye, Boyd saw Adams move toward the door. "Wait, take me instead."

"You?" Turner scoffed. "No one cares if you die, Sinclair. Stone has clout as the acting director of the FBI. I would have preferred Weatherby, but Stone will have to do. He'll remain my hostage until I'm out of here."

Boyd knew that once Turner was out of the building, he'd kill Stone and anyone else who got in his way. Yet while Turner had spoken, Boyd eased a little closer. He watched Turner's trigger finger, wondering how comfortable the guy was with using a gun. He knew from the VP's background he didn't serve in the military. Not that much skill was needed when you had the barrel pressed up against your target.

Still, he could see that Turner's hand was tight around the gun handle, using force to keep it pressed against Stone's head. His finger was lax on the trigger as if he didn't really want to pull it. Boyd knew it was far easier to hire people to do your dirty work than to actually kill them yourself.

A factor he hoped, and yes, reverently prayed, would work in his favor.

Although he must have killed at least one agent to

obtain the gun. Boyd inched just a little closer as Turner turned toward the door, dragging Stone with him. He keenly watched Turner's gun hand. He didn't want Stone to die, but he also didn't want Turner to get away with plotting to assassinate the president and Xi Jin Ping.

As Turner moved toward Adams, he lightened the pressure of the weapon against Stone's head, and Boyd saw his chance. He leaped forward, closing the gap as he reached for Turner's gun hand. In his peripheral vision, he noted that Stone closed his eyes, expecting to be fatally shot. But Boyd used all his strength to wrench the gun up toward the ceiling, even as Turner finally pulled the trigger. The resulting gunfire was loud, but Boyd's strength was far superior to the older, weaker man's.

Adams quickly joined the fray. Boyd did not let go of Turner's gun hand, keeping it pointed upward. He grabbed Turner around the neck with his free hand, closing off the guy's windpipe.

A gurgling sound emerged from Turner's throat. Boyd didn't let up, not until the VP relaxed his grip on the weapon. Once Boyd had the gun, he tossed it over to the corner of the room, then assisted Adams in securing Turner's hands behind his back.

Stone broke free, his gaze wide as he rubbed the spot on his head where the gun had been seconds earlier. "I—thought I was a goner."

"I know." Boyd cast him a sympathetic look. "It was a risk I had to take. No way could we let him walk out of here."

"I agree, which is why I thought I was a dead man." Stone looked at Boyd with admiration. "I'm not sure how you did that, but thanks."

Boyd nodded and glanced over at Lina. She was pale

but managed a small smile. "I knew you'd do that, risk yourself to save everyone else."

"I had to." Adams and another Secret Service agent had Turner in a tight grip. The VP stared at Boyd with a venomous gaze but didn't say anything.

"Nicely done, Boyd," Jordan said with a grin. "You're a great addition to my team."

Stone stepped up to Turner. "You're under arrest for treason, planning to assassinate the president, and likely other charges that we'll uncover once we know the entire truth."

"Oh, he's probably responsible for the death of NSA Agent Tillman. Sun found him dead in his home. And Tillman's ID was used to access secure information."

The acting director of the FBI grimaced, then nodded at Adams. "We'll add murder to the list. Let's get him out of here."

Adams and another Secret Service agent took Turner out with Stone accompanying them. They left one Secret Service agent behind, a guy named Charlie Durango.

"Slick move," Durango said with a nod.

Boyd simply shrugged, then crossed over to Lina. "I'm sure they'll lift the lockdown soon."

"We only have one of the traitors," Lina said, glancing at her mother, Sam, and Jordan. "We still need to talk about Tao Cho Nyan."

"He's Xi Jin Ping's problem," Boyd said.

"The attempted attack against Xi Jin Ping took place here," Lina said. "I don't think the president wants China to know about this."

He nodded slowly. "You're right." He turned toward Jia and Sam. "Do you think you can talk to Xi Jin Ping?"

"Yes," Jia answered. "And this news is better coming

from me than from you as I understand the Chinese mentality and can speak fluently about what I overheard. However, I need to know what you saw on the video feeds."

Boyd filled her in on what they'd learned. "I realize it's not much, but the fact remains that Xi Jin Ping's beer was poisoned."

"Yes, I agree." Jia looked at Sam. "I need to do this."

"Of course," Sam agreed. "But I'm going with you."

"Me too," Lina quickly added.

"Hey, don't keep me out of this now," Jordan drawled.

Boyd looked at Durango. "You need to get all five of us in to see Xi Jin Ping."

Durango grimaced but used his earpiece to communicate to the agents who were guarding the Chinese leader. "Okay, we'll be there shortly." Durango gestured toward the door. "Okay, let's go. They're in the diplomatic reception room in the center of the White House."

"Are you keeping Tao Cho Nyan in a separate place as Xi Jin Ping?" Boyd asked as they all left the yellow conference room.

Durango nodded. "Yes. That was the directive from Adams."

"Good." Boyd exchanged a glance with Lina. He hoped Jia would be able to convince Xi Jin Ping of the danger.

He wanted nothing more than for the danger to be over. Even though he didn't want to leave Lina.

Despite all his talk of not being in the market for a relationship, she'd broken through the barriers around his heart.

JANUARY 31 – 10:14 p.m. – Washington, DC

Jia did her best to stay focused on completing their mission. Sam took her hand, and she smiled at him, thinking it was entirely possible God had sent this man to her for a reason.

If only Li Na would find a way to forgive her. Maybe after the shock wore off, her daughter would agree to see her again.

When they arrived in the diplomatic reception room where Xi Jin Ping and his wife were being held, Jia noticed the Chinese leader regarded her with keen interest. Maybe he was glad to have a friendly face here amongst the overwhelming presence of the Americans.

She highly doubted he'd be so happy once he knew why she'd come. In China, relaying bad news never reflected well on the messenger.

Jia stepped forward and bowed respectfully. While she wasn't a huge fan of the current leadership, she knew Xi was a better choice than having Bo Dung Manchu or Tao Cho Nyan taking his place. "Good evening, Your Excellency," she greeted him in Mandarin.

"Good evening," Xi returned with a brief nod. "What brings you here?"

"I am sorry to say I bring distressing news." She lifted her head and, despite their customs, boldly met his gaze. "I worked undercover for many, many years within the Six Red Dragons run by Bo Dung Manchu and learned of a plot to kill you."

"So I have been told by the American government," Xi said. He narrowed his gaze as if unpleased with her fortitude. "Why should I listen to you?"

Jia inwardly sighed and forced herself to play the game. "Your Excellency, while I am a mere woman, I overheard a plot to kill you and the President of the United States. I learned Mayleen, one of my sister's twin daughters, was being taught about the first family, studying Kali Copeland's facial expressions and movements. I understood the implication of this especially after my sister was murdered here in the US. The daughters were switched, and Mayleen was to assist in killing the president. We believe Tao Cho Nyan is involved as he has much to gain by your untimely death."

This news caught Xi Jin Ping by surprise. His eyes widened, and he looked thoughtful. "You have proof of this?"

"The American government has arrested their second-in-command, Vice President Eric Turner, for his role in the assassination attempt." Jia held his gaze. "We watched video in which there was a brief meeting between Turner and Nyan."

Xi waved a hand. "That is hardly proof of such a heinous allegation."

"Ah, but Nyan also brought your beer to the table," Jia said evenly. "The same beer laced with strychnine, a very deadly poison. Tell me, Your Excellency, who else would wish to harm you?"

Xi stared at her for a long moment. Then he glanced at the others who'd accompanied her. "How exactly did you learn of this plot?"

Jia knew she was treading on dangerous ground. The Chinese were a paranoid group in general, and Xi Jin Ping was the most paranoid of all. He would not be pleased to learn of her deception, even if the knowledge she'd gained had helped to save his life.

"I became a member of the Six Red Dragons with the intent of learning more about their criminal acts. Bo Dung Manchu is a very greedy man. He wanted to grow his organization even larger than it already was. I heard him speaking to a man I believe to be Nyan about this plan to harm you and the President of the United States."

Xi Jinping's dark gaze bored into hers. "You spied on him." His tone was full of disdain.

She inclined her head. "Only to stop him from taking deadly action against you, Your Excellency. And I was nearly killed for hearing that much. I risked my life because my loyalty is to you."

That part was a lie, and she hoped God wouldn't hold it against her. She didn't really have any loyalty to the country of her birth. Oh, there were plenty of good people who lived there, but the corruption was very bad.

"How many others have you spied on?" Xi demanded.

"Only Bo Dung Manchu. He is a greedy ambitious man who wishes to be in your shoes, Your Excellency." She purposefully refrained from mentioning how she'd been forced to kill Hui Genghis Chen in order to escape being raped and tortured after he'd found her listening to Manchu's conversation. She didn't trust Xi Jin Ping's grace to extend that far.

And she was still a Chinese citizen, having met and married Tony Parker while she was studying here in DC.

That time of innocence seemed like a million years ago. She had many regrets, yet looking back, she didn't think she'd have made a different decision. Pretending to be dead to get to the very group that killed Tony was all that had mattered. Especially when she discovered her sister was part of the group as well. And now she could see things had worked out exactly as they were meant to.

Something Li Na may not understand.

"How can I believe you?" Xi asked, looking at her with distrust. "Maybe you are secretly working for Manchu?"

She swallowed a flash of impatience. "Many attempts

were made to kill me and Sam King as we left Beijing. Attempts the Vice President of the United States knew about. Because he and Nyan were working together. You were here in America, so you may not realize what transpired back in Beijing. Believe me, their reach is wide in our homeland, Your Excellency."

Xi didn't say anything for a long moment.

Jia bowed again. "I have told you what I know, Your Excellency. The decision of what to do with this information is yours. I humbly advise you to choose wisely."

With that, she turned away. Jia caught Li Na's intense gaze and tried to smile. She knew Sam understood Mandarin, but she did not believe her daughter did. "I did my best to convince him of the danger," she said in a low voice.

"I heard the entire conversation," Boyd said. "You did a good job."

Jia blushed. Interesting that Boyd understood Mandarin. And the way he looked at her daughter was also intriguing. It was similar to the way Sam smiled at her.

"Bring Tao Cho Nyan to me!" Xi shouted in English. "I want to face the man who tried to kill me."

Jia let out a pent-up breath. It seemed Xi Jin Ping had decided to believe her.

And why not? He could easily replace Nyan with someone else. There were plenty who would seek favor with Xi Jin Ping.

She nodded at Sam and silently prayed the US would grant her asylum here rather than send her back to Beijing.

Despite Xi Jin Ping's decision to believe in her, she did not think he would bother to keep her safe.

If she was forced to return to China, she faced certain death.

JANUARY 31 – 10:31 *p.m.* – *Washington, DC*

"I don't think bringing Nyan here is a good idea," Sam said in a low tone to Adams. "We need to keep Nyan separated from Xi Jin Ping."

"I agree. Besides, Nyan isn't leaving the US, he'll stay as a guest in our federal prison while we investigate his role in all of this." Adams glanced over at Xi Jin Ping who was now chattering away in Mandarin. "I'm sure China will want him to stand trial in their court system, but we get first dibs."

"Good." Sam couldn't deny a sense of relief. He reached for Jia's hand. "I have another favor to ask."

Adams eyed him warily. "Yeah?"

"Jia must be granted asylum here in the US. It would not be safe for her to return to China."

"I agree," Boyd spoke up. "After all, I have to believe Jia contributed to the chatter about the threat posed by the Six Red Dragons."

Adams glanced at Jia. "Is this true?"

Jia nodded. "Yes. I was able to get some communication to Sam prior to my cover being blown. It was how he came to meet and ultimately rescue me."

"You rescued me, Jia," Sam protested. "And while our role may be considered minor, the initial intel that Jia sent out helped put the president on alert."

The head of the Secret Service blew out a breath. "Okay, we'll work with Stone to make that happen."

"Thank you." Sam glanced down at Jia, who was staring at her daughter. He would have liked some time alone with Lina to let her know how brave her mother was for what she'd accomplished over the years, but the way Boyd was standing guard, he suspected that wouldn't happen anytime soon.

"Thank you," Jia said, turning her attention to Adams. "I would appreciate being allowed to stay in the US."

"Will you be safe here?" Boyd asked. "We know the Chinese mafia has a long reach."

Jia lifted her hands. "Who can say? My hope is that Xi Jin Ping will take care of Manchu and those working for him."

"Wait a minute, are you saying your life is in danger?" Lina asked. "Even here?"

Sam was glad to see that Lina cared enough about her mother's situation to ask. "Your mother was forced to kill a man in order to escape," Sam said quietly. "His family along with other members of the Six Red Dragons will seek retribution."

Lina's expression was troubled. "Well, then, she needs to go into witness protection."

"No, I refuse." Jia turned to her daughter. "I would like to spend some time with you, Li Na."

Lina looked uncertain, then nodded. "We can do that, very soon. But I want you and Sam to be safe. That's the most important thing."

Sam couldn't help but smile. "I will do whatever is necessary to keep Jia safe. However, you should know, your mother is very capable of saving herself. And me."

"Thank you," Jia said, her dark eyes bright with tears. "Thank you, Li Na."

For the first time since the two had seen each other, Lina reached over to touch her mother's arm. Then she quickly embraced her. "I'm glad you're here."

"Me too," Jia whispered.

. . .

JANUARY 31 – 10:42 *p.m.* – *Washington, DC*

"Sinclair, the president wants to speak with you and Lina."

Lina reluctantly moved away from her mother to look at Boyd. He didn't seem overly impressed with Adams's statement. Boyd sighed and rubbed the back of his neck.

"Okay, let's do this." Boyd took her hand, and she reveled in his strength. "But when this meeting is over, can we leave? I gotta tell you, it's been an incredibly long day."

Just hearing Boyd say the words made Lina realize how exhausted she was too. She sent one last glance over her shoulder at her mother, surprised and glad to see Sam holding her mother close.

Lina knew she needed to forgive her mother for leaving all those years ago. Her grandparents had loved her, and she'd had a good life. One in which she'd excelled in science and received her PhD in microbiology.

While she'd survived and thrived here in DC, her mother had been living in fear within the Six Red Dragons. It made her sad to think about what her mother must have gone through. And it also made her proud to know her mother had helped bring down the largest, most powerful faction of the Chinese mafia.

The trip to the library within the executive residence didn't take long. Lina secretly marveled at the various rooms she'd been in.

When they walked in, Lina was shocked to see Kali was with them. The chopper trip to and from Richmond must not have taken very long. The girl was dressed in a typical Chinese tunic and pants, and she sat close to her mother's side.

"Mr. President, ma'am." Boyd nodded at them. "Kali, I'm glad to see you're okay."

"I heard you helped save my dad," Kali admitted, smiling shyly at Boyd. Lina could tell the girl still had a case of hero worship for Boyd.

And honestly? She couldn't blame Kali one bit.

"They drugged her, Boyd," Eloise said darkly. "I'm so upset with myself for not realizing that girl was an impostor. And Kali's twin sister too! How terrible is that? I know it was only a day and a half, but I still should have known."

"I still think I should get to meet Mayleen," Kali said.

"No!" her parents said simultaneously.

"She's been arrested, Kali. She's not your sister in any way that counts," Eloise said.

"Boyd, Lina, we owe you both a debt of gratitude," President Copeland added, stepping forward to offer his hand. "Without you, this evening would have ended much differently."

"It's part of the job, sir," Boyd said, shaking his hand.

Lina smiled. "I'm glad I could help, but it was all Boyd and Jordan who made this happen."

"Yes, I know." The president's gaze turned serious. "Boyd, I'd like you to come back to work for the Secret Service. We really could use someone with your talent."

Lina didn't know why the offer surprised her, but it did. She glanced at Adams, who was nodding in approval.

Boyd hesitated, then glanced at her. She could see the indecision in his eyes.

"Please, Boyd," Eloise said. "I'd feel so much safer having you guarding us."

"Me too," Kali added.

Still, he hesitated. "I'd like a few days to think about it," Boyd finally said.

Lina was surprised. "What's to think about?"

Boyd turned to look at her. "My future depends on you, Lina."

"Me?" Her voice squeaked. "What do you mean?"

His mouth curved into a smile. "I know it's probably not the time to tell you this, but I've fallen in love with you, and I think we should decide our future together. Whatever career path I take, either returning to the White House or staying with Security Specialists, Inc., impacts you too."

Love? She blushed, knowing the president and his family were listening to this. "I—really? I thought you weren't interested in, well, you know, family stuff."

"I wasn't before, but I am now. Very much." Boyd gazed into her eyes. "I love you, Lina. You probably need time, which is understandable. But you should also know I've never said those three words to any other woman. Ever."

She was humbled by the emotion she saw in his gaze. "I'm happy to hear that, Boyd. Because I love you too."

"Thank You, God," he said and swept her into his arms and kissed her.

EPILOGUE

February 1 – 12:00 a.m. – Washington, DC

"Happy Chinese New Year," Lina said with a half-hearted smile. "It's nice to know we saved the day."

"Exactly," Boyd agreed. He was sitting beside her at Jordan's house, where they'd been taken courtesy of the White House Secret Service, in a limo no less. Lina told herself not to get used to the extravagance.

"Actually, it's noon in China at the moment," her mother pointed out. "I must say I am impressed at how quickly the US government acted with assistance from Xi Jin Ping. It is a relief to know Manchu and several of his men have already been placed in custody."

"And Mayleen is telling everything she knows in hopes of getting a lighter sentence," Boyd added. "I still can't believe she sneaked the strychnine in in bottles marked as makeup."

"Me either. Doug Weatherby is being held responsible for the leak inside the NSA, which was really caused by the former VP using Tillman's access," Jordan said. His gaze turned serious. "It's unfortunate Sun discovered Tillman was dead in his home. Another victim of this terrible conspiracy."

"What about Yates?" Boyd asked.

"His condition has stabilized," Jordan assured him. "The surgery was a success, although they were forced to infuse several units of blood. Last update was that his vitals are stable and he was beginning to wake up."

"I'm glad," Lina murmured.

"I can't believe Turner was that power hungry as to work with the Chinese mafia to become the next President of the United States," Sloan drawled. "Guy must be certifiably crazy."

"I think he let his previous failures to become elected get to him. His first attempt was when he was a few years older than Copeland is now. Based on what little I saw when I worked on the First Lady's detail, Turner truly believed he deserved the role, more so than Copeland. And that belief was cemented in stone when the president often sought his counsel in matters of high importance." Boyd shook his head. "Good thing he's going to jail for the rest of his life."

"Idiot," Jordan muttered.

"It's really over," Lina agreed. Despite the late hour, everyone had come together. Lina smiled at Jordan, Diana, their young son Ben, and thirteen-year-old Bryn. Sloan and Natalia were there, too, with their young daughter. Sun and Mack were also present, and from the way Sun rested her hand on her lower abdomen, Lina guessed she was expecting too. The Security Specialists, Inc. team seemed to be family oriented yet determined to carry out their important mission of keeping the country safe.

Finally, her gaze rested on her mother and Sam King. They'd had some time to talk on the drive to Jordan's, and while it was still difficult to believe her mother was alive all this time, Lina understood that she had played an instrumental role in identifying and responding to this targeted terrorist threat. When she'd told her mother how proud she was of all she'd accomplished, the woman's eyes had filled with tears. They'd embraced tightly, and Lina knew she'd welcome having her mother and Sam in her life.

"I heard the president asked you to return to the Secret Service." Jordan eyed Boyd from his seat next to his wife and children. "He and the First Lady were very impressed with your work on this case."

"Yes," Boyd admitted. He tightened his arm around her shoulders. "I guess tonight's events made up for the incident in Manhattan."

There was a moment of silence before Sun spoke up. "Well gee, Boyd, don't keep us in suspense." The petite North Korean woman stared at him expectantly. "What did you decide? Are you taking your old job back or staying with us?"

"Just for the record, we'd like you to stay with us," Sloan added.

"Yes, we would," Natalia agreed.

"You know my feelings on the matter," Jordan piped up. "We can really use someone who speaks and reads Mandarin. But I'll respect your decision either way." He grinned. "It might be nice to have a friend working inside the White House."

Lina knew Boyd had already made his decision, after asking for her opinion. She only wanted what was best for him, but he'd insisted they were a couple, and while each job had its pluses and minuses, he wanted to do what was best for the both of them.

"Both Lina and I have decided I should stick with you

guys," Boyd said with a wide smile. "Lina understands and accepts the danger, as I do."

"Thank goodness," Natalia said with obvious relief. "We were worried you'd prefer the glitz and glamour of the White House."

"Not in the least," Boyd said firmly. He leaned over to kiss Lina again, making her blush. "I do need a favor, though."

"What kind of favor?" Mack asked.

"I know I just started a few weeks ago, but I'd like a week off to help Lina straighten some things out. We believe the Institute for Nanoscience will likely remain closed for a while, but we still need to make sure her position there is secure."

"Done," Jordan spoke without hesitation.

Diana nudged him. "You might want to point out that we're all officially on standby for the next week because the president wants us available in case he needs help with tracking more evidence against Turner and Tao Cho Nyan."

"I'm working on that aspect of the case," Mack said, waving his hand. "I'm going through their phone records and computer files. Sun's helping me. We'll find what we need."

"Mack is teaching me everything he knows," Sun teased, kissing his cheek.

Lina couldn't help being impressed with the teamwork they displayed and the respect they were given by the President of the United States.

She didn't think life with Boyd working for an organization known to get involved with terrorist threats would be easy, but she didn't care.

The job was important and bigger than everyone in this

room. Which was exactly why her mother had made that fateful decision twenty-five years ago.

"I love you," Boyd whispered in her ear. "I'm grateful God brought us together, Lina."

She beamed at him. "And I love you too." She kissed him again, feeling very blessed to have God's grace and love surrounding them forever.

DEAR READER

Thanks so much for reading *Target for Treason*, the fourth book in my Security Specialists, Inc. series! The idea came to me, and after brainstorming for a few days, I decided I just had to write it. I hope you enjoyed Boyd and Lina's story.

If you liked this book, please consider giving a review. These reviews are critical to authors, and I would very much appreciate it.

I'm truly blessed to have such wonderful readers! Please know I'd love to hear from you. I can be found on Facebook at https://www.facebook.com/LauraScottBooks, on Twitter at https://twitter.com/laurascottbooks, and on Instagram at https://www.instagram.com/laurascottbooks/. I can also be reached through my website at https://www.laurascottbooks.com. If you're interested in hearing about my new releases, consider signing up for my newsletter. You'll receive a free novella that is not available for purchase through any platform. It is exclusive only to my newsletter subscribers.

Until next time,
Laura Scott

SEALED WITH COURAGE

Aubrey Clark approached the low-income two-story apartment building with trepidation. The East Village suburb of San Diego had the highest crime rate of the metropolitan area. If not for her very real concerns about ten-year-old Lucas Espinoza, and the lack of response from the two phone messages she'd left for his mother, no way would she walk here alone in the dark on a chilly evening in late February.

She shivered, keeping her gaze alert for trouble as she approached the building. No surprise to find the place was in a sorry state of disrepair, peeling paint, sagging eves, several cracked windows, and broken concrete. Aubrey had been there once before to talk about Lucas's progress with learning sign language, but that visit had been during the daytime.

Maybe she should have waited until tomorrow. She'd held her adult sign language class that evening, so couldn't come until afterwards. By tomorrow, though, she could have come right after her kids left for the day, when it was still light out.

Too late to change her mind, now. Hesitating on the sidewalk, she peered at the ground level corner apartment Lucas shared with his mother and her latest boyfriend, Jose.

As a teacher at the school for the deaf, she enjoyed her elementary school kids. Maybe because losing her husband ten years ago, meant giving up the idea of having a family of her own. When she'd noticed the bruises on Lucas's arms, she'd used sign language to ask what had happened. He'd flushed and claimed he'd fallen off his bike.

No way did she believe that. For one thing, she doubted the boy owned a bike, his clothes were threadbare, and his shoes were several sizes too big. Secondly, the bruises had looked to her like fingerprints digging into the boy's skin. She'd tried to ask Lucas about his relationship with Jose, but the child had shaken his head, vehemently denying any trouble.

As required by law, she'd made a report to Child Protective Services. The social worker agreed to investigate Aubrey's concern.

Then Lucas hadn't shown up at school for two days in a row.

She swallowed hard and set her shoulders. Since the start of the school year, Lucas's mother, Nanette Espinoza, had been friendly and seemingly interested in learning sign language so she could communicate with her son. Nanette had even come to a few of her adult classes, but then had stopped attending, claiming she had to work.

The bruises Lucas sustained were concerning, but as the social worker had pointed out, they weren't broken bones. She assumed the social worker had seen far worse injuries. Aubrey wanted to believe the child was home with the flu.

But she didn't.

Her steps slowed when she glimpsed movement through the window. A short and burly Hispanic man appeared upset, waving his arms around in anger. Was that Jose? Aubrey found herself moving closer to the window, keeping her gaze focused on his mouth. Initially she had trouble understanding what he was saying, because she could only see his profile. Then he turned just enough that she could read his lips.

You'll tell the police he ran away!

She sucked in a harsh breath. Was he talking about Lucas? Had he done something to the boy? Had he killed him?

Do you want to disappear, too?

The man abruptly stopped talking and stared through the window, his gaze colliding with hers. She gasped and quickly ducked down then belatedly realized what a stupid move that was.

The windows were closed. She should have just waved and pretended to be out for a walk. The man in Lucas's apartment didn't know she could read lips.

A door slammed loudly. Aubrey panicked. Was he coming after her? She jumped up from her crouch and began to run, praying for God to keep her safe.

"Aubrey? Wait! What's wrong?"

A man emerged from the shadows, making her screech in alarm. Then she saw the dog standing beside him.

"Mason?" She recognized Mason Gray and his Belgium Malinois, Bravo. Mason was a former Navy SEAL who was taking her adult sign language class. What he was doing here in the East Village was a mystery.

A string of Hispanic curses echoed behind them.

The boyfriend was coming for her!

"Hurry, we need to go!" She instinctively used sign

language as she spoke, as Mason was deaf in one ear. She couldn't be sure he'd heard the man's curses.

"Stay to my left," he said curtly. Bravo happened to be on a leash in his right hand, so that worked out fine for her.

Mason broke into a jog. Aubrey did her best to keep up with him, although her idea of running was dashing from the garage to the house to avoid the rain.

As if sensing her difficulty, Mason grabbed her hand and tugged her down one side street, then another. She blindly followed his lead, unfamiliar with this area of the city. She had faith in Mason and Bravo, although she didn't know much about the man other than he used to be a Navy SEAL. He rarely talked about himself, and frankly didn't ask anything about her, either. All his focus seemed to be centered on learning sign language.

Yet she instinctively trusted him.

It didn't take long for her breathing to grow labored, her heart pounding so hard she thought it might burst out of her chest landing on the road with a squishy plop.

"Can we rest a minute?" she gasped.

Mason didn't answer, so she tugged on his hand. That made him look at her. Since he still held her hand, she used her free hand to spell the word as she spoke. "Rest."

He glanced behind them, then slowed to a walk. Bravo trotted beside him sniffing the air.

She put a hand to her chest, willing her pulse to return to normal.

"Are you okay?" Mason asked. His gaze was impossible to read in the dark. They slowed so that they could face each other to speak. When they stopped, Mason cocked his right ear toward her to hear better.

"Yes, I am now, but what are you doing here?" She

didn't understand how he'd been there to help. "Do you live in East Village?"

The corner of his mouth quirked in what might have passed for a small smile. "No. I was following you."

"Following me?" She stared at him in shock. "You mean, like a stalker?" The question popped out before she could pull it back.

"Not a stalker, just a concerned citizen." His gaze bored into hers. "I was worried when you left the class and headed this way alone, rather than taking your usual path toward your home. What happened back there?"

That he'd paid that much attention to her comings and goings was a discomforting surprise, but his question made her shiver. Now that she was no longer alone, those moments in front of Lucas's house replayed over in her mind.

You'll tell the police he ran away.
Do you want to disappear, too?

"I—uh, need to report a missing child to the police." She spoke slowly and loudly so Mason could hear, unwilling to let go of his hand to use sign language. She'd been blessed to have a cochlear implant placed seven years ago, and she'd mentioned the possibility of Mason qualifying for one. He seemed interested, but had also hoped his hearing would return.

For his sake, she hoped it did, too.

He scowled. "Missing child? Who?"

"Lucas Espinoza. He's a ten-year-old boy in my fifth grade class." She thought about how vulnerable the deaf boy would be if someone had kidnapped him. It would be incredibly difficult for the child to communicate to anyone even if he was able to escape.

Yet she feared Lucas wasn't just missing. If he was, why

the conversation where Jose instructed Nanette to claim he ran away? Why not be honest about the fact that he was missing?

No, she had a very bad feeling Lucas might be dead. Killed by Jose, or someone he knew.

Tears pricked at her eyes. Maybe she shouldn't have reported the bruises to CPS. Maybe she should have tried to talk to Nanette, first.

Dear Lord, what had she done?

"Aubrey" Mason gave her hand a tug to get her attention. "What happened to Lucas? How do you know he's missing?"

"I read the man's lips." She recounted how Lucas hadn't shown up for class, so she'd come to talk to the boy's mother, when she saw the argument through the window. "He saw me standing outside, and then I heard a door slam. That's when I started running."

Mason's expression turned grim. "Okay, we'll report this to the police, but not until we get you someplace safe."

She nodded, glancing around the dimly lit deserted street. Getting far away from this area seemed reasonable.

Thankfully, Mason continued forward at a slower pace so that she could keep up. Yet as they walked back toward the neighborhood where she lived, she couldn't seem to banish Lucas's face from her mind.

If the boy had been badly hurt, or worse, she'd never, ever forgive herself.

Great, the pretty lady thinks I'm a stalker. Mason couldn't really blame her, since most normal people didn't see danger lurking around every corner.

Then again, his life had been anything but normal.

The fact that Aubrey had been in danger, only proved

he'd made the right decision in following her. To be fair, he'd have preferred staying in the shadows. But when she'd dropped to her knees, then jumped up and ran her features alarmed, he'd rushed forward, revealing his position.

Bravo looked up at him, his tongue lolling out of his mouth. The Malinois had been a working dog on their SEAL team. When their last mission had caused Mason's left ear drum to rupture, he'd fought hard to get Bravo retired with him. Thankfully Bravo was six and a half years old, and they typically retired dogs when they turned seven, so he'd been granted permission to bring his partner home. Still, despite his age, Bravo was the most athletic dog he'd ever worked with, and that short run was nothing compared to the physical exertion he usually offered his partner.

That would have to wait until, later. A missing child was serious business. Yet he wasn't comfortable having Aubrey in this section of town. He navigated the streets with her in tow, doing his best to move slowly enough for her to keep up. Since losing the hearing in his left ear, he'd become more attune to his other senses. He could see her chest rising and falling with exertion, sweat dampening her temples where wisps of blonde hair escaped from her ponytail. She wasn't conventionally beautiful, her mouth a little too wide, her nose upturned at the end, but that hadn't prevented him from feeling the kick of attraction.

Inappropriate attraction. She was his sign language teacher, nothing more.

When they reached South Park, he paused near a bench and gestured for her to sit down. "We can rest here for a few minutes."

Aubrey dropped gratefully down on the seat. "I'm sorry I'm not in better shape," she said loudly enough for him to hear.

He almost said something foolish about how he liked her shape just fine, but managed to refrain. No need to live up to his stalker moniker. He sat beside her, so that his right ear was closest to her. All those years of keeping Bravo to his right because he happened to be left handed and held his weapon in his left hand, was hampering him now. "Do you often visit your student's homes?"

She winced and shook her head. "No. I just—Lucas is special. He's bright and could do really well for himself in spite of being born deaf. I was hoping to help him obtain a cochlear implant, but now..." her voice trailed off.

"Look, we'll call the police, I'm sure they'll investigate his disappearance." He idly rubbed Bravo's sleek pelt. His K-9 partner happened to specialize in tracking scents, but that was when Mason had been a SEAL.

Now he was a civilian trying to adjust to his new injury and his new life.

And doing a piss-poor job at both.

Aubrey put her hand on his arm to get his attention. He noticed she did that a lot, as if she knew first hand that it was easier to listen when you caught a person's attention, first. "Thanks for coming to my rescue."

"No problem, but I am concerned about your safety. Any chance that guy knows where to find you?"

"I don't think so," she said, although her brow puckered in a slight frown. "I personally haven't met Jose, only Nanette, Lucas's mother."

When he'd shown up early for his adult class, he'd noticed the kids called her Ms. Clark. If Lucas happened to mention her name, this Jose guy probably knew who she was. That's how Mason had learned her name even before he'd taken the first sign language class, where she'd introduced herself as Aubrey.

A pretty name for a beautiful woman.

He rubbed the back of his neck. Maybe he was a stalker. No question the woman had caught his attention. Not that he'd planned to do anything about it. He was a forty-two-year-old retired SEAL with no clue how to live outside of the Navy.

She touched his arm again. "To be honest, I can't say for sure the man in the apartment was Jose. I'm assuming he was Nanette's boyfriend, but he could be anyone."

"Why don't you go ahead and call the police?" He suggested. "The sooner they get out to investigate the better." After spending twenty-two years doing the most difficult job on the planet, it went against the grain to hand the situation over to the authorities. Of course, he didn't have the credentials to do that work any longer.

Aubrey pulled out her phone. "I've never called 911 before," she said as she hit the buttons.

He listened to her side of the conversation. She was calmer now and gave the information in succinct sentences. Her enunciation was careful, and he'd wondered about her somewhat monotone speech patterns. When he'd learned she'd been born deaf, and had been given a Cochlear implant, he'd been impressed with how well she'd adapted.

And that she'd dedicated her life to helping those who couldn't hear.

"Thank you," Aubrey finally said. She lowered the phone and touched the end button. Then she glanced up at him. "She's sending two officers to talk to Nanette Espinoza."

"You don't look happy about that," he noted.

She sighed. "I don't know how much credence they're putting in my ability to read lips. But I know what I saw."

"I believe you." He stroked Bravo again, then reached

for Aubrey's hand. Keeping their hands joined, he addressed his dog. "Bravo, this is Aubrey. Aubrey is a friend, Bravo. Friend."

Bravo sniffed their hands for a long moment before his tail wagged back and forth.

"He's a beautiful dog."

"Thank you. We've been home for a few months now, but he's still a highly trained military K-9, and can be aggressive at times." Something that came in very handy when tracking terrorists, not so much while walking amongst the citizens of San Diego. "You need to be careful around him."

"I understand." She smiled as Bravo licked the back of her hand. "Well, I guess it's time for me to head home."

"Bravo and I will escort you, just to be safe."

She nodded and stood. She may have said something, he couldn't be sure. Not hearing statements and other sounds, was extremely frustrating. At first he'd railed in anger that this had happened to him. Then he pulled himself together and decided to set an example for the rest of his teammates. Kaleb, Hudson, Dallas, Dawson and Nico hadn't emerged unscathed, either. They'd all suffered during that last deployment, barely escaping a dicey situation that had claimed the life of one of their teammates, Jaydon Rampart. His fault, Mason silently admitted, as team leader. It was his job to bring them all home.

A job he'd failed, in more ways than one.

Still, as one of the oldest and active SEAL teams, their retirement had been a foregone conclusion by the time they'd returned stateside.

Even without their various injuries and problems, they would have been forced out.

Being a SEAL was a young man's game. Granted their

experience and expertise had carried them along for a few years longer than most, but he'd always known they were operating on borrowed time. He was forty-two, the oldest member of their team.

And there was no doubt that if they'd have retired earlier, Jaydon would still be alive.

Aubrey touched his arm again. "I live this way."

He knew where she lived, which again, made him stalker-like. Yet he hadn't been able to help himself. Frankly, he knew where all the adults who took the sign language class lived, only because he spent a lot of time walking the streets with Bravo, rather than sleeping. And deep down, he'd needed to know everything about the people surrounding him in the small classroom. "Okay."

"...followed me..."

He tried to piece together what she'd said. "I'm sorry if I came across as a stalker, but I do a lot of walking at night, it helps me sleep."

She looked at him and he tipped his head to hear better. "I was wondering why Jose, if that's who it was at the apartment followed me," she repeated carefully. "He probably doesn't know I can read lips."

"Oh." He wondered if he'd ever get used to being sixty-five percent deaf. "You're right in that most people don't understand the ability to do that. Although it could be there was something else happening in that apartment. A crime he thought you witnessed."

"I hadn't considered that possibility." She turned right at the next intersection. "That only makes Lucas's disappearance more dire."

"I know." He didn't like the thought of a ten-year-old deaf kid being taken or worse, hurt. Doing nothing chafed, but then again, he had his own issues to deal with. And he wasn't a SEAL, any longer. "Hopefully the police will find him."

"I intend to keep praying for Lucas until he's found."

Praying? He shied away from talk of faith and God. When he'd been younger and going through the arduous BUDS SEAL training, he'd prayed for strength and endurance every single day. But over the years, he'd remained focused on training and preparation for each mission.

Until the underwater bomb had exploded too close to him.

They walked without speaking for several long moments. When he saw the small robin's egg blue bungalow that she owned, he instinctively slowed his steps. Oddly enough, for a man who preferred to be alone, unless you counted hanging with his teammates, he'd enjoyed this brief time with Aubrey.

"Thanks for walking me home." She paused on the sidewalk. "See you at class."

"Sure." He gave Bravo the hand-signal for sit, and the dog dropped to his haunches. The SEALs used hand signals a lot, which is why he'd decided to learn sign language. He regarded Aubrey for a moment. The interior of her small house was dark, but he didn't like leaving her like this. "I'll wait here until you're safely inside."

As he said the words, his peripheral vision picked up some movement. His other senses were highly focused since losing more than half his hearing. The small black car slowed, the passenger window lowered. Mason was moving by the time he saw the gun barrel.

"Get down!" He launched himself at Aubrey, knocking her to the ground. Bravo barked wildly as gunfire echoed around them. Mason rolled to the side, instinctively reaching for his Sig Sauer, only to remember he'd left it at home because the school didn't allow firearms.

In a flash the vehicle disappeared around the corner. Bravo's frenzied barking caused several lights to turn on in the houses on either side of Aubrey's. He figured there were at least two faces pressed against the windows, watching.

Furious at being shot at, he lunged to his feet, then reached down to draw Aubrey upright. "I'm sorry, are you okay? Did I hurt you?"

"Who—was that?" she wheezed, putting a hand to her chest. He'd no doubt hit her hard enough to knock the breath from her lungs.

Good question. Things had happened so fast, he hadn't gotten a good look at the shooter, or the driver.

Had to be the same guy she'd seen in the apartment. Why? He wasn't sure, but his gut warned him that Aubrey's concern over a missing child had gotten her involved in something very dangerous.

Bravo whined beside him, and he took a moment to check the K-9 for signs of injury. Thankfully, the dog seemed fine, but he scowled in the direction the car had disappeared.

That idiot had nearly killed his dog, and Aubrey. He'd been vested in this situation based on principal, no kid should be in danger. But now?

This had just gotten very personal.